Beautiful Before God

a novel

Jeff Paschal

Beautiful Before God
ISBN: Softcover 978-1-955581-69-1
Copyright © 2022 by Jeff Paschal

This novel's story and characters are fictitious. A few established institutions, public offices, public figures, and public officials are mentioned, but the characters, names, and places involved are wholly imaginary and any resemblance to actual persons, living or dead, or to actual places and events is purely coincidental.

Parson's Porch Books is an imprint of Parson's Porch *&* Company (PP*&*C) in Cleveland, Tennessee. PP*&*C is an innovative organization which raises money by publishing books of noted authors, representing all genres. Its face and voice is **David Russell Tullock** (dtullock@parsonsporch.com).

Parson's Porch *&* Company *turns books into bread & milk* by sharing its profits with the poor.

www.parsonsporch.com

Beautiful Before God

Acknowledgments

In the spring of 2020, I was surprised to find myself unemployed, living in the middle of a global pandemic, and with lots of time on my hands. What to do?

Write a novel.

I'd done some writing before newspaper columns for the *Cleveland Plain Dealer* and the *Greensboro News & Record* newspapers, a few essays in magazines and biblical commentaries, and easily more a thousand sermons over the course of about thirty years as a pastor.

All well and good, but writing a novel was a different, larger literary critter for me--daunting but mostly fun. I've been inspired by Anne Lamott who once warned, "You're going to feel like hell if you wake up someday and you never wrote the stuff that is tugging on the sleeves of your heart…" Likewise, Kurt Vonnegut advised, "The arts are not a way to make a living. They are a very human way of making life more bearable. Practicing an art, no matter how well or badly, is a way to make your soul grow, for heaven's sake."

I hope this novel is entertaining. It's not a theological treatise; it's a love story with flawed characters who get into trouble—a lot. But for people who know me, you won't be shocked that the story (first draft completed just before Christmas 2020) at least touches on some of the great issues of our day.

I'm deeply grateful to my volunteer editor, Susan Bruce, who spent many hours improving the text and correcting errors that a professional novelist would not make. Thank you, Susan!

Thanks also to my friend, Mary Ellen Lawson, for examining one section of the novel for technical accuracy, and to David Tullock and Parson's Porch Books for their fine publishing work.

My family members and friends, especially my wife, Beth, have been sources of great encouragement and love. So, with thanksgiving and love, I dedicate this book to family and friends--expected and unexpected.

"…Belief is believing in God; faith is believing that God believes in you."
Andre Dubus

"...all courage was a form of constancy... it was always himself that the coward abandoned first. After this all-other betrayals came easily." Cormac McCarthy

"...Enemies are, of course, the necessary concomitant of any robust life, the very proof of its strength." John Irving

"At this time Moses was born, and he was beautiful before God..." Acts 7:20

Introduction

2020

The Rev. Dr. Moses "Mo" Campbell had been tossing and turning in bed for several hours. He rolled over once more, facing away from his wife who sighed because he had disturbed her sleep again. Then he reached over to his bedside table and turned his charging cellphone toward him—2:00 a.m. "Damn!" he thought, "Of all nights."

He tried taking long, slow, deep breaths. This didn't work. Next, he turned to counting backwards from 100. No luck. And then he prayed in silence, "Lord, I must be up by 6:00 a.m. to get ready for the meeting. You know I have a general idea of what I'm going to say, and I suspect it's going to get me into trouble. But I believe you want me to say it. So, I must say it. And I *will* say it. Now, on top everything else, with no sleep I'm already going to be exhausted, and probably have a headache. Could you help me out, Lord?"

Mo heard no answer, not a voice from heaven, not even a quiet, calming word in his head, just the sound of his wife beginning her soft snoring again. Damn! He finally drifted off to a fitful sleep around 3:00 a.m. and was awakened by the simultaneous vibration of the fitness tracker watch on his wrist and his cellphone's musical alarm that sounded like a marimba concert at 6:00 a.m.

"Good morning," said his wife in a voice as gentle as a cat's purr, "I'm going to stay in bed a few more minutes."

"Okay. Good morning," he mumbled. Groaning, he rubbed his tired scratchy eyes, rolled out of bed, stopped by the bathroom, and then headed to the kitchen where the coffeemaker, set for 5:45 a.m., had already brewed the first pot of Maxwell House. He downed his first cup of black coffee while scanning the newspaper on his iPad and eating a piece of whole wheat toast with butter and Smucker's peach preserves on it. Then he ate a bowl of Raisin Bran and knocked back the second cup of coffee and a glass of water and two ibuprofen tablets to try head off the mild headache that was already threatening to mushroom into a migraine thunderstorm. Looking at his watch, Mo knew he didn't have time for his morning run, but he decided to go for a quick walk outside, just ten minutes to clear his head and calm his nerves as he strode down country roads listening to the songbirds and crows and spying the occasional deer leaping and crashing through the roadside underbrush.

When he returned to the house, he showered, and put on black dress shoes, black slacks, and a dark blue dress shirt. His wife met him in the kitchen. "Don't you look nice," she said and gave him a longer than normal hug, and a kiss on the lips. Her last words before he grabbed his iPad and headed out the front door were, "Remember, I love you, and no matter what happens, I support you. We're in this together." "Thanks," he said as he looked into her eyes, "I love you too."

Mo climbed into his Toyota Prius, its odometer reading 197,856 miles. He thought, "If we pamper it, I'll bet we can another hundred thousand miles out of this baby."

The thirty-minute drive to First Presbyterian Church in Coopersville was smooth—light traffic, the sun coming up behind rolling hills. Farms with cows, horses, sheep, goats, alpacas, and chickens dotted the landscape. Mo listened to 80s pop music as he imagined what he might say and how others at the meeting might respond. He pictured himself speaking with a combination of passion and dignity he felt reflected the gravity of what was happening. And in his mind, he saw the other commissioners to the meeting listening carefully, nodding their heads in agreement, and then debating how they might move forward as a body of believers to address the grave danger that threatened the country and the world.

Mo was a pastor in the national denomination known as the Presbyterian Church (USA). It was one of the more progressive Christian denominations in the country, and Presbyterians in the U.S. had a long and remarkable history. Presbyterian colonists, with their distaste for royalty and their emphasis on freedom, had been so instrumental in instigating the American Revolution that it was also called, especially by British King George III, "The Presbyterian Rebellion." Modern-day Presbyterians used a representative democracy form of church government (polity) for their individual congregations and the larger denomination. It was no coincidence that it was like the United States' form of government. In fact, the Declaration of Independence and the U.S. Constitution had been influenced by Presbyterians with their stress on liberty, equality, and shared power, and their suspicion about dictatorship or monarchy. So Mo came by many of his political leanings and commitments as a logical extension of his heritage.

Worship prior to the meeting was set to commence at 9:30 a.m. sharp. And Mo pulled into the parking lot of First Presbyterian Church, Coopersville at 9:25 a.m. By the time he had signed in as a clergy commissioner, picked up paperwork for the meeting, said hello to a few friends, and made a quick restroom stop, the gathered worshipers had already finished the call to worship and the first hymn and were launching into the prayer of confession. "Crap!" thought Mo, as he squeezed into a pew in the back of the church, giving a sheepish nod to other folks in the pew. "Sorry," he mouthed softer than a whisper. The rest of the service proceeded without incident. When it came time for the sermon, he wasn't surprised when the preacher spoke about the need for "Christian unity." And Mo thought, "Yep, with everything that's going on right now, once again this is what we hear in a sermon, instead of actually addressing the real issues and the dangers we face." Though he tried to calm himself, Mo began to feel lightheaded, a sign that his blood pressure was rising like an overheated car radiator.

When the service ended, the Moderator said, "The 206th meeting of Good Shepherd Presbytery is now called to order." Good Shepherd Presbytery covered several neighboring counties and was a body of laity (ordained as elders) and clergy (ordained as ministers) that met several times a year at various churches to conduct church business and share ministries. Those who attended the meetings with the right to speak and vote were called "commissioners," and they were expected to vote their conscience, seeking to discern God's will rather than trying to please a constituency. The meetings themselves were somewhat formal and followed Roberts Rules of Order for the most part.

As usual, at this meeting the Moderator, the Rev. Angela Turnbull, had the Stated Clerk (who also served as Parliamentarian) certify a quorum. Requests for new business were considered. A docket for the meeting was adopted. First-time elder and minister commissioners were announced, asked to stand (if able), and then welcomed with polite applause. Special guests were introduced. Committee reports were made. Seminary students were examined as part of the ordination process. The names and faces changed, but the meetings were quite similar around the country. To an outside observer, it was like a meeting of Congress, except God, rather than the Constitution, was the guiding star around which everything was supposed to be considered. It was formal, because, as the Bible said, all things were to be done "decently and in order." And few denominations got the "decently and in order" part of meetings better than Presbyterians.

The Good Shepherd Presbytery meeting was moving along well. In fact, participants were pleased because some of the committee reports were shorter than usual, and the meeting itself was running fifteen minutes ahead of schedule. If things continued this way, maybe the meeting would adjourn ahead of schedule, and folks could head home early. Wouldn't that be nice?

The last report on the agenda before adjournment was the report of the Justice and Peacemaking Committee chaired by the Rev. Wilbert Wallace, an overweight, balding, good-natured, 60-something-year-old pastor who waddled down the church aisle to the microphone and arrived slightly out of breath from the walk. He began his report, highlighting efforts to address systemic racism, sexism, and discrimination against LGBTQ+ folks. He mentioned how a workshop on "Christian Unity in the Purple Church" had been well-received and had built deeper understanding in the presbytery. Mo noticed several people nodding in agreement. As Pastor Wallace concluded his report, the presbytery Moderator asked if there were any questions for him from the commissioners.

Mo stood and was recognized by the Moderator, who asked him to state his name and church. "I'm Mo Campbell, pastor of Memorial Drive Presbyterian Church in Sidwell. Bill, could you tell us what the committee is doing to respond to the ongoing dangerous and destructive behavior that is coming from President Trump and the elected officials who are enabling and covering for him?"

Bill's mouth dropped open, and he paused a moment before replying, "Um, well, our committee doesn't deal with partisan politics. We are a 'purple church,' you know. We explore larger issues in more nuanced ways…" His voice drifted off.

Mo jumped in, "Larger issues in more nuanced ways? Are you kidding me? This guy and his sycophants are doing everything in their power to destroy the planet and abolish democracy. Yet we say nothing. Our failure as this body of elected leaders in the church to hold President Donald J. Trump publicly accountable for the consistently immoral abuse of his office is nothing but cowardly bullshit and a damned shame."

As the words left his mouth, Mo was a bit surprised at his own word choices. He'd known he was going to speak, but he wasn't exactly certain what he was going to say until he said it. And now that he had said it, it felt like the moment when he was a teenager and he'd taken the first step off a twenty-foot cliff to leap into a local reservoir posted "Danger: No Swimming or Trespassing." There was that moment of exhilaration followed by "Uh oh. No going back now."

Meanwhile, the presbytery had its own feelings about what he'd said. Almost a full astonished second passed as the holy space was filled with the sounds of "Oh, my God!" and people gasping as if they had been doused with ice water. But then practically in choreographed unison, several ministers and elders leapt to their feet. Their voices echoed around the church sanctuary, bouncing off high ceilings, stained glass windows, and hardwood floors, as they asked to be recognized by the moderator.

"I stand for a point of order, Madam Moderator," said a stone-faced commissioner as he looked toward the Moderator who stood behind the pulpit, "I cannot believe the vulgar language I just heard in this sanctuary. The speaker is terribly out of order, and he owes this entire body a sincere apology."

"I agree," said the Moderator, giving a quick confirming glance at the Stated Clerk of the Presbytery. "Dr. Campbell, do you apologize?" she asked, locking her eyes on his.

Standing, Mo spoke, his voice quivering with anger, "No, Madam Moderator, I do not. I am not out of order. Our *presbytery* is out of order."

There were more gasps and murmurs, along with clergy and elders shaking their heads in amazement.

Another commissioner who stood nearby was recognized by the Moderator. He said, "Madam Moderator, this is not the first time Dr. Campbell has acted in such a disrespectful way towards this body. I move that this most recent incident be turned over to the Permanent Judicial Commission for consideration of formal ecclesiastical charges."

The Moderator said, "It has been moved that the Permanent Judicial Commission consider formal charges against Dr. Campbell. Is there a second to the motion?" Several voices rang out, "Second!"

"Is there any discussion before we vote?" asked the Moderator.

And there was much discussion, but we will come back to that.

Chapter 1

1965-1980

The Rev. Dr. Moses Witherspoon Campbell had always seemed a thorny fit for the ministry, what Presbyterians called "the Ministry of Word and Sacrament." For one thing, unlike many of his colleagues, he had not been reared in a family populated by generations of ministers, ministry thus sort of a continuation of "the family business," though always much more than that, of course.

Born in 1965, people sometimes did wonder how Moses got his name that seemed so appropriate for his profession. It wasn't because his parents thought he was destined to be a faith leader of any kind. Nor did he receive his name because his parents entertained any grandiose notions of his destiny. No. Their reasoning was more modest. Moses was named Moses because his pregnant mother had been reading the Bible one day, as her pastors had recommended, (she tried to read through the entire Bible every few years). And she came across this line in the Book of Acts, "At this time Moses was born, and he was beautiful before God…" "What a lovely phrase!" she whispered. Then she thought to herself that her baby would certainly be beautiful to her. So, surely he or she would also be beautiful before God. Moses' mother decided then and there that if her firstborn were a boy, she would like to name him Moses. And that's what she and her husband named their son, though most people called him Mo for short.

Mo grew up to become the very first minister in his family. So, he knew nothing of the various somber "pastor" voices and facial expressions that some of his contemporaries invoked on Sunday mornings or at funerals or weddings or in counseling sessions. Nor was he the recipient of insider recommendations to serve the largest and most prestigious congregations. And he had not grown up observing how to deflect the occasional disappointed or furious parishioner by offering a pliant clerical appeal, "I see your point. We'll just have to pray about this." Or how to answer a difficult question by not really answering the question, "Yes, that's certainly troubling. It will require lots of careful thought." These were not familial gifts passed down to Mo, and their absence became more and more obvious as his strange life unfolded and God's peculiar use of that life became clear.

But Mo did indeed come from a family of believers, and generally decent people, though they were not particularly observant about regular attendance in Sunday school and Sunday worship. They did not sit on any of the various congregational committees, much less the congregation's main governing body, known in their denominational tradition as "the session." Nor were they mixed up in the numerous church controversies and squabbles you might overhear from the mouths of unhappy parishioners.

Dear God, another sermon on increasing financial stewardship from the membership? Was Pastor McIntyre oblivious to what the congregation needed and wanted?

Did you hear how Nadine insulted Camilla at the Christian Education Committee meeting on Wednesday night? The tone of her voice--it was appalling.

Why is the Property Committee recommending the church spend so much money on a new sign by the road? For heaven's sake, everybody knows how to find the church!

The Campbells avoided all this church drama. Instead, a couple of times a month, three times if they were being especially dedicated, the family showed up for worship. They took seats not in the front pews, which seemed uncomfortably close, as if the preacher might suddenly ask them a question mid-sermon, though that would never happen. This was an educated, dignified Presbyterian church, not some backwoods, snake-handling, speaking in tongues, slain in the Spirit, hand-clapping bunch of zealots! But neither did the family sit on the back pew that tended to be occupied by congregants who wanted to make a quick getaway after the service to grab a restaurant table for lunch or head to the country club for a round of golf or a swim, though this was all frowned upon, being Sunday, after all.

So, the Campbells sat in the middle pews, not even really establishing a favorite pew, *their* pew as other church members sometimes claimed for themselves like western states pioneer frontier territory they had scouted by horseback and staked property rights upon with flags thrust into the earth. "I claim this pew for my clan!" No. They just took a spot somewhere in the middle of the sanctuary two or three times a month.

Sunday school held at 10:00 a.m., an hour before worship, was a similar undertaking for them. Two or three times a month, Mo's father, Stephen, an insurance agent for the Winnetka Insurance Company, and mother, Melinda, an elementary school teacher, might attend an adult class. But they rarely commented during the lesson, preferring instead to listen to what the teacher and the other participants might have to say. Mo and his elder sister, Tabitha (everybody called her Tabby) went to the classes for children, and, as they grew older, the youth class. As a small child, Tabby listened, sometimes wide-eyed to the various biblical stories and she asked questions. "What? You mean God decided to kill the whole world with a flood? Why? What could they have done that bad to get everybody killed, even the babies? And how did they get all the animals on the boat? And what did they do with all the animal pee and poop?"

Mo was different. During these children's Sunday school classes, he was inclined to look out the classroom windows to identify various robins, bluebirds, cardinals, sparrows, squirrels, chipmunks, and other wildlife that might be seen flying, hopping, or chittering about. He marveled at their boundless energy and constant movement, the intricacy and variety of their beauty, a rainbow of color moving outside the window, unplanned and uncontrolled by human beings. And they were certainly more interesting to him than what was being read and discussed. On one occasion, the teacher, Mrs. Goforth, stopped her Bible lesson in mid-sentence and said to Mo, "Moses Campbell, please get yourself focused on the Lord again." Surprised and embarrassed, Mo answered in a chastened, courteous voice, "Yes, ma'am. I'm sorry. I meant no disrespect. I was focusing on the ways God speaks through the creatures God made, but I'll also focus on the ways he speaks in the Bible."

As was the practice of Mrs. Goforth, at the beginning of each class, after the opening prayer, each student was expected to recite a Bible verse from memory. And once a particular verse had been recited by a class member that morning, the verse was considered taken, and not to be recited again that Sunday. Mo always silently prayed that nobody used "Jesus wept" (the shortest verse in the Revised Standard Version of the New Testament) before he had a chance to say it, because he was hard-pressed to come up with another verse. As a back-up selection, he sometimes quoted Psalm 24:1, "The earth is the Lord's." In Mo's view, generally Sunday school was something to be endured, not so much as say, prisoner of war camp torture but more like regular cleanings of his teeth by the dental hygienist, Sally, whose busty beauty almost completely offset the unpleasantness of the twice-yearly task. Almost.

Only once in his early years in church did Mo ever recall having what Christian theologians might categorize as a clear "revelatory experience of the holy." And, of all times, it came as part of the mundane of church life, what was called the confirmation process. During this six-month period conducted every two years, the confirmands, mainly students in the 8th and 9th grade, received additional Christian instruction on Wednesday evenings 6:00-7:30 (a meal included). They prepared to confirm their faith publicly and become active church members, as well as ready to receive Holy Communion in worship for the first time. Confirmands learned the essentials of Presbyterian church history, theology, and worship, the Bible, and a bit about their own congregation--First Presbyterian Church of Dover, South Carolina, established in 1833, a congregation of about 200 members in a town of around 13,000 people, located in the "Upstate" (western) section of South Carolina, the third oldest church in town just behind the Southern Baptists and the United Methodists whose churches were not only established earlier but now were much larger.

At the end of the confirmation process, the students were required to meet with the session. It was comprised of the pastor, Dr. McIntyre, and twelve respected laypersons in the church who were ordained as elders. The confirmands were to be examined about the "historic faith" of the church universal, Presbyterian beliefs and practices, and their own faith. Mo had heard that the session members, especially Dr. McIntyre, sometimes asked questions designed to trick you. He'd even heard rumor from Tabby that one year a confirmation student was voted down by the session because he had not memorized all the ancient Apostles' Creed and some elders thought he exhibited "a bad attitude." (None of this was true. The session members themselves were often forgetful of Presbyterian beliefs and what it meant to be a Presbyterian. *How many sacraments do Presbyterians celebrate? Seven. Oops. I mean, two. What are the original languages in which the Bible was written? Latin and Greek. No. Hebrew and Greek, with a few phrases of Aramaic thrown in for good measure.*)

In fact, in the more than 140 years of the congregation's existence, the thought of rejecting a confirmand for lack of knowledge or bad attitude had never crossed a single session member's mind, even for a millisecond. The session members (mostly people in their 60s, 70s, and 80s with a few "young people" under 60 sprinkled in) were just happy to see some kids joining the church. But Mo knew none of this, and he prepared for the session's examination poring over his notes and study materials as if his very soul were somehow at stake.

The evening of the examination finally arrived, and the confirmation class and the session assembled in First Presbyterian Church's fellowship hall. It was a large room with stained glass windows featuring a variety of biblical scenes (Jesus teaching large crowds from a boat, Jesus "The Good Shepherd" carrying a sheep, little children surrounding Jesus and being blessed by him). There were a couple of long wooden fold-out tables prone to pinching your fingers during set-up and take-down. And in the corners of the room were a few strategically placed massive wooden chairs that looked like thrones complete with worn maroon velvet seats and ornate hand-carved, high-rise wooden backs and arms. Nobody sat in these chairs during meetings. That would have seemed vain. But they remained in the room as historical pieces and could be moved and used for Vacation Bible School plays or for the annual Christmas pageant.

Mo and his father and mother arrived around 6:45 for the meeting scheduled to begin at 7:00. Don Thompson, one of the other two confirmands was already there with his family. He slouched in his chair at the table, gave a "what's up?" nod and flashed a crooked grin at Mo.

"How ya doing, Mo?" he asked.

"Fine," said Mo, "a little nervous."

"You're kidding, right? Nothing to it."

"I hope you're right."

"Have you ever known *any*body to be turned down?"

"Well, no, but I've heard it happened one time."

"That's a bunch of bull. Stay cool."

"Okay."

At 6:58, Bob Sullivan. and his family rushed in, a little out of breath, but with relieved smiles. "Down to the wire," said Dr. McIntyre, laughing along with Bob's parents. Bob puffed his cheeks and blew out his breath as he sat down and gave a nod to Don and Mo, who nodded and smiled. At exactly 7:00, Dr. McIntyre said, "This meeting of the session of First Presbyterian Church is now called to order. We extend a special word of welcome to our confirmands and their families. We're glad you're here and we're honored by your presence. Let's begin our time with prayer. Let us pray. O Lord, you have created everything that is, seen and unseen. And you have created us, your children, just a little lower than the angels, full of the potential to adore you and serve you. We gather now with these confirmands. They have spent these months learning about you and your word, about your holy church, and about their solemn responsibilities as followers of Jesus Christ. You know their hearts and minds completely, O God. As we gather and engage in examination, give us, finite, sinful people that we are, a sense of their hearts and minds as well. We pray it all in your blessed name. Amen."

In the middle of this prayer, Mo noticed cold sweat dripping from his underarms onto his undershirt. And at the same time, he became aware of a presence he could not name, familiar yet alien at the same time, and some sort of electricity in the air. And then he felt his attention concentrated as the questions were asked, a seriousness mingled with a kind of gladness and peace, a sense of reality beneath the reality he normally experienced. This sensation only lasted for a few moments and then things went back to normal. But for a while, something was different. And he would remember this feeling for the rest of his life and notice that it returned from time to time, not something that he could conjure up by sheer force of will but something that came unbidden and startling. A presence in the future that would sometimes humble him, other times move him to tears in gratitude, and still other times stir in him a barely controlled rage about injustice.

After the examination ended, Dr. McIntyre looked out at the gathered elders who made up the session, and he asked, "If there are no further questions, is there a motion that these confirmands be accepted into membership?"

"So moved," said elder Bob Stephenson.

"Is there a second?" asked Dr. McIntyre.

"Second," said elder Mary White.

"Is there any discussion?" asked Dr. McIntyre. He gave a cursory glance at the group and then said, "Hearing none, all those in favor of the motion, say 'Aye.'"

"Aye," said all the elders.

"Any opposed?" asked the pastor. No one spoke. And Dr. McIntyre said, "The motion carries. Congratulations and welcome!" The gathered elders broke into applause.

Don looked at Mo and said, "See, what did I tell you? Nothing to it." Mo said, "Yeah, you were right. No big deal."

Chapter 2

1980

The following fall, now a 10th grader, Mo graduated from the junior high school Sunday school class to the senior high school class, and his attention shifted. He no longer looked out the window as much. Now he spent his time in typical teenage boy fashion--silently weighing the physical merits of the girls in the class with him. He was impressed by the three 10th grade girls who sat together across from him. There was Regina Stuart with her wide blue eyes always appearing to be astonished, long blonde hair, round face, accompanied by strikingly large breasts. She was the quietest of the three. Beside her sat brown-eyed Denise Townsend; she had a petite upturned nose and a thin mouth, along with a slim figure. She was a bit more talkative than Regina. And then there was Annie McDonald, red hair, and blue eyes (which Mo later learned is the rarest hair and eye color combination in the world), dimpled cheeks, narrow nose, and a beautiful curvy shape. She was easily the most outgoing of the three girls.

But what was truly remarkable about Annie was not her physical appearance; it was the way she related to Mo.

"Hey, Mo!" she would whisper with a wicked little smile during class when the teacher was turned around while writing on the blackboard, "I see you looking over here. Whatcha looking at? You gettin' your eyes full?"

Mo reddened, pursed his lips, and said nothing as he looked at the floor while shaking his head side to side. He thought, "Yeah, you caught me looking at you, but you don't know what I'm thinking. My thoughts are one thing I can always keep private if I want to. But maybe one day I'll tell you what I was thinking."

For a couple of weeks, the Sunday school class studied the Book of Exodus. They concentrated on the section in which God speaks to Moses in a burning bush telling him he has observed the suffering of the Israelites held in slavery. The teacher, Mrs. Peterson, said, "Notice the strange twists and turns of the story. God calls Moses to tell the cruel Pharaoh 'Let my people go!' But Moses whines to God, says he isn't good at public speaking, and that he stutters. Finally, God gets so exasperated at him that he says, 'Fine! Your brother Aaron can be the spokesman!' So, Moses and Aaron go to Pharaoh (sort of a group effort), but for some reason the Bible does not say anything about Aaron doing any talking to Pharaoh. Does Moses suddenly discover some courage on the way to the meeting? We don't know. All the Bible records is Moses and Pharaoh talking, and God sending plagues, each one worse than the other, whenever Pharaoh changes his mind about releasing the Israelites. And it all ends with the final plague—the terrible deaths of the Egyptian first-born--and then Moses leading the Israelites through the Red Sea to freedom and eventually to the brink of the Promised Land. It's a Promised Land Moses will see from a distance, but not be allowed to enter himself. Troubling, isn't it?"

"'Troubling' is a mild way of putting it for the Egyptians *and* for Moses too," thought Mo.

After class was over Mo passed the three girls in the church hallway, "Hey, Moses!" Annie yelled, her voice sing-songy and laughing. "If you want us to get out of the way, just hold your hands up high and part the Red Sea!" She raised her hands above her head, motioning the sea to open. And Mo, his face now crimson again, stammered, "So, so funny, Annie." But this just encouraged her. "Is that all you've got to say? Maybe you could get your brother Aaron to speak for you. Moses, do you have a big staff?" And so it went, Annie picking on Mo and flirting with him at the same time.

Chapter 3

Annie was an exceptional high school student, particularly in English classes. She eventually became editor of the school newspaper, "The Dover Dabbler," and a member of the tennis team. She was feared especially for her fierce backhand that caught more than one slack-jawed opponent holding her racket to defend against catching a tennis ball in the face. Annie also won second runner up in the homecoming court, losing out only to Margaret Sullivan (1st runner up) and Susan Leslie, the homecoming queen, whose legendary form earned her the whispered, unofficial title of "a woman among girls."

Annie dated a little bit, usually going out with guys she found interesting, not just handsome, or athletic. But she and Mo never went out. He was too nervous to ask her, preferring instead to ask girls he assumed were less likely to turn him down. Yet for all Mo's shyness, he kept an eye on Annie. And though she would not have admitted it at the time, she kept an eye on him too.

In the summer after high school graduation, Mo and Annie ran into each other at an end-of-summer party held in early August. Normally, the two travelled in different social circles (Annie with the popular kids and Mo with the kids who were not exactly outcasts, but not popular either). This party was being thrown by several parents of kids who were getting ready to head off to college, and Mo was invited because he had been on a few dates with Regina from the church Sunday school class. Mo and Regina got along ok, but both knew nothing serious would develop between them, because their conversations were often filled with long awkward silences. Still, instead of being lonely, it was nice enough just to have somebody to hang around with and to make out with. Later in life, it occurred to Mo that he and Regina had not only enjoyed a friendship but learned a little bit about sex from each other. Rather than something to regret, their mutual fumblings were times for patient teaching each other about sexuality.

The party was being held at a firehall rented by the parents, who also tried to operate as discrete chaperones—in the background enough that the kids could enjoy themselves, but visible enough that they did not enjoy themselves too much. Mo showed up wearing a dark sport jacket, with a white shirt (collar up), bowtie, black pants, and black shoes. Regina (a fan of Madonna) arrived in a black sequined top that was no match for her bosom that threatened at any moment to explode from its temporary detention center.

She also wore a black skirt that strained at its seams, and sparkling silver stiletto heels that not only accentuated her hip movements but also made her every step seem like a tightrope walk adventure.

Mo and Regina greeted each other with a quick hug.

Mo said, "How's it going?"

"Good," said Regina, "And how are you?"

 "Good," he said. These were some of the highlights of their conversation.

They waved and said hello as other kids came in, some almost immediately dancing, others taking places standing along the walls or situated near the refreshments and punch bowl. The deejay played "Billie Jean" by Michael Jackson and "Every Breath You Take" by The Police. Regina's energetic dancing to each song placed her clothing in jeopardy. Safer were the slow songs, "Tonight, I Celebrate My Love" by Roberta Flack and "We've Got Tonight" by Kenny Rogers.

Then, right on schedule, the deejay decided to play "YMCA" by the Village People. And everybody belted out the refrain, complete with letters formed by arm motion, "It's fun to stay at the Y-M-C-A!" It was that first Y jabbing upward movement that provided Regina's bosom its long-awaited freedom as the top button of her blouse popped off, exposing a black lacy bra. Before most people realized what had happened, Regina pulled her top together in front of her with one hand and hurried to the ladies room.

Mo decided this might be a good time to get some punch and snacks. But as he headed toward the table, the deejay switched to another slow song "Hello" by Lionel Richie, and Mo felt a tap on his back. He turned and there stood Annie.

"Wanna dance?" she asked.

"Uh. Yeah, that'd be good" he said.

Annie led him to the dance floor and offered her hand. Mo wasn't much of a dancer but at least knew how to do the modified slow dance of holding his partner's hand with his left hand and holding her close to him with his right around her waist.

As they shuffled around in a slow circle, Annie stood closer to Mo than she had ever been, and he smelled her perfume and noticed the fullness of her lips. It made him a little bit disoriented, and it took him a moment to realize she had asked him a question.

She said, "So, what're you doing in the fall?"

"What?" he asked.

"What are you doing in the fall?" she repeated.

"College," he said.

"Yeah, I figured you might be," she said. "Where are you going? And what are you majoring in?"

"I'm going to Garden College in Charleston and majoring in biology."

"As much as you love animals, I'm not surprised," she said. "Are you and Regina going to keep dating?"

"Well, you know Regina is heading off to USC in Columbia. So, I don't think we'll see too much of each other. We've already decided to just be friends and see other people. So, who knows how that'll go? I think I'm going to be busy anyway—running cross country in the fall and track in the spring, working part-time, the usual. What about you?"

"I'm going to Garden College too, majoring in English," she said.

"No way! How cool," he said. "I know you're into literature, and I like the things you've put in 'The Dabbler.' You have a way of being funny, but also making me think."

"Thanks," she said, smiling. Then, still smiling, she gave him a sideways glance. "You know I like to pick on you because I like you, right?"

"Yeah, I thought so, or at least I hoped so," he said.

"Do you know why I like you?" she asked.

"Um. I'm not sure," he said.

"Because you're kind and you tell the truth," she said.

"Thanks," he said. "I try."

The music for their slow dance ended, and Annie said, "Keep in touch, okay?"

"Okay," he answered, as Regina emerged from the restroom, her top now reinforced with several industrial strength safety pins. Her head shaking side to side, she walked over.

"You alright?" Annie asked.

"Yeah, I'm so embarrassed, but fine otherwise," said Regina exhaling and rolling her eyes.

"I was keeping Mo warm for you," said Annie.

"I appreciate that," said Regina, laughing. "Somebody needs to."

Chapter 4

1983

Mo and Annie did not see each other again that summer. In the fall, they both enrolled at Garden College in Charleston. As an English major who also happened to have parents who were grammar sticklers, Annie tested out of having to take English 101 (basic English grammar). And she leapt right into several literature and composition courses, a heavy load for a freshman, but she still found time to date a little. First, there was Andrew, a thin, pale, bespectacled, fellow redhead in her Introduction to English Composition class. He managed to get a date with Annie by accidentally knocking her books off her desk as he squeezed by her to find a seat in the lecture hall. "Oops! Sorry!" led to "Hey, could I make it up to you by taking you to dinner on Friday?"

After a few dates with Andrew, there was Ryan--olive-complexion, beefy, dark-haired, and a member of the wrestling team. He liked to wear t-shirts a size too small to show off his biceps, shoulders, and chest muscles ("pecs," as he called them while flexing). At first, he seemed to have a genuine interest in Annie. "What made you decide to become an English major? Who's your favorite author? What's your favorite book?" But soon daily conversations were dominated by his reciting of how many pounds he'd curled, benched, squatted, overhead pressed, and how many repetitions, and how sore he was, details about his matches, and endless talk about the need "to make weight" for his next bout. And though he was pleasant enough, Annie just wasn't that interested.

And then there was Greg. He was a U.S. history major, a lacrosse player from New York State, and athletic without feeling the need to talk about his fitness daily. He and Annie enjoyed conversations not only about what was happening in the world but even some crossover talk about the development of the English language in America, and how U.S. history helped shape U.S. language and how the language influenced U.S. history. Annie felt a connection with Greg that she had not felt with anyone else she had dated. She began to trust him. And finally, on a Friday night not long before the Christmas break, Greg asked his roommate to be out of the dorm room for a few hours so that he could be alone with Annie. And he and Annie made love for the first time.

After exams, Annie headed back to Dover and Greg left for New York State. And not long after Annie and Greg returned to campus, Annie missed her period. She was a little bit worried, but figured it was unlikely she was pregnant. After all, they'd used a contraceptive. But finally, after a few anxious days, Annie bought a home pregnancy test, and it came back positive. Her heart skipped a beat, but she immediately tried to calm herself down thinking, "I probably didn't do the test right. Besides, I've heard that sometimes these things are not that accurate." But after a few more days, she visited the campus health center and the doctor confirmed that Annie was indeed pregnant.

She felt nauseated at the news. It didn't seem real, more like a bad dream she expected to wake from any moment. She prayed in silence, "Dear God, help me. Show me what I should do."

During an evening walk around the campus, Annie told Greg.

Greg said, "Pregnant? Are you sure? We only did it once, and we used protection."

"Yeah, I know," she said, "but protection doesn't always work and once is all it takes."

Greg scowled, silent for a moment. Then he said, "Well, I'm not ready to be a father. You need to take care of it."

"Fine! I will," Annie said, her eyes flashing. "Thanks a lot." Hurt and anger swarmed and buzzed like an enraged nest of wasps inside her, and she turned to go.

"Wait," he called, "I can help a little." But she ignored him, and kept walking away, back to her dorm room. She tried to study a little, but it was hard to concentrate. Finally, around midnight she went to bed, but she kept remembering and replaying Greg's comment, "You need to take care of it." He obviously didn't give a damn about her. "Why didn't I see that before?" she asked herself over and over before she finally was able to sleep a few hours.

The next afternoon Annie drove home to Dover. She had grown up in a modest ranch house in a middle-class neighborhood. Her father was a postal worker, and her mother was a guidance counselor at the high school. After dinner with her parents, Annie sat on the couch in the living room, and told them what had happened. They both seemed stunned for a few seconds. Then Annie's dad sighed and spoke first.

"We love you," he said, glancing at Annie, and then nodding at his wife. "We're disappointed, but we love you and we'll support you and the baby. Would you like to keep it, or would you like to put it up for adoption?"

Annie said nothing for a few seconds.

Then she said, "Neither."

"Neither? What are you talking about?" said her father, his voice rising.

"I want… I want to get an abortion," said Annie.

"An abortion?" said her father and mother at the same time.

"Yes," said Annie. "Greg's not committed to me. And this is not the time for me to have a baby. I've thought about it, and prayed about it, and I'm going to get an abortion."

"Out of the question," said her father.

"It's my body," she said.

"But it's more than your body," said her mother.

"Yes, but it's *in* my body," she answered, "And it's my choice."

"It's a sin," said her mother.

"I don't know if that's true, mom. I just don't know. But maybe it's a sin for me to have a baby I'm not ready for, a baby whose father isn't ready for it either, a baby we aren't ready to love yet."

"Well, we won't pay for an abortion," said her father.

"Okay," Annie said, her jaw set and her eyes brimming with tears. She rose to her feet. "Then I'll have to find the money some other way. Good night." She went to her room and closed the door. Breathing fast, the tears now escaping her eyes, she tried to calm herself down by taking slow deep breaths, and softly repeating, "I'm going to be okay. I'm going to be okay." After a few minutes, Annie got ready for bed. She read a little in her Bible, and came across a passage that spoke to her, "Hear my prayer, O Lord; let my cry come to you. Do not hide your face from me in the day of my distress. Incline your ear to me; answer me speedily in the day when I call." Psalm 102:1-2. "That's my prayer," she thought. "I'm going to be okay," she said again. Finally, she put the book down, and around 1:00 a.m. fell into a fitful sleep.

The next day, after her father and mother had gone to work, Annie went into their bedroom. She knew where they kept emergency money in a small metal tin in their closet hidden inside one of her dad's old army boots that he never wore anymore. Typically, there was $300 in it. She took $200, figuring that if her parents checked, they would still see some money there on top and not investigate further.

Annie phoned her Sunday school friend, Denise Townsend. Denise had stayed closer to home to go to Simpson County Community College and get an associate's degree in business administration. She did this partly to placate her overwrought parents struggling with the reality that their only daughter was all grown up. She also hoped a couple of years at a community college would save her some money. Denise not only planned to transfer to a four-year college for her bachelor's, but she planned to try to squeeze a little more cash from her parents to help with graduate school, especially if she promised to go somewhere nearby.

"Hey Denise, it's Annie. How are you?" she said, trying to sound normal.

"I'm fine," said Denise. "How are you? Are you loving Charleston? I'm *so* jealous."

"Charleston's great. It's so beautiful and there's so much to do," she said.

"That's right. Rub it in," said Denise chuckling. "What else is going on? You dating some cute guys?"

"Um, Denise," said Annie, her voice breaking, "I'm in trouble."

"What? What's going on?"

"I don't want to talk about it over the phone. Can I come over?"

"Of course. I don't have any classes today."

"I'll be over in about 15 minutes."

"Okay."

Annie pulled her little green Ford into the driveway of a two-story colonial-style house with white siding. Denise met her at the front door. She immediately noticed that instead of being met by typical Annie—happy, confident, and ready with snappy comments--the person at her door had bloodshot eyes filled with tears. Denise swept Annie into her arms in a big hug, and thought, "This must be bad." After a few moments she said, "Oh, you poor thing. Come on inside." Denise led Annie to a chair in the kitchen and gave her a cup of tea.

"Okay. What in the hell is going on?" she asked.

Annie sniffled, but finally got her breath and said, "I'm pregnant."

"Oh, damn," said Denise.

"Yeah," said Annie.

"Well, you know I love you, girl."

"I know," said Annie. "And I love you too."

"So, what are you going to do?" asked Denise. "Because you know I'm with you whatever you're planning."

"I don't want to keep it," she said. "It's not the right time for me, and the guy I had sex with isn't ready to become a father either. I just want to end this pregnancy."

"You mean you want an abortion?" asked Denise, her eyes widening a little.

"Yeah."

Denise took a deep breath, paused a beat, and then asked, "How can I help? Do you need me to drive you down to the clinic?"

"Yeah. Would you do it? I know it's a lot to ask."

"Of *course*, I'm your friend," Denise said, leaning her head to the side.

"But you know the protesters will be there, and they'll have lots of nasty things to say," said Annie, sighing and then pausing to take a sip of tea.

"I'll bet they will," said Denise, crossing her arms, "But I'm not afraid of those twits with their signs and hateful comments. Bunch of damn hypocrites."

"Yep," said Annie rolling her eyes as she imagined the scene. "You're a good friend. You're the best"

"I know," said Denise with a slight smile. And Annie gave a small laugh.

Annie had called the day before for an appointment. And just before lunch, they arrived at the women's clinic--a plain-looking one-story brick building attached to some other offices. On the front window it read, "Planned Parenthood." As they got out of the car, a few protestors met them outside in the parking lot. A middle-aged woman, heavy makeup, and her dark hair in a bouffant, held a sign with a photo of a late stage aborted fetus on it. She shouted, "Mother, don't kill your baby! Look! See who you'd be killing! Please don't kill your baby!"

But Annie saw things differently than this woman and the other protesters. A couple of years earlier, she had visited her mom's sister, Aunt Hazel, who had lived in New York City since the 1960s. Her aunt was a liberal Christian, a free spirit, an artist, a painter who specialized in watercolors. She supplemented her income by waitressing at an Italian restaurant in Manhattan. Aunt Hazel had no children of her own, but her level of interest in Annie measured somewhere between parental and big-sisterly. She celebrated Annie's every success, no matter how minor, and listened to her life's adventures with the intensity of a child sitting beside a campfire, hearing a ghost story. Annie enjoyed their visits, but she especially looked forward to time with Aunt Hazel whenever Annie's own life was running dry. Then, her aunt's attention was like a spring rainstorm that causes the desert landscape to explode into a flowery paradise, as if by some sort of timelapse magic.

One evening, they sat in Hazel's tiny apartment kitchen after dinner, eating mint chocolate chip ice cream, laughing, and telling stories. Then her aunt took Annie's hands in hers and looked her in the eye.

"Annie, my dear," she said, her voice gone suddenly serious, "I'm going to tell you something hard that I want you to remember."

"Oh, okay," said Annie, puzzled and her voice hushed. She looked her aunt up and down for signs of any illness. "I hope you're alright."

"Oh, I am. Don't worry," said her aunt with a kind smile, her voice gone soft and steady. She continued. "Many years ago, when I was a young woman, I had gone on a date with this guy I'd met at the restaurant. He was a little older than I, but he was good looking, had a nice sense of humor, and we hit it off on our first date. So we were all set to go on a second date. He asked me to meet him at his apartment so he could give me a quick tour of the place, and then we were going to leave from there to go to dinner and a movie. But as soon as I came in the door, I started getting a bad feeling from him. He smelled like he'd already been drinking a lot. He began to show me around the apartment, room by room. But then suddenly he got aggressive, and said 'Baby, just gimme a taste before we go out.' And he pushed me into his bedroom, pinned me to the bed, and raped me. Afterwards, he got dressed, acted like nothing had happened, and said, 'Thanks, baby. You about ready to go get some dinner?' Well, I threw my clothes on, ran from the apartment, and took a cab home. I never went to the police. I figured I was a grown woman, and I was so ashamed that I hadn't been more careful. For years and years, I blamed myself, until I finally realized it wasn't my fault at all. It was his fault, just his.

"Within a few weeks, I also realized I was pregnant. Through some of my co-workers, I found a medical school dropout and paid him $200 to perform the abortion in a makeshift operating room in his apartment. The place was a pigsty, I guess from the remnants of previous abortions, and it stunk like a sewer. The guy was a creep who felt me up as part of what he said was a 'preparatory medical exam.' And then the abortion itself hurt like hell. After it was over, I went home, bleeding heavily. And soon I developed a raging infection and spiking fever and ended up in the hospital. Doctors managed to save my life, but they said I would never be able to have children."

Annie's eyes had filled with tears, and she said, "Aunt Hazel, that's awful. I'm so sorry."

"Thanks, Annie," said her aunt in a gentle voice. "I'm doing okay now, but it's been a hard journey."

Annie nodded. "I can't imagine," she said. She paused a moment, her mind racing, and then she said, "Aunt Hazel, I'm not judging you, but I'm wondering something. After you found out you were pregnant, did you ever consider keeping the baby or putting it up for adoption?"

"No," said her aunt, shaking her head, her voice firm but calm. "And if I had been forced to bear by rapist's child, I would have felt as though I had been raped again, over, and over. Annie, I know you are religious, and I am too. I don't believe that as soon as a sperm and an egg come together in conception there's a human being. And I know there's nothing in the Bible that says that either. I just cannot imagine God would have wanted me to be forced to deliver. I don't think God would have wanted that for me or for the child. And people who say pregnancy from rape is somehow part of 'God's plan,' and 'we just need to accept it,' make me want to vomit. Annie, I told you this story, because I don't want you ever to forget. Yes, you belong to God. But in this life, at least, your body belongs to you, and what goes on in your body is your decision. And nobody else's."

So when the protester with the bouffant yelled at her, Annie thought, "Lady, you have no idea. You don't know me. You don't know my story." She was tempted to shout something back at the woman, because though she felt what was growing in her was more than just a few random cells, it was also miniscule, an embryo, and not a full-fledged person. It was a being with the potential to become a person. And Annie thought that every person born deserved to be truly wanted and loved, not just tolerated, or heaven forbid, hated, and mistreated as some unwanted children were. So, she heard the woman's comments, but she did not accept them as true. "Big hair lady, you have no clue," she thought. And Annie did not answer her. Other voices cried out a cacophony of abuse. "Whore!" "Slut!" "You're going to hell! Turn around before it's too late."

Annie and Denise kept moving, though after another person yelled, "You'll never forgive yourself!" Denise slowed and started to turn and shout something back. But under her breath Annie said to her, "It's okay. She's wrong. Let's keep going." And then they were ushered inside the clinic by a volunteer.

Denise took a seat in the waiting area. Annie walked up to the sign-in window, filled out the required paperwork, paid with cash, then sat down beside Denise, thumbing through magazines, not really reading them, just glancing at pictures and headlines. After about ten minutes, a nurse came out into the waiting room and said, "Annie?"

Annie stood, and Denise stood with her and asked, "Do you want me to come back with you?"

"No. Thanks. I'm fine," she said, her voice steady.

"Okay, if you're sure," said Denise.

"I am," she said. "I'll see you in a little bit. You're a good friend."

"I know," said Denise. She and Annie smiled.

Annie walked back with the nurse, changed into a gown, climbed onto the medical table, and put her feet into the exam stirrups for the procedure. The doctor, a slim, fifty-something-year-old man with salt and pepper hair, came in and explained details of the process and how Annie might feel later.

Giving her a kind look he asked, "Do you have any questions?"

"No," she said, her voice softer than she expected.

"Are you ready?" he asked.

"Yes," she said.

"Okay," he said and moved into place, "You're going to feel some pressure. Try to keep breathing and it won't hurt as much, and we'll be finished quickly."

Annie kept breathing. She did feel some pressure, something like a menstrual cramp, then worse, and then it was all over. She got her release instructions, (a little cramping and spotting were to be expected, but no heavy bleeding).

Then she put on her clothes and went to the waiting area where Denise gave her a little hug.

"How're you doing, hon?" asked Denise.

"I'm okay," said Annie, suddenly feeling very tired. "Could I stay at your house tonight?"

"Absolutely," said Denise.

The next day, Annie drove back to Garden College, picked up missed assignments from her professors, and continued with her studies. As she thought about the abortion over the next few days and weeks, she did not feel guilt. She still believed the embryo was a potential human life, but not actually a full-fledged human being already. And she reasoned that if she had been wrong and had taken human life with the abortion, then this person (he or she) was now safe in the arms of God. And Annie had always learned in church that she herself was imperfect, a child of God trying to make the right decisions, sometimes getting things right and sometimes failing, but no matter what, she too was safe with God.

Chapter 5

After a few weeks back at college, Annie began to date again. Her relationships were now more casual than before. And though some of the guys she went out with urged her to sleep with them, she decided she would not agree to that level of intimacy until she felt a deeper level of trust and commitment in the relationship. And she kept her heart guarded with a wrought-iron fence around it.

Annie never learned how word got out, but as the semester went on, rumors began swirling around campus that she had gotten an abortion. Over time she was viewed as a tramp by some of the co-eds who came from fundamentalist Christian traditions that made no allowance for abortion, even in cases of rape or incest. Annie saw the furtive glances and heard the whispers from female students. "There's abortion girl."

With some of the male students she became even more of a potential bedroom conquest. Their strange and stupid reasoning was that if Annie had had an abortion as the rumors claimed, then she must be promiscuous, wild in bed, and would probably do just about anything. At least that was their twisted way of thinking. In truth, Annie was comfortable with her body, and refused to accept being treated with contempt in bed or anywhere else for that matter. Her faith had taught her that she was precious, and her sexuality was a good thing, not something shameful.

But between the catty behavior of the fundamentalist women and the predatory attitudes of the men, Annie's life became an open-air prison of stress and loneliness. Fewer people related to her at all. And her circle of female friends that had been easy-going and fun, gradually disintegrated, as her friends got tired of being around someone who had lost most of her joy.

Annie dated rarely as she viewed the men around her with suspicion about their true motives. So, she focused more and more on her studies, especially her writing. She used her pain as a burning fuel for her poetry and short stories. And Annie's professors were astonished at the depth of writing that came from such a young person. They did not know the terrible price she had paid for each word she wrote.

One night, Annie came back to her dorm room after putting in several hours of study in the library working on a short story. As she came down the dorm hallway, she noticed many of the doors to the rooms were uncharacteristically closed. Then she saw why. On her dorm room door someone had written in bright red lipstick BABY KILLER!

Annie felt the adrenaline kick in and her heart began beating wildly in her chest. She heard muffled laughter from behind some of the doors. And for just an instant she was afraid. But then she wasn't.

She turned towards some of the closed doors and yelled, "Any of you coward so-called *Christians* want to say something to my face? Here I am!"

There was some whispering behind the doors, but no doors opened.

"Here I am!" she yelled again.

She waited, then opened her door and stepped into her room, slamming the door behind her. Breathing hard, she fought back tears of rage. *Who did they think they were? What made them think they knew her and that they had the right to control her decisions?* She was so angry she wanted to hit someone. But hitting was not in her nature. And gradually she was able to take some deep breaths and slow down a little bit. There was some Budweiser in the mini fridge that she and her roommate, Clara, shared. Her hands shaking, Annie took one out and drank it down in four gulps. Then she took a white washcloth, wetted from the bathroom sink, and wiped the words off her door, leaving the washcloth streaked with red.

Annie went to bed around midnight. She tossed and turned as she kept thinking of what she wanted to say to the cowards. But around 2:00 a.m. she finally fell asleep, and in her dreams instead of reproach or threat, she felt God's peace. When Annie awoke at 6:00 a.m. she had a sense that God had something for her to do. She wasn't sure what it was yet. But she knew God had something for her to do.

Over the rest of the semester, other messages, about one a week, were scrawled on Annie's dorm room door. "Slut." "Whore." "Going to hell." And several the fundamentalist women students continued with a campaign of whispered insults, snickering, sideways glances, and ostracism.

Chapter 6

As a biology major, Mo had no classes with Annie, but word of the abortion and how other students were treating her eventually got back to him, and he was enraged. Mo was acquainted with the wildly inconsistent behavior of fundamentalist Christians. He'd observed that they could be some of the most generous people you could imagine. *A tornado swooped down and destroyed your home? How terrible! We'll help you rebuild, and in the meantime, come and live with us. You don't have food or clothing? Here, have some of ours.*

Then there was what the fundamentalists called "missions" or "mission." As far as Mo could tell, often this seemed to mean sending missionaries or regular church members to poor countries to tell others about the gospel of Jesus Christ by helping with building projects, such as churches or houses, or providing food, clothing, and money. But it also meant handing out evangelism pamphlets and Bible tracts with scary pictures and dire warnings about God's judgment. This included talking to passersby on street corners about the consequences of failing to make a verbal confession of Jesus as Lord before it was too late. There might be a revival event held in a large public space, such as a stadium. Sweaty preachers pointed fingers, shouted about God's love, and threatened listeners with eternal hell, unless they "got right with God," and "made a decision for Christ before it's too late" and thus "got saved."

Even at 18 years of age, this emphasis on eternal damnation for people who'd not made a spoken confession of faith in Jesus seemed bizarre and cruel to Mo. "What about Jews?" he thought. "We were always taught in church that they are God's chosen people. Are they just out of luck? And what about Muslims and Buddhists, and all the other religions, and even atheists?" He had an atheist friend who had moved down from Ohio. He was a nice guy, but had zero interest in going to church with Mo. Was a loving God going to send him to hell to burn in agony forever? It made no sense to Mo.

On the other hand, what was a loving God to do with especially wicked people--the child rapist and murderer, the prison cell torturer applying electric shocks to a shrieking young woman, the war criminal committing genocide, the embezzler stealing a retired couple's life savings? Would there be no consequence for them, and others like them? Would they simply cease to exist--poof? Or would they waltz into heaven? Mo didn't know. But he knew he hated the arrogant certainty of the fundamentalists, their overconfidence not only about who was going to heaven and who wasn't but also their arrogance about other things. The "clean" language people were supposed to always use. What people should wear. Who people should date and what they were allowed to do on dates. The certain damnation of homosexuals. And, especially, their utter confidence that once a sperm and egg came together in conception this was a human being whose rights trumped the pregnant woman's, and whose rights trumped common sense. So, some fundamentalists felt smug that they were doing God's work by bullying women who got abortions. And some of these fundamentalists were now bullying Annie.

Mo knew something about bullies from his own life. He had a large scar on his face, a crescent moon just below his right eye from when he had fallen face-first down some concrete steps as a child. And despite the stitches, the wound had gotten infected and finally left a crescent moon railroad track scar. So some of the kids picked on him. He remembered in third grade, being picked on by a larger boy at recess. The kid laughed at him in front of a group of other kids.

"Look at that moon scar under your eye. I'm gonna call you Moon Pie!"

Mo's tried to ignore him, but he felt his eyes beginning to well up. The boy said, "What ya gonna do, Moon Pie? Cry?"

"Leave me alone," said Mo, his jaw set, as he turned and started to walk away.

But the boy yelled, "Make me!" and pushed him from behind so hard that Mo fell sprawling into the grass. And for a moment, time seemed to move in slow motion for Mo. He scrambled to his feet, and before he could think and his astonished tormentor could react, he balled his right hand into a fist and swung a big looping punch that connected on one side of the other boy's nose. The bully bent forward, moaning, and crying, both hands to his nose, as bright red blood poured from his left nostril onto his shirt and even onto the grass. The boy's nose was not actually broken, but it hurt, and the blood terrified him. Fortunately for Mo, a teacher had witnessed the entire event, knew it was self-defense, and inwardly celebrated that the bully had finally gotten what was coming to him. Mo himself was amazed at what his fist had accomplished. And for the rest of his life, he remembered that sometimes the bully backs down if you punch him hard in the nose.

Sometimes.

His sophomore year in high school, Mo had the misfortune of attracting another bully—Nathan Saunders, a fellow sophomore, a wide-receiver on the football team who outweighed Mo by about 20 pounds of added muscle. There seemed to be no reason for the bullying. Nathan just cruised around the school with a kind of cheerful malevolence, aware of his ability to inflict pain, and often looking for something nasty to do. He decided one day that he didn't like Mo and he thought his scarred face would be amusing to mock. He also noticed that the easy-going Mo was not likely to fight back if attacked. So, he began picking at Mo on a regular basis. An elbow to the ribs while walking down the hallway. Books knocked from Mo's hands on another occasion. "Faggot!" he yelled at Mo in front of other students, as he and his friends laughed, and Mo looked down, red-faced, shaking his head side to side.

One day while walking down a mainly deserted hallway, Nathan and a couple of his friends came upon Mo. The two friends blocked Mo's escape route in either direction. The few other students who happened to be in the hall were careful to avoid seeing what was going to transpire. When he saw that both exits were guarded by the bully's accomplices, Mo stood his ground and Nathan walked up and with a two-handed push to the chest knocked Mo down and sent him sprawling, sliding across the linoleum.

"Get up, ugly! I'm gonna do it again!" he yelled.

Mo got up and Nathan, sneering and laughing, knocked him down again. "Get up! Let's see what ya got, faggot!"

Mo got to his feet, but before Nathan could knock him down again, there was movement at the end of the hallway behind Mo. It was David Woodard, the center on the football team, all 6 feet, 4 inches, 285 pounds of him. "Great," thought Mo as he looked back and forth. "Just what I need, another bully."

Grim-faced, David walked toward Mo, and then kept going past him straight towards Nathan whom he grabbed by the shirt with his left hand while pulling back his right fist ready to punch. Nathan started to struggle and push back, but a glance into David's eyes now turned black with fury made him decide otherwise.

Nathan started to speak in a high voice, "Hey, David, we, we're on the same team…"

But David cut him off. "Shut up, you stupid son of a bitch! I see you going around school picking on people smaller than you. You think you're a badass, because you *finally* made the team. But you're just a bully, and I fricking *hate* bullies. Tell me why I shouldn't kick your ass right now? Tell me!"

"Okay. Okay," said Nathan, his voice still an octave higher than normal. "I'm sorry. I'll leave him alone."

"No," said David. "You're not just going to leave him alone. You're going to leave *everybody* in this school alone, or I will find you by yourself sometime, and I *will* kick your ass. Got it?"

"Got it," said Nathan, his voice still pinched soft and high.

Finally, David released his grip and Nathan took the opportunity to make a quick departure. Then David looked around the hallway and saw Nathan's two friends who had retreated a safe distance. "You two wanna come get some?" he asked. The two shook their heads no and exited the hallway.

David turned to Mo. "You alright, man?"

"Yeah," he said. "Thanks."

"No big deal. I hate bullies. My parents told me if I ever acted like a bully, they would absolutely kill my ass. And they said I better not look the other way when somebody was getting bullied either."

The few other students who had been watching, some with open mouths, went about their business, but several of them were smiling and snickering. The air was suddenly lighter.

Neither David nor Mo ever spoke of the incident again. But each gained respect for the other. Mo admired David's willingness to stand up for someone else. David appreciated Mo's refusal to back down, even though there was no way he was going to win the fight. From that day on, David and Mo who had been distant friends since elementary school, became better friends, and eventually, best friends. Mo turned into a real fan of the football team that, with a record of 0-10 (and 0-11 looking quite likely), was awful. But he came to the games and rooted for the team and enjoyed seeing how David did in each game. For his part, David took an interest in the cross country and track teams (both ranked in the top ten in the state) and looked to see how well Mo did. David would often sit with some of the cool kids in the hallways before school started and he would yell for Mo (who was not one of the cool kids) to come over and talk. He loved to give Mo gentle punches on the arm or chest and put up his fists to fight. "Whatcha got? Whatcha got?" he would tease. And Mo would play along, putting up his fists to throw a few easy punches that David caught in his grizzly bear paws while laughing. "Man, you are way too tough for me!"

Chapter 7

So, when Mo heard about what was happening to his friend, Annie, an animal fury arose in him, a ferocity he had not felt for some years, and he knew he needed to do something about it. He began looking for Annie in the cafeteria during meals. Mo tried showing up early and showing up late but didn't see her. But finally he happened to see her at dinner one evening, just a few minutes before closing. Only a few students remained in the room, eating alone or in small groups at tables. Annie was sitting by herself in a corner near a window. Her long red hair was pulled back in a ponytail. She wore a dark green shirt, cut-off blue jean shorts, and sandals. She was just as beautiful as Mo remembered her from the dance the last time they had talked. But her head drooped, and her eyes also looked puffy, as if she had not slept well in a while.

Food tray in hand, as Mo got near her table, he spoke as gentle as a whisper, "Annie."

She slowly looked up, and then her mouth opened with a startle of recognition. Her face broke into a wide smile as she leapt to her feet. Mo set his tray on the table as Annie wrapped him a tight hug. He noticed how wonderful she felt pressed against him, and he also noticed that she held the hug a lot longer than he expected. Finally, she stopped squeezing.

He stepped back and said, "You look beautiful."

"Thank you," she said. "You look nice too."

"Thanks. How are you?" he asked.

"Fine," she said, glancing down. But her eyes began to fill with tears.

"Hey, that doesn't look 'fine.' May I sit with you?"

"Sure," she said, motioning toward a chair at the table, as she sat back down.

"Annie, I've heard some rumors. What's going on?"

"It's a long story," she said. "What have you heard?"

"Well, I'm just going to come out and say it. I've heard that you had an abortion, and now a bunch of idiots are making your life miserable."

"Yeah, that's pretty much the gist of it," she said, grimacing and nodding her head.

"I'm your friend, and I want to support you. Okay?"

"Okay."

Annie and Mo caught up as they ate dinner together. She told him about dating different guys, and he said he had heard about that. Inwardly, she was surprised and pleased that he was keeping track of her, but she said nothing about it. Just as she began to tell him about what had happened with Greg, a cafeteria worker's voice came over the loudspeakers, "The cafeteria is closing in ten minutes. Please finish your meal and bring your trays to the dishwasher area. Thank you."

Mo said, "I really want to hear the whole story. Could I walk you back to your room?"

"That'd be great," she said. Mo swallowed the rest of his meal in three bites. He and Annie dropped off their trays, and then headed out into the night. It was early spring and a cloudless evening. The air was still a bit chilly, and the stars spread across the night sky like a million fireflies a billion light-years away. The couple walked beside each other not holding hands, but when Mo noticed Annie shivering, he offered her his zippered Garden College jacket, and she accepted.

"So, tell me the rest of what happened, please," said Mo.

Annie told him the entire story and he listened while tossing in short curses and comments.

Greg's reaction to her pregnancy--Mo murmured "Worthless."

Annie's parents' response--Mo shook his head and said, "I'm so sorry."

Denise's kindness--"I'm not surprised. She's a good friend."

The trip to the clinic and meeting the protesters--"Damn it!"

The actual procedure--"Oh, that sounds tough."

And finally the response of the fundamentalist Christian co-eds and the predatory male students--"Oh, my God. I just want to punch somebody."

When she had finished talking, it occurred to Annie that Mo was the first person she had really told the whole story. And he had listened, not given advice, or passed judgment, just listened. It felt as though for the first time in weeks that she wasn't facing an impossible situation all by herself. She had an ally, a friend.

"Mo, thanks for listening to me, and not judging me," she said.

"Judge you?" he sputtered. "I could never judge you. I'm not good enough for that myself. And I'm glad to listen to you. Thanks for telling what's going on. I may have to kick somebody's ass."

"Whoa! Whoa there, cowboy. I appreciate your sticking up for me, but I don't want you to get into trouble helping me. Okay?"

"Okay," he said. "Let's sleep on it and think about what's the best way to handle these cowards."

"Thanks," she said. Then she smiled and continued, "I have to watch out for you, Mo. I can't have you killing Egyptians and burying them in the sand, you know."

Mo laughed. "I know. Still picking on me, aren't you?"

"Always. Do you remember why I said I pick on you?" she asked.

"I do," he said, smiling. "Let's talk tomorrow." Mo and Annie exchanged phone numbers, and then gave each other a long goodnight hug. As Annie walked down the dorm hallway, she thought to herself, *I have a friend--an angry, protective friend--but a friend. And maybe something more.*

The next morning Mo phoned Annie and asked if they could have lunch or dinner together in the cafeteria.

"I have some ideas about these jerks," he said. "And I want to hear what you think."

"Okay," she said. "You're making me a little bit nervous."

"Don't worry," he said.

"Alright, let's talk about it at dinner. Same place in the cafeteria, but 30 minutes earlier so you don't have to eat your dinner like a wolf that's been starved for a week."

"Ha! You should see me when I really eat fast," he said.

"Um, that's okay. I'll take your word for it," she said.

"See you tonight," he said.

"See you then."

Chapter 8

That evening after they picked up cafeteria trays piled high with steaming hot Garden College meatloaf, mashed potatoes, and brown gravy, (guaranteed to add "the freshman 15" in just one sitting) they sat alone in their corner of the dining hall. Mo wore his usual blue jeans, (his best, properly weathered pair, of course), and a shirt with the rock group KISS on it. Annie wore a knee-length red skirt with a dark blue top that fit snugly. Mo noticed that, unlike the evening before, she was wearing some makeup—a touch of mascara, a dusting of rouge, and some lip gloss. Her hair was let down straight, with just a hint of curl at the bottom. Mo's mind flashed back to when he and Annie had slow-danced together, and for a moment once again he was disoriented by her beauty. "So, tell me about these plans of yours," she said.

"Okay," he answered. "You're dealing with two sets of problem children, right? So, we need a strategy for each one."

"Alright," she said.

"What do fundamentalist women hate?" he asked. "I don't know. Books with lots of big words and no pictures?"

"Behave," he said laughing. "What do they hate? They hate the opposite of what they love. And what do they love? They love feeling so virtuous, so superior to the rest of us lowly sinners. Right?"

"Yeah. I guess so."

"So, what do they hate?" asked Mo. "They hate being shown to be just as flawed and sinful as the rest of us. They hate to be embarrassed while they're trying to appear so morally superior."

Annie considered this for a moment, and then said, "I agree. So, what's the plan?"

"I'll get to that," he said. "Remember, we're also dealing with these nasty guys. I have a solution for them, but it will take some patience on your part. Will you be patient?"

"It depends," she answered. "What do I have to do? And is it going to get me kicked out of school?"

"No. Of course not. Would Mo lead you astray?" he asked with a sly smile.

"Maybe. Remember those 40 years wandering in the wilderness? What is it?"

"Simple," he said. "You just pretend I'm your boyfriend."

Annie burst out laughing. "You realize it *is* 1983, right? I'm not a damsel in distress, and I don't need a damn knight in shining armor to protect me."

"I know, I know, but seriously, hear me out," said Mo. "I don't have to *be* your boyfriend. I just need to *look* like I'm your boyfriend. You know, hanging around with you a lot, doing things together, that sort of stuff, nothing sexual."

"Oh my God, you are such an idiot!" she said, rolling her eyes, but also smiling a little. "I can just tell guys 'no' when they hit on me."

"I know," he said. "But this is even better. It just makes things even more simple and clear. It makes it easier. You don't have to make excuses. 'I'm busy,' 'I have to study for an exam,' and stuff like that. You just say to them, 'Sorry, but I have a boyfriend. His name is Mo.' And that's end of the story. Are you willing to try it? I promise not to try to take advantage."

Annie shook her head back and forth, rolling her eyes again, but smiling a little, and holding back a laugh. Then she finally said, "Okay. I'll try it. But don't get any ideas. Now what about the fundamentalist women?"

"I have a plan," he said, "and I'll need your help. Are you free Friday night?" Mo then began to outline the plot with Annie. After he'd finished, Annie raised her eyebrows, puffed her cheeks, and blew out her breath as she said, "Boy! I would not want you on my bad side. But they deserve it, and it just might work."

Chapter 9

For the rest of the week, Annie and Mo ate meals together, walked around the campus as a couple, and were careful to be seen giving each other goodnight hugs, but no kissing.

Friday night finally arrived, and Mo met Annie in her room on the first floor of the women's dormitory, a nondescript redbrick building with carpeted halls, sturdy upholstered furniture, bathrooms shared between suites, and a big TV stationed on an entertainment center shelf in the common room. As promised, in two small bags Mo had brought the items needed for the plan. It was 10:00 and they just needed to wait a couple of hours before launch. Annie played some albums on her stereo—Michael Jackson, Hall & Oates, Duran Duran—loud enough to enjoy, but soft enough still to talk. Annie sat on her bed, and Mo sat in a desk chair facing her.

Reaching into one of the bags Mo said, "While we're waiting, I've brought a game to play, if you'd like."

"Okay," said Annie. "It's not Spin the Bottle, is it?"

"Not yet," he laughed. "Here's how it works. I've brought these index cards that I've written questions on. There aren't any 'yes' or 'no' questions. These are all open-ended questions. You pick one at random and then I pick one."

"Sounds like 'Truth or Dare,'" said Annie.

"Well, not really," said Mo. "There aren't any embarrassing questions and there are no dares. There're just questions to get to know each other better. I mean you *are* my girlfriend; you know."

"Shut up," said Annie, but a small smile crept out.

"Try it. If you don't like it, you can stop," said Mo. He shuffled a deck of about thirty index cards with writing on one side of each of the cards. He held out the deck to Annie, writing side down, and she picked a card.

"Talk about your favorite place to go on vacation and why it's your favorite," said the card. Annie pressed her lips together, put her left index and middle fingers to her lips, and squinted her eyes for a moment. Then she said, "The Outer Banks of North Carolina. Now Charleston is nice too, but it's kind of built up and feels so busy. So I love to go to the Outer Banks because it's so quiet and peaceful, not that many people there, mainly just wide beaches, sand dunes, sea oats, and the ocean that seems to go on forever. I don't want to sound hokey, but it feels like a holy place, a place where I can slow down and listen and hear God." And as she spoke, Annie noticed Mo staring at her, listening, concentrating, and his undivided attention was balm for her wounded soul. Unlike some of the men she'd had actual dates with, she already got the sense that he cared about her. It made her excited and nervous.

"Okay. Your turn," she said, "But you have an advantage, because you know what the questions are."

"True," said Mo, "Maybe you'll want to come up with some of your own questions for me."

"Maybe," she said.

Mo took a card from the deck and read it aloud, "If you could drive any kind of car, what would it be?"

"Ooh. I'll bet you want to drive something like a Porsche or a Mustang, something fast, right?" asked Annie.

"Nope," said Mo. "I want to drive an electric car that doesn't take gasoline."

"An electric car?!" said Annie. "You mean like science fiction, stuff like that?"

"Yeah," he said.

"Why would you want something like that?" Annie asked.

"Because I hate all the pollution that cars make, smog, and all the stuff that gas-powered cars harm, not just the air but also the land and the water and the wildlife. Besides, how cool would it be not to have to stop and put gas in the car all the time?"

Annie smirked. "So how would you power it? Giant batteries? A long extension cord?"

Mo offered her a serene smile, "That's fine. Make fun of me all you want, but scientists are already working on prototypes. Just wait. You'll see."

"You're kind of weird," said Annie, turning her head to give him a sideways glance and a crooked smile.

"Thank you," he said.

"You're welcome," she answered.

They played the game for about an hour, and then decided just to talk and ask questions of each other beyond what was printed on the cards.

Mo asked, "What was it like to grow up in your family?"

"It was pretty good," said Annie. "Middle-class family, decent house, not rich, not poor, you know. I'm an only child. So, I guess I got spoiled a little bit. At least that's what my parents used to say when I got into trouble. My dad worked for the post office and my mom was a school guidance counselor. Daddy could be kind of gruff, but underneath it he was as kind as a Bassett Hound—big bark, no bite. Of course, my mom, being a guidance counselor, did a little bit of psychoanalyzing of me, but she really didn't overdo it most of the time. According to her, everybody has some sort of mental illness, the only question is how severe and debilitating your illness is!

"You probably know mom and dad were both active at First Presbyterian. They went to church almost every Sunday, served on committees, all that stuff. They made me go to church too, and they said I could decide to skip church once I had graduated high school. But I still go because it helps me and it's a habit. I guess all in all I was lucky. My parents were sometimes strict, but they loved me, and they still do."

Mo nodded and agreed, "Uh huh."

Then Annie asked, "And what about you? What kind of a family produced such a crazy person?"

Mo chuckled. "I'll have you know, I come from only the finest stock," he said drawing himself up in mock dignity. "And I think you already know, my dad sold insurance—house, car, motorcycle, and even some life insurance. The motto around our house was, 'We hope nothing breaks, (including you) but if it does, we'll give you money.' My dad always thought that was funnier than it is.

"You know my mom taught elementary school because you were in her class one year. I suspect that's why she is prematurely gray."

"Hey!" shouted Annie, laughing. "I was a sweet little girl, and I'm sure your mom would confirm that."

Mo rolled his eyes, smiled, and said, "As I was saying before I was so rudely interrupted, my mom was a long-suffering elementary school teacher who helped even the most difficult children. She did enjoy her work and she did help me with my homework more than once. She and my dad got along most of the time. They loved Tabby and me, but I think Tabby edged me out for the favorite child role. Besides, she's smarter.

"As far as church goes, our family was not into it as much as yours was. We were not 'every week' kind of people. My parents are mellow, and they stayed, and still stay, miles away from church drama. They would sprint away from even the whiff of controversy. My mom always said, 'church should be a sanctuary, not a battleground.' I will say that overall I enjoyed church, and especially Sunday school, as I got older."

Annie gave a fake cough and cleared her throat while raising an eyebrow. "Yeah, I know you enjoyed Sunday school," she said while giving Mo the side-eye.

"Changing the subject. Here's one," said Annie, "When you die, what do you want people to say about your life?"

Mo thought for a second and then said, "Mo was one of our greatest presidents and it was amazing that he had time to find a cure for cancer at the same time. No wonder he won the Nobel Prize."

"So funny." said Annie shaking her head and laughing. "Modest too."

Garden College had a curfew at midnight. Persons of the opposite sex were supposed to be out of each other's rooms by then. But this was often ignored, and Annie knew it was especially ignored by Savannah Stephenson, the ringleader of the women who had been picking on her. With the self-confidence of an angry toddler on a sugar high, Savannah practically gave orders to the other women on the hall. Whatever Savannah wanted, she got, and this applied to the blasphemous "in the name of Jesus" hazing given to Annie. The other women might as well have saluted and shouted, "Yes, drill sergeant!"

Savannah's roommate went home every weekend. So Savannah's boyfriend, Cliff, stayed over from Friday night until Saturday mid-morning almost every weekend. It was against the college's rules, of course, but people pretended not to notice, because it was Savannah.

At just a few minutes after midnight, Annie, serving as a lookout, made sure nobody was looking. And Mo walked down to the dorm hall janitor's closet, pulled out a master key he had "borrowed" from one of the janitors, opened the circuit box, and turned off the power. The hallway and rooms went dark. A few puzzled and angry voices could be heard coming from within the rooms. Quickly feeling his way, Mo tiptoed to Savannah's room door. He leaned two objects against the front of the door. Then he knocked and stood back. At the sound of the knock, Cliff had hidden in Savannah's bedroom closet. But after a moment, the door to Savannah's room opened, and the objects toppled into the room.

"What in the hell?" Savannah said as she bent down and picked up the objects. And at that moment, just as she straightened up, Mo lifted his Polaroid camera and took a flash photo of Savannah wearing her sheer nightgown and holding a half-empty bottle of Jack Daniel's Whiskey and a box of Trojans lubricated condoms. A few feet behind Savannah, but still within range of the camera, was Cliff peeping his head out of the bedroom closet. While Savannah and Cliff were still blinded and confused by the flash and the darkness, Mo and Annie ran down the hall and outside. Once outside, they sprinted about fifty yards to a tree line on campus where they stopped, breathing hard, and then they burst into laughter.

In the darkness with the half-moon's illumination, they watched the Polaroid for a few seconds as it finished developing, like magic, right before their eyes. There in the photo stood Savannah looking groggy and drunk holding the Jack Daniels bottle and the Trojans. Cliff looked like he was trying to see what was going on and trying to hide at the same time.

"We did it!" said Annie, still breathing hard, and hugging Mo. "That was so mean, *and* so fun."

"It was," he said. "But she deserved it."

"And you deserve this," said Annie as reached a hand toward his face and kissed him on the mouth.

Mo thought, "Wow! That was amazing. Thank you, God!"

After a few minutes to make sure the coast was clear, Mo and Annie went their separate ways back to their rooms as if nothing had happened. Neither slept well that evening. They were too excited not only with their "plan" but about what was happening between the two of them.

The next afternoon, Savannah found a typed note and a photocopy of the picture in an envelope that had been slipped under her door. She opened the envelope and read the note, "The abuse stops now, or the photo gets mailed to your parents and your pastor."

Annie never got another message on her door.

And she no longer needed to pretend that Mo was her boyfriend. Because he was.

Chapter 10

Over the next couple of months, spring brought her abundant charms to Charleston. Icy winds turned to warm breezes bearing the scent of salt water. Leaves weighed the trees heavy with green. Flowers burst from their buds and their fragrance was like walking into the perfume section of a department store. The city and the beaches lured Mo and Annie for long walks to see sunrises pushing away the night and blazing sunsets that made it seem as though an inferno burned across the entire horizon. They played 1950s "beach music" on the stereos in their dorm rooms, and Annie did her best to teach Mo how to dance "the Carolina Shag." He improved enough not to step on her toes very often.

When college was finally out for the summer, Mo and Annie headed back to Dover. Annie worked as one of the lifeguards at the country club. More than one male swimmer walking poolside tripped while gawking at her beauty. The lifeguarding job also gave Annie some spending money (some of which she put back into her father's old army boot to replace what she'd borrowed). Her parents had been angry about the abortion, but they loved Annie and they were proud of her, and it was rare that she did anything that really went against their wishes. As the months had passed, they had forgiven her and come to respect that the abortion was her choice, not theirs. She was not merely their daughter; she was a woman, her own person.

With her summer evenings free, Annie had time to do some writing and to hang out with Mo and some of her friends from high school. These were fulfilling days that she recorded in her journal. One entry read, "They say that youth is wasted on the young, and maybe that's true. I suppose I don't really appreciate how good my life is now. Yet I do at least sense some of it. How life seems so full of possibility as I imagine I'm just getting started on what promises to be a long journey. How my body is young and strong, and my aches and pains are few. And how I am still moved by the beauty of the world around me, and grateful for the people dear to me, especially Mo."

Mo meanwhile spent his early mornings knocking out a few miles running on the asphalt, as well as on a few trails, getting ready for cross country in the fall. He was not a gifted runner, but he still enjoyed the discipline—pushing himself with hard workouts that left him thirsty, tired, and sweating as if his runs took him across the Sahara. He also hoped for the elusive "runner's high" a kind of euphoria, a feeling of power and of being able to keep going forever. It was a state that he and other veteran runners sometimes experienced when exercising at a pace that challenged without overwhelming. You didn't hit the "runner's high" sweet spot all the time, but when you did, you felt free, and afterwards you craved having that feeling again.

For his summer jobs, Mo mowed yards and trimmed trees and bushes in the neighborhood. Other than disturbing the occasional yellowjacket or wasp nest and getting stung, he appreciated being outside, getting a tan, and adding a bit more upper-body and lower-body exercise to his training, while getting paid for it. Like his distance running, it was also time when he could think about his life, and he could work through anything that made him angry. "Take that!" he thought as he whacked off some stray tree branches. "And that!" as he lopped an over-sized bush down to size.

But, of course, mainly what Mo thought about while he worked (and often when he ran) was Annie. How in the world had he gotten so lucky to be dating a woman that smart, funny, kind, and gorgeous? Thinking about Annie made even the South Carolina rainforest heat days go by a lot faster.

The only real problem was that Annie seemed so perfect to him that he sometimes wondered, "What in the world is she doing with me? Now that things have settled down at school, I know she could date a better-looking guy and somebody with more money and better grades. But, for some reason, she likes me, and apparently she has liked me since we were in Sunday school together as kids. It's strange, but I'm not complaining."

Mo also did summer part-time work with the South Carolina Wildlife Commission, studying various local reptiles and amphibians. Biologists were beginning to make the connection that when these animals, especially toads and frogs with their absorbent skin, diminished in an area, there was the danger that human-made pollution was killing them. And when the frogs and toads disappeared because of pollution, human beings themselves were also in danger.

As part of his work, Mo was tasked with assessing the health, number, and species of snakes in the area. This was a good fit, because though many people had a terror of snakes, Mo did not. In fact, one of his childhood memories was of being startled on a fall Saturday afternoon when he found a snake crawling in his backyard. Mo had seen snakes on TV, but he had never encountered firsthand a creature move with such a strange and undulating motion. He was mesmerized.

"Mama, come here! Hurry!" he'd shouted. His mother had rushed outside and caught the little snake, her fingers gently wrapped around it just below its head. She lifted it up for Mo to see. It was maybe 10 inches long from head to tail, and about the thickness of a beginner's wooden pencil around.

"It's a Garter Snake," she said. "You can go ahead and touch it. It won't hurt you." So Mo had petted the snake and he noticed that it wasn't slimly as he had expected. Its scales were cool and slightly rough on the outside.

"Can I hold it?" he asked.

"Sure," said his mom. "Just be easy with it. You don't want to hurt it."

Mo held the snake and noticed its surprising muscular strength even in such a small creature. After a few minutes, his mom said, "Okay, it's time to let this little guy go. He'll need to find a place and start hibernating soon."

Chapter 11

A few days after letting the snake go, Mo came home from elementary school to find a paperback copy of *Reptiles and Amphibians: A Guide to Familiar American Species* in the Golden Nature Guide series placed on the study desk in his room. Beside it was a note that read, "Enjoy learning about my relatives and me! From your friend, the Garter Snake." Mo pored over the 150 plus pages of common names, color pictures, descriptions, range maps, facts and fables about turtles, lizards, snakes, alligators, crocodiles, frogs, toads, and salamanders.

Mo discovered that South Carolina was home to a vast array of reptiles and amphibians. In the "Upstate" part of the state where he lived, there were Green Snakes, Garter Snakes, various black snakes, toads, tree frogs, Bullfrogs, salamanders, American anole lizards (sometimes called American Chameleons because they often changed color, occasionally matching the surface they were resting on), snapping turtles, box turtles, and painted turtles, and this was just a start.

There were no alligators in the Upstate, but there were a few in "the Lowcountry," the eastern part of the state, and especially in the southeastern part of the state. The state was also home to a few venomous snakes. The Eastern Diamondback Rattle Snake, the Water Moccasin (also known as the Cottonmouth, because the inside of its mouth was white like cotton), and the Eastern Coral Snake with its red, yellow, and black bands. The Eastern Coral Snake could be distinguished from similar looking Milk snakes by this saying, "Red on yellow, kill a fellow. Red on black, venom it lacks." Later in life when Mo took kids camping, he used his own variation of the saying to remind them to check for signs of dangerous dehydration, "If the pee is yellow, kill a fellow. If the pee is clear, no need to fear."

In the Upstate there was only one venomous snake, the Copperhead, which was the color of a copper penny. These snakes were very common in the area, and you might see them along roadsides where they slithered to find warmth, but often found themselves run over by vehicles. The Copperhead's bite was painful, but rarely deadly to human beings.

Mo learned that the non-venomous King Snake not only ate lizards, mice, and birds but also Copperheads, Coral Snakes, and Rattlesnakes. How odd, he thought, that these venomous snakes were no match for a non-venomous one that used the element of stealth and surprise against them. The *King* Snake, seemed an apt name in Mo's mind.

But Mo's favorite snake was the Eastern Hognose Snake so named for its turned up "hog snout." It was non-venomous but pretended otherwise. If you bothered it, it would coil up, hiss, and finally strike (though its teeth were small, and it had no true fangs for people to worry about). If this acting job didn't work, the snake would become even more dramatic and roll over on its back, tongue lolling out, and play dead. If picked up and turned right side up and set on the ground, it would roll onto its back, tongue out, and play dead again. "And the snake Oscar goes to…"

Mo thought, *Well, I guess if you can't be a badass death-dealing venomous snake, the next best thing is to pretend to be one. Maybe there's a lesson in there for me too.*

Chapter 12

Mo and Annie found respite from the broiling hot days of summer when evenings came, and they enjoyed the cool of the town's old movie discount theater "The Red Bird" where they ate mountains of buttered popcorn washed down with oceans of soda. One night they watched the science fiction thriller "Alien" and when the alien burst from a hapless crew member's chest Annie jumped and pressed up against Mo who jumped too. They also took in "Apocalypse Now," and afterwards had a discussion over ice cream at "Michael's Ice Cream and Burgers," a local hangout.

"I have an uncle who was in Vietnam," said Annie. "I want to be supportive of him, but I'm not so sure about whether our country should have gotten involved over there or not."

Mo said, "Yeah, I hear you. I'm not sure either. In fact, I'm not sure about whether we should go to war period."

"You mean you're against all wars?" asked Annie. "Seriously? Are you a pacifist?"

"I didn't say that. I'm just not sure," said Mo. "One of the messages I took from the movie is that there are rules about how wars are supposed to be fought--you know, the Geneva Convention, no torture, no attacking civilians, that sort of thing. But once a war breaks out, like Vietnam, all the rules just go to hell and people go batshit crazy."

"Yeah, the movie definitely made that clear," said Annie, taking a bite of her burger and patting her mouth with a napkin.

"The other thing," said Mo pausing to swallow, "is that the pressures of war sometimes create heroes who're brave and who make dramatic self-sacrifices for others. You know, like the guy who throws himself on a hand grenade to save his buddies. But war is also just cruel and insane, and it makes otherwise decent, sensible people turn cruel and insane. It rewards the side willing to do the craziest and most destructive things to win the war.

"I mean we just saw Captain Willard sent out to 'terminate by extreme prejudice' Colonel Kurtz who'd gone rogue and slipped into insanity and decided to do whatever it took to win. But I think the movie hinted that Willard's actions and Kurtz's actions were both 'sensible' in wartime thinking.

"And I just can't get out of my mind the scene when Colonel Kurtz was talking about how the American military had gone into a village and given Vietnamese children vaccines against polio. But after the unit left, a crying man from the village came running after them to tell them what had happened. The unit returned to find that each vaccinated child's arm had been amputated by the Vietcong at the site of the vaccination. The colonel saw this as an example of the enemy's willingness to do anything to win. But I keep thinking, dear God, the unintended consequences of even trying to do something to help innocent people. Why does doing good have to be so damn hard?"

"I tried to forget that scene. It's just horrible," said Annie. "But what about World War II? Don't you think we had to go to war then? If we hadn't gone to war, Hitler and the Nazis would have won, and so would've the Italians and Japanese. The whole world would have been living under dictators instead of being free. Don't you think we have to go to war sometimes?"

"Maybe. Probably," said Mo, taking a sip of his Coke through a white and red plastic straw. "I just think we jump into too many wars, and when we get into them it turns into hell. And I wonder what God thinks about it all. I mean it's hard to imagine Jesus leading an infantry charge or dropping a bomb, or saying, 'Good job doing the Lord's will. You killed a bunch of people.'"

"Oh, come on," said Annie, frowning. "That's not really a fair way of putting it. Do you think Jesus would want the Nazis running everything with their 'master race' Third Reich crap? For God's sake, they killed 6 million Jews in the concentration camps. How many more people would they have killed if we had stepped aside and said, 'Go right ahead and kill these people. We've decided to be pacifists.'?"

"Okay, now who's being unfair?" asked Mo. "You were in Sunday school with me. You know it's more complicated than that."

"I know," Annie said. "So, what are you saying then?"

"I'm saying I just don't know. That's all. I just don't know. The movie made me think, and I'm going to keep on thinking about the whole issue of war" he said.

"Fair enough," she said. "It was a good movie, wasn't it?"

"Yes," he said.

"How about a comedy next week?" she said.

"You bet. Between 'Alien' and 'Apocalypse Now,' we've seen enough blood for at least a week," he said.

The next week they watched the comedy "Meatballs" with Bill Murray. The conversation at Michael's afterwards was a just a tad bit lighter.

Chapter 13

Over the summer, Mo "muscled up" from all his yard work. And because he wasn't naturally afraid of snakes, as many people were, in his work with the Wildlife Commission he was taught how to catch snakes with practically automated speed and precision. See the snake. Pick up the snake with the metal snake hook. Drop the snake into the bucket. It was over in seconds.

Of course, being in the Upstate, the only venomous snakes Mo dealt with were the Copperheads. But his boss, a forty-something-year-old, big-bellied, married, no kids, lifelong Upstate resident named Mr. Merriweather, noted Mo's unruffled snake-catching ability. So he decided to groom him for future work by taking Mo along on a couple of day trips to the southeastern part of the state. There he would also capture the more dangerous Eastern Coral Snakes, Cottonmouths and, the deadliest snake in North America, the Eastern Diamondback Rattlesnake.

The Coral Snake was not normally aggressive, and, despite its bright colors, was hard to find. But the Cottonmouth usually stood its ground and opened its mouth to show the white "cotton" inside announcing, "Don't bother me. I will mess you up." The Eastern Diamondback Rattlesnake also refused to back down when confronted. Instead, it coiled up and sometimes offered a warning rattle before striking. Its rattles were made of keratin, a substance like human hair, and each time the rattlesnake shed its skin, the rattle was enlarged. With deadly venom and its sheer size, up to 8 feet long, the Eastern Diamondback was a terrifying creature to encounter in the wild, much less to catch. The venom from just one bite was strong enough to kill four people.

The day for his trip to the southeast part of the state came, and when his alarm clock went off at 4:25 a.m. Mo groaned, rolled out of bed, and put on a T-shirt, long pants, and leather boots. He also grabbed sunglasses and a fisherman's hat to put on once they arrived on site. He wolfed down a bowl of cereal, gulped a cup of water, and a cup of coffee, made a trip to the bathroom, and headed out the door by 4:45, arriving at the Wildlife Commission office by 4:55. Mr. Merriweather was already standing outside waiting. He spat some chewing tobacco juice on the pavement and gave Mo a crooked smile.

"Damn, son! You look like shit," he yelled, laughing. "You just get out of bed?"

"Yes, sir," said Mo, looking down, rubbing the back of his head.

"Well, don't you worry. I'm driving. You can take a nap. You might need some more beauty sleep if you're gonna keep that pretty girlfriend of yours."

Mo was used to his teasing. So, he just shook his head, laughed, and got in the truck. Mr. Merriweather kept his word. He didn't talk much. And eventually Mo got groggy, leaned his head back against the headrest, and slept about 30 minutes. He awoke to the sound of soft country music on the truck radio, The Marshall Tucker Band, from Spartanburg, SC, playing "Heard It in a Love Song." Mo looked outside and noticed that the scenery was already changing. The red clay and rolling hills of the Upstate were gradually turning to the flat landscape and sand of the Lowcountry. Faster moving muddy brown Upstate rivers were giving way to slow-moving narrow creeks filled with black water that might conceal who knows what. Maple trees, peach trees, and pecan trees were replaced by pine trees and oaks with Spanish Moss hanging down to create an exotic, step back in time, kind of atmosphere.

About 2 ½ hours after they'd left, Mr. Merriweather turned the truck down a dirt road out in the country. And after a few minutes, he finally parked in a sandy, pull-off spot near a wooded area, little-used, in one of the smaller state parks.

Mr. Merriweather said, "Excuse me while I uncoffee myself," as he ambled a short distance into the woods to take a leak. Mo followed suit but went in the opposite direction to give them both some privacy. After they returned to the truck, Mo and his boss unloaded snake-catching hooks, tongs, and buckets. Then they began making their way, as quietly as they could, through the wooded area toward the creek.

They had hardly begun their search when they saw movement on a bank near the water, a large snake, dark, with a pattern hard to make out, sunning itself on a rock. As they got near, the snake coiled and opened its mouth to reveal solid white inside. This was a Water Moccasin, a Cottonmouth for sure. Mr. Merriweather got between the snake and the water. And with a long-handled snake hook he gently began to pick the snake up. "Get the bucket ready, Mo," he said. Mo, who had been carrying a large, white plastic bucket (like what you might buy for mixing paint, because that's what it was), held the bucket at arm's length from his boss.

"Mo," said Mr. Meriweather in a patient voice, "I know you're a little nervous. What do you need to do now?"

"Oh, yeah," said Mo, shaking his head, a little bit disgusted with himself. "Set the bucket down" he said as he set the bucket on a relatively level spot, then stepped back as his boss deposited the snake with the gentleness of someone cradling an uncooked egg into the bucket.

"You got the top?" asked Mr. Merriweather. "Go ahead and grab hold of the handle to set it on top of the bucket. Then screw it closed without exposing your fingers to the snake. Okay?"

"Yes, sir," said Mo as it took him a couple of times to get the top to catch in the grooves to screw it down. His gloved hands were a little bit shaky.

"Good job, son," said Mr. Merriweather. "It kinda gets the old ticker going, doesn't it?" And Mo noticed that his heart really was thumping in his chest.

During the rest of the morning, they found a Brown Water Snake (non-venomous) and a Green Snake (so safe you could just catch it with your bare hands). Then they walked back and took a break for lunch by sitting on the tailgate of the truck. Mo's mom had packed him lunch in a paper bag the night before—a Peter Pan peanut butter and Welch's Grape jelly sandwich on white bread, Wise barbequed potato chips, an apple, Dannon blueberry yogurt, a can of Pepsi, and a napkin with a smiley face drawn on it.

Mr. Merriweather took one look at the yogurt and the napkin with the smiley face and started chuckling from his belly.

"Damn! With yogurt breath and that smiley face, these snakes might just turn themselves in instead of having to be caught," he said.

Mo just smiled and shook his head.

Merriweather eyed Mo and turned a bit more serious.

"So, what're you planning to do after you graduate from college?" he asked.

"I'm not sure yet," said Mo. "Maybe I'll be a biologist or a herpetologist."

"Ooh. You know the fancy word for people who study snakes," said Merriweather teasing him again. "I think you'd be good at it," he paused, wiping his mouth with his sleeve, "if that's what you're supposed to do with your life. Have you ever thought of doing anything else or is your mind all made up?"

"Well, no. I guess my mind isn't all made up yet," Mo said, his words slow and his voice quieter.

"Like what?" asked Merriweather.

"I'd rather not say."

"Come on. I won't make fun of you."

"Alright, then. I can't explain it very well, but sometimes when I was a little kid in Sunday school, I would look out the window at the trees and the plants and the birds and the animals and I just felt this weird connection with them."

"Okay. Well, that explains the biologist possibility," said Merriweather.

"But" said Mo, looking down at the sand and weeds, "there was also something more. It wasn't just the connection with them but a connection with the One who made them and who keeps them alive and who keeps everything alive and everything in some sort of order."

"Oh. So, you're thinking of becoming a minister," said Merriweather raising his gaze from staring at the tall grass near the woods to look Mo in the eye.

"Yeah, but that doesn't make any sense," said Mo squinting a little, "because I'm not good enough to be a minister. I mean my other favorite thing about Sunday school as I got older was looking at the girls in the class. And though I pray a lot and read the Bible almost every day, I also cuss all the time, and drink too much sometimes. So, this is just a crazy thought. I'm pretty sure I'm going to be a biologist."

Merriweather burst out laughing so hard that he began to cough. He tapped on his chest as if to settle himself and eventually stopped coughing. After he recovered enough, he finally said, "So you're imperfect. You're a sinner. Join the club. All ministers are sinners. And I'll look forward to hearing your first sermon."

After lunch they moved to another area, not close to water, but a section of the park alternating forest and patches of saw palmetto, a bristly-looking plant with dark berries. They had walked for about thirty minutes when Merriweather tapped Mo's shoulder with one hand and pointed with the other. About ten feet ahead in a sunny spot lay the largest snake Mo had ever seen in the wild. It had to be at least seven feet long, maybe eight, with scales shaped like diamonds, an Eastern Diamondback Rattlesnake, the largest and most dangerous snake on the continent. And it was not in a good mood. As Mo and Merriweather got within a few feet, the snake coiled ready for action, and the sound of its rattle sent chills down Mo's spine.

Merriweather showed a thin smile and said, "That'll wake you up from an afternoon nap." He handed Mo the snake hook. "I'll get the bucket this time," he said, as he set the open bucket down on a level spot nearby.

Mo took a deep breath as he moved slowly toward the creature and the rattling got louder, and the snake struck towards his boots, causing no damage.

Merriweather said, "You can do this. It's just like the others, just bigger and meaner."

As Mo moved the hook toward the rattler, it struck again with a seething primeval rage, but then Mo got the hook underneath the middle of the snake and lifted it off the ground. Though his adrenaline was flowing, he also noted how heavy the snake was as he used both hands to lift and maneuver it over the bucket and drop it in as the rattling continued with the bucket serving as an amplifier. Merriweather took a hook, caught the bucket's metal top handle, and placed the top on the bucket before screwing it down, being very careful not to expose his fingers to the snake at any time. The rattling continued, now muffled by the snake's temporary enclosure.

Mo took a big breath and blew it out.

"Man," he said. "*That's* a snake."

"Good job," said Merriweather. "The next one will be even easier."

Chapter 14

As summer continued, Mo and Annie worked their part-time jobs, took in some movies at The Red Bird, and followed this with visits to Michael's for ice cream and the occasional burger. Michael's was known for its specialty burgers, and Mo's favorite was The Cherry Bomb. It was two beef patties, fried sweet onions, lettuce, tomato, Duke's Mayonnaise (this was a restaurant in the South, so no other brand of mayonnaise would be considered), Heinz Ketchup (because everybody knew it was the best), with eight maraschino cherries placed between the top bun and the two beef patties. When you bit into the burger, the red juice from the cherries exploded and mixed with the Heinz Ketchup, sweet onions, and tomato to make an oddly satisfying and messy local delicacy.

Annie preferred The Hocus Pocus burger, available only at certain times of the year. At first glance, it appeared to be regular fast-food fare—a burger with one beef patty, lettuce, tomato, uncooked onions, Duke's Mayonnaise, Heinz ketchup, and Texas Pete Hot Sauce. But the owner of Michael's (Michael Ramone, a transplant from Lubbock, Texas) also owned several acres of land that he began to farm once he moved to the country just outside Dover. He soon discovered that his crops were being devoured by hordes of rabbits. Without enough natural predators to control them, such as the abundant coyotes of his native Texas, the rabbits multiplied into a virtual rolling sea of varmints laying waste to his corn, beans, and tomatoes.

Michael's solution was to sit on his back porch some evenings with a .22 rifle with a high-powered scope and shoot rabbits. At the end of an evening of leisurely back porch hunting, he would grab a wheelbarrow and bring all the rabbit carcasses in. Then, while downing a six-pack of Budweiser, he'd skin them, and prepare them as filets to be cooked and added as an additional item inside The Hocus Pocus burger. As Michael advertised it on the menu, "Nothing up my sleeve. Nothing in my hat. Hocus Pocus. Presto Change-o! A rabbit in your burger!"

Mo thought this was the dumbest slogan he'd ever heard, but people came from miles around just to say that they had eaten this concoction. Annie thought the slogan was hilarious, and she especially enjoyed that when you talked to Michael about the rabbit meat being one of the patties in the burger, he added with a wink, "And we put the Texas Pete hot sauce in there just to keep you hopping."

Of course, as it is with many college students, Mo's and Annie's summer was a curious and mixed passage of time. There was their sometimes-monotonous daily work in weather so hot and humid it felt like the tropics. And then there was pleasant time together many evenings as they got to know each other more and more. Annie had gotten bored with her lifeguard work quickly, but at least she had collected a cute assortment of freckles on her face and what passed for a slight tan for someone with her milky complexion. Sitting in the lifeguard's chair all day, had also given her some time for reflection about life in general and her life. Though she would not fit the conservative or fundamentalist Christian mold, Annie took her progressive Christian faith seriously, and she believed that she needed to do something with her life that would benefit more than merely herself or her family. She began to think it would be important for her to combine her gifts and love of writing and literature with some way of helping people, especially people who were facing struggles. Annie didn't know exactly how this might play out yet, but she knew these were some of the goals and values she held for her life.

For his part, Mo was still puzzling about things he and Mr. Merriweather had talked about. He had time for thinking during his early morning runs over the hilly South Carolina Upstate, but even early in the day, the heat and humidity made the time exhausting--not the ideal conditions for serene contemplation. So, Mo was looking forward to fall.

Chapter 15

Like many college students, Mo and Annie did not attend church every Sunday. But they did attend at least two or three times a month, sitting beside each other in the balcony above the back of the church--a comfortable distance away from their families. Oddly enough, both enjoyed traditional Presbyterian worship with its formality, beauty, and emphasis on responding to God with all the intellect we human beings can muster.

Typically, in the printed worship program, called "the bulletin," there were meaningful corporate prayers of thanksgiving, intercession, and confession that the entire congregation prayed aloud. Mo and Annie were also glad to join the congregation in singing hymns, many of them majestic and hundreds of years old, from a hardcover hymnal. They appreciated hearing the volunteer choir and they listened carefully to the scripture readings, as well as the pastor's thought-provoking and sometimes humorous sermons.

Though Mo appreciated Holy Communion, Annie especially looked forward to it, and she wished it were celebrated every Sunday, instead of just quarterly as was their congregation's practice. "If we believe Christ is present with us in Holy Communion, why are we so stingy about how often we have a meal with him?" she once asked Pastor McIntyre, who mumbled something about church members having to prepare the elements and clean up afterwards, and how some church members felt that weekly observance of the sacrament would make it feel "less special." To this answer, Annie responded with an eyeroll and a sigh.

Most Presbyterians did not believe that the communion elements of bread and grape juice were suddenly physically changed into flesh and blood by a miracle. But they did accept that something mysterious and wonderful did indeed happen in communion, some sort of spiritual nourishment, unity with God and loved ones who had died, a kind of connection with other people of faith (and Annie believed, even people of no faith at all).

Mo preferred the times when there was a baptism during worship. Baptism in the Presbyterian tradition was sometimes administered to adults and might even be accomplished by immersion. But this was unusual. Most Presbyterians were baptized as infants or as small children, sprinkled with water by the pastor as the ancient baptismal words were spoken. Though this sacrament was lovely, you never knew what kids might do—fidget, cry, laugh, talk, grab the pastor's eyeglasses, or just sleep through the whole thing.

With their sometimes-hectic lives, Mo and Annie even valued the moments of meditative silence in the sanctuary just prior to worship starting, and they liked the pauses for silent reflection during some of the prayers. All in all, they were grateful for the steady rhythm and discipline of worship, and they felt renewed by the ancient Sunday morning drama of life, death, and resurrection enacted each week.

Their little home church was also blessed to have several unusual strengths for a congregation its size. A few years before he left for a position with a large, prominent congregation in Columbia, SC, First Presbyterian employed John Stephens, a young, gifted organist and choir director who could play practically all the organ literature. John was a gangly six feet tall, with large thin hands, dark hair, a ghostly complexion (probably from being inside practicing so much) and he was not even thirty years old. Unlike some church organists who turned Sundays into dour affairs slogging through melancholy organ and choir music week after week, John turned each week into something music lovers (and even music tolerators) could enjoy. He made sure the choir was not stuck singing from just one era of music. One week they might sing something from the Classical period. Another week, the Romantic period. Another week they might offer an African American spiritual. Still another week, the congregation might be treated to contemporary Christian music from the 20th century, sometimes even with piano and percussion accompaniment. Worshipers would sometimes say, "I wonder what John is going to surprise us with this week."

Without turning into an arrogant or rude conductor, John also demanded strong singing from his choirs. He had a way of seeing potential in his choir members, especially the least talented among them. Through kindness and encouragement, John helped them reach their full potential. Especially he was known for accepting almost any singer into the choir, and then having the weakest singers stand near the strongest ones to imitate them. And John never, *never* embarrassed one of his singers, because he saw the music not merely as a performance that might garner him accolades but as an offering of worship to God.

Unless the church were during the somber, penitential ecclesiastical season of Lent, before the service began, John might whip out some of the more challenging organ literature. At the end of the service, he played music so joyful and inspiring that the congregation often stayed seated to listen and then stood to applaud when the selection was complete.

Annie caught John after worship one Sunday. "That was absolutely beautiful," she said.

"Thank you," John answered in a soft voice, giving a slight shy bow. "I appreciate it, and I'm glad you liked it."

"Do you take requests?" Annie asked with a smile.

"Well, that depends upon the request," said John. "I don't want to sound snobby, but it needs to be something that fits into worship well. What do you have in mind?"

"How about Bach's Toccata and Fugue in D minor?" she said.

"Ooh! The tune that gets used in *Phantom of the Opera* and lots of other scary flicks. That's tough. You're not making it easy for me, are you? But it'll fit as a postlude," he said, with a big grin on his face. "Give me a few weeks to practice."

"We're going back to college in month," she said.

"When's your last Sunday here?" he asked.

"The 14th," she said.

"The 14th it is!"

Annie walked away beaming.

Though Mo appreciated the music and other elements of worship, he really paid attention to the sermons more than anything else. Did the preacher connect with the congregation or was he just staring down at his notes? Did the sermon have an interesting beginning, maybe even some relevant humor (not just a tacked-on joke)? Was he able to follow the flow of the sermon and did it make sense? Did it have any engaging stories, memorable images, and powerful writing? Was he challenged by the sermon, comforted by it, and even sometimes moved by it?

Over time, Mo started jotting notes about the sermons onto the worship bulletins so he could remember the various points later. And to his surprise, he gradually began to construct his own sermons in his mind. Various ideas and illustrations would float into his consciousness, and eventually he'd write them down in a little notebook.

The whole thing was puzzling to him, because, as he had told Mr. Merriweather, he knew he was not good enough to be a minister. And he still loved studying biology and being outdoors in creation. Yet there was this peculiar presence, this urging, a voice he knew but did not know, a voice as familiar as on the day of his confirmation, but a voice uncontainable, bidding him somewhere he could not predict, and he was not certain he wanted to go.

Chapter 16

A couple of weeks prior to their return to college, Mo's and Annie's friend, Regina, was driving home around midnight after a get together with college friends at Michael's. She was a mile from home, waiting at a stoplight, and when the light changed to green, she stepped on the gas, and never saw the Red Mustang traveling at 60 miles an hour as it ran the stoplight and crashed into her driver's side door, killing her instantly. Regina was 20 years old.

Early the next morning, Annie got a call from Denise who spoke in a soft, quivering voice, "Annie, I've got some bad news."

"Oh, no. What is it?" asked Annie.

"Regina was killed in a car wreck last night," said Denise.

"Oh my God, no," said Annie, crying. "What happened?"

"She got t-boned at the traffic light at the intersection of Wrightman and Clevenger Road. It looks like the other driver was speeding and ran the light and hit her on the driver's side, just caved the whole door in. She probably died instantly," said Denise.

"Oh my God, I can't believe it," cried Annie. "I can't believe it. I was just talking to her the other day. She was so excited about getting back to school. She had this new guy she was dating. I can't believe it." She continued to weep.

"I know," said Denise, "I know." Then after a minute she said, "Will you tell Mo?"

Annie sniffled, and then said, "I will. He's going to be so sad."

"I know," said Denise.

It was a Saturday morning and Annie decided that since Mo was already coming over to take her to breakfast, she would tell him about the news in person. When Mo pulled into the driveway and got out of his car, Annie walked out to meet him. And as she got near, he could see from her smeared makeup and teary eyes that she had been crying.

Fearing something awful, he asked, "Annie, what's wrong?" as they walked toward each other.

Her face crumpled, "Regina's dead," said Annie. She and Mo collapsed into each other's arms, crying.

"Dead?" he asked. "Dead? What happened?"

Her voice catching, Annie said, "Car wreck. Her car got hit at the stoplight at Wrightman and Clevenger Road. The other driver must have been flying and hit Regina's car on the driver's side. Just smashed it in. Police think she died instantly. The other driver is in the hospital, but they think he's going to be okay. Oh, Mo. I just can't believe she's gone."

"I can't either," he said. "She was our friend, and she was such a good person."

The funeral was held Saturday morning at 10:00 a.m. at First Presbyterian Church. As sometimes happened with the death of a young person, the sanctuary was packed for the service, not only with family members, but with dozens of college and high school students, and Regina's former teachers. A few of the pews down front, near the pulpit, had been roped off, reserved for the family. As the service began, from the back of the sanctuary, speaking into a wireless microphone clipped to his black clerical robe, Dr. McIntyre announced to the congregation, "Please stand," as he motioned with his hands for all persons to rise. Then he led the family in a slow procession down the center aisle to their pews. When all the family had sat down, Dr. McIntyre told the congregation, "Be seated, please" as he motioned for them to sit.

He then took his place in a seat behind the pulpit. And when John Stephens finished playing the organ prelude, Dr. McIntyre rose from his seat and slowly climbed up the steps to stand behind the pulpit that was maybe seven or eight feet above the main sanctuary floor. He looked down on the pulpit's lectern, adjusted his typed notes, and glanced at a small black volume, titled *The Worshipbook--Services*. Among other things, it contained "Orders for the Public Worship of God" and one of those orders was the "Witness to the Resurrection—Funeral Service."

Dr. McIntyre's movements were unhurried, careful, as if he had done this many times before and he all the time in the world. A couple of people in the sanctuary coughed into the silence. Then Dr. McIntyre looked up from the pulpit, his face solemn. He scanned the people seated before him. And then he spoke.

"We have gathered this morning, during tragedy, to grieve as a community of faith, to hear God's promises to us found in scripture, to reaffirm our faith in the resurrection through Christ our Lord, and to give thanks for the life of

Regina Margaret Stuart. Please stand and take part in the responsive liturgy you will find printed in your worship bulletin." The congregation stood, and Dr. McIntyre began to read, "Jesus said: I am the resurrection and the life. If anyone believes in me, even though he die he will live, and whoever lives and believes in me will never die…"

But Regina is dead, and she believed in you, thought Mo.

Dr. McIntyre continued to read, "Come to me, all you who labor and are overburdened, and I will give you rest."

Rest? Regina was just getting started. She didn't need to rest. She needed to keep living.

"Our help is in the name of the Lord," read Dr. McIntyre.

"Who made heaven and earth," answered the congregation.

"Praise the Lord," said Dr. McIntyre.

"The Lord's name be praised," answered the congregation.

No! What help from the name of the Lord are you talking about? And where was Regina's help? And if you made heaven and earth, couldn't you at least have made that car swerve a few feet in the other direction?

The service continued with a unison prayer of confession of sin. But Mo didn't feel like confessing. So, he just stood with everyone else, but without speaking or even pretending to speak. Annie gave him a sideways glance and a slight frown. Finally, after singing the funeral hymn "Near to the Heart of God," Dr. McIntyre invited the congregation to sit. He prayed a brief prayer of illumination, asking God to grant the congregation and him insights and hope from the Bible and the sermon. Then he read four scripture readings. Three of them were old standards used in funerals. "The Lord is my Shepherd…" (Psalm 23), "Who shall separate us from the love of Christ?" (Romans 8), and "…We shall all be changed…For this perishable nature must put on the imperishable…" (1 Corinthians 15). But there was another reading, the first reading, Mo had never heard before, and one that seemed an odd choice to him. As Dr. McIntyre explained before the reading, the speaker of this passage (Lamentations 3:19-21) begins by complaining to God *before* he expresses trust in God. He says to God, "Remember my affliction and my bitterness, the wormwood, and the gall! My soul continually thinks of it and is bowed down within me. But this I call to mind, and therefore I have hope: The steadfast love of the Lord never ceases…"

As he moved into the funeral sermon, Dr. McIntyre said, "On this day, this tragic day, we should begin with honesty. We are heartbroken about Regina's death, bewildered that this gentle and kind young woman who had so much to offer the world, and whose whole life lay ahead, is now gone from us. Appeals such as, 'Heaven just gained another angel,' or 'God had a purpose,' or 'She's in a better place,' may be well-meaning, but they just don't cut it for many of us. We are angry, angry that life is sometimes filled with unfair, senseless tragedy, and before we say anything else maybe we say to God, "Remember my affliction and my bitterness, the wormwood, and the gall!"

And with those words, Mo realized his own frustration and anger. *Why, God? Why?* And then he became aware again of that presence he had felt at his confirmation several years earlier. A voice said to him, "I know you are angry. So am I. Take that anger of yours and use it for something good. Take me on if you dare. Come and wrestle with what it means to be a human being serving as my instrument of justice and love in this broken world. Your given name is Moses. Don't you think it's time for you to live up to your name?"

I thought you were supposed to be comforting, said Mo.

"I am," said the voice. "But comfort comes in different forms. And sometimes the best comfort is a challenge. Are you ready?"

I don't know, he said. *I'm not good enough.*

"'Good enough,' has nothing to do it with it," said the voice. "Weren't you paying attention in Sunday school and worship at all? You know the stories—Abraham, Nathan, Paul—all of them terribly flawed, all of them sinners. Right, Mo?"

Okay, he said. *But you will have to help me.*

"Of course."

The rest of the sermon, at least what Mo could recall, focused on the promise that no matter how terrible things get, God will never abandon us. God will be with us in tragedy, injustice, and even death. And finally, we all be together, transformed in the life to come. So, despite our grief and anger, we support each other, live in hope, and entrust Regina to God's merciful care.

Mo had his own way of thinking about it. What is our final reality? A speeding car spattering a young woman's head against the car window? Or all of us together, made perfect? Both are true, but which is the last word?

Chapter 17

On Mo's and Annie's final Sunday in church before heading back to college, Dr. McIntyre preached about Genesis 32:22-33, the story of Jacob wrestling one night, all night, with God who appears in the mysterious form of a man or perhaps an angel. The writer of Genesis says their wrestling match ended not as we expect, with God's obvious, easy victory ("See, I won with both hands tied behind my back!") but in a *draw* with Jacob injured and limping from God knocking his hip out of socket. Yet despite his painful injury, Jacob refused to let go of God, refused to stop wrestling with God until God promised to grant him a blessing. And what was the blessing? A new name, Israel, which means in Hebrew "the one who strives with God."

Dr. McIntyre ended his sermon, "This is also our calling as the people of God, not to get comfortable with God but to argue with God, to wrestle with God and to wrestle with what is going on in the world today. Our calling is to refuse to accept injustice with, 'Well, that's just how things are.' No. We are called to wrestle. And, if we do, if we wrestle with God and the beautiful but broken world God made, like Jacob we're going to get hurt, because such wrestling creates deeper living. And deeper living demands something from us, even as we dare to demand something from God. And in the wrestling with God, we will discover the blessing, the richest, most meaningful and rewarding life possible, life as God's struggling, striving servants. So, dear friends, what do you say? Wanna wrestle?"

And Mo thought, *Jacob, I think I know how you felt. And Lord, don't you think you're over-doing this call to ministry thing?*

At the end of the service, Annie and Mo sat and listened as John played "Toccata and Fugue in D Minor" by Bach as the postlude. Every member of the congregation also remained in the pews, transfixed by musical dynamics that moved from a whisper to massive chords that shook the sanctuary, from sedate tempos to such a frenzy of notes that it seemed even the organist's two hands and two feet would not be enough to play them all. The piece was played with such precision and passion that when the final notes sounded, it was met with a standing ovation from the congregation and a couple shouts of "bravo!" thrown in for good measure.

When he and Annie returned to campus the next day, Mo knew what he had to do. He walked from his dorm room down to the registrar's office. The registrar, "Miss Nancy," as the students called her, was an attractive 56-year-old woman, who chewed grape-flavored bubble gum and listened to country music all day, every day. "Miss Nancy" had worked at the college for 22 years and figured she had heard every tale of woe that a college student could experience or imagine. Mo said to her, "I need to change my major."

"You do?" she asked, crossing her arms. "Now why would you go and do a crazy thing like that?" a smile tugging at her lips.

"I can't say," he answered, thinking that if he told her that God had spoken to him, she would think he had lost his mind. "It's just a feeling," he continued.

"Well, what is this *feeling* causing you to want to change to?" she asked.

"I want to switch from majoring in biology to majoring in religion and minoring in biology," he said.

"That's quite a switch," she said. "But you're only a sophomore. So, I think it's doable. You won't need any more science courses for a while, and you'll need to pick up lots of religion courses, and some language studies, maybe Hebrew, or New Testament Greek, or Latin, or German wouldn't hurt either. What do you hope to do with this religion major?" she asked.

"I can't really say right now," he said.

"You can't really say right now," she said, a dubious frown creasing her face. "Have you discussed this with your parents?"

"No, but I will," he said. "And it's my decision anyway."

"I suppose, but they are the ones paying the bills. I want your word that you will talk to them this week, agreed?"

"Agreed."

Chapter 18

Mo left the registrar's office with a revised schedule for the semester and a new advisor, Dr. Edward Tiraboschi, a forty-something-year-old professor who had come the previous year from a small liberal arts college in central Ohio. The professor stood about six feet tall, thin as a blade of grass, an owlish face framed by thick glasses. He was fond of wearing brightly colored bowties with his sports jackets, dress shirts, and dress pants. Mo climbed three flights of creaky, old wooden stairs to get to his office. The door was closed and a plastic name plate on the outside said, "Dr. Edward Tiraboschi, Assoc. Professor of Religion." Mo knocked. A voice inside boomed, "Come on in! It's unlocked!"

Mo opened the door and saw Dr. Tiraboschi seated in a leather desk chair with rollers. Stacks of books were strewn around the room, and there were stacks on his desk, but in a space in between the desk stacks the professor stared down at a solitary book.

"I'll be with you in just a sec," he said, not looking up. "I'm just finishing up this page." He continued to read for another full minute, occasionally shaking his head up and down and saying, "mm" and "hmm" as he read. Finally, he grabbed a store receipt he'd been using as a bookmark, put it between the pages, and said, "Kierkegaard. Fascinating. Do you like his work?"

"Um. I haven't read any of it," said Mo.

"Oh, forgive me," said Dr. Tiraboschi as he stood up, smiled, and reached out to shake Mo's hand with a bone-crushing grip. "I should introduce myself. I'm Dr. Tony Tiraboschi. Most of my students just call me Dr. T, for short, and it's easier to pronounce. And you are?"

"Moses Campbell, but most people call me Mo," he said.

"It's good to meet you, Mo. How might I help you?" asked Dr. Tiraboschi.

"I just switched my major from biology to religion, with a biology minor. And the registrar said I should come and see you, because you're my new advisor," said Mo.

"Cool!" said Dr. Tiraboschi. "And you've caught me at a good time. I've got a few minutes. Have a seat." He motioned toward a sort of brown tweed-colored couch occupied by a black and white tuxedo cat sleeping on one end on a pillow. When Mo sat, the cat got up and strolled over to him, purring, and rubbing against him with its head.

"Oh, that's Sylvester," said Dr. Tiraboschi. "He's friendly. Do you like cats?"

"Yes, sir," said Mo.

"Well, then, you're gonna love Sylvester," said Dr. Tiraboschi. "But please don't call me 'sir.' I feel old enough already being called doctor and professor!"

"Yes…" said Mo, catching himself just before he said "sir" again. It was ingrained in him from childhood. "Yes."

Dr. Tiraboschi smiled. "So, tell me a little about yourself," he said. "Where are you from?"

"I'm from Dover, South Carolina. It's a little town about four hours from here. It's in the Upstate," Mo said.

"Of course, I've heard of it. There's an egg-shaped metal covered bridge over a river there, right?"

"Yes, that's it," said Mo. "The bridge is sort of an off-white, egg color. You enter and exit from the pointy ends of the bridge, and, of course, it curves up as you go over the river, and curves down as you get to the other side. It's the only egg-shaped metal covered bridge in the country. The county is one of the top chicken egg-producing counties in the country, and there is a state egg festival held there each year. So, you can see why it's held in Dover.

"There're all kinds of egg-based dishes to eat, vendors selling egg-themed crafts, and games based on eggs. My favorites are some of the different egg-toss games. There's the standard game, you know, where groups of two people compete by standing at a distance from each other tossing an egg to each other, each couple gradually moving farther apart trying to see who can throw and catch the egg the farthest without breaking it, and especially without breaking it and having it splatter all over them. That's fun. But there's also the super-charged version of the egg toss. People use homemade contraptions to launch eggs across the Dover River (an eighth of a mile wide where they launch) and then they use other homemade contraptions to try to catch them without breaking them. And each year the longest distance launching and catching without breaking wins $500 and bragging rights to the Eggs-strava-ganza Egg Toss. I think some genius kids from MIT entered one year and won, but usually it's just some smart locals."

"Sounds eggs-salent," said Dr. Tiraboschi with the flicker of smile.

"Eggs-actly," said Mo, "You're cracking me up."

"Okay, I'll stop, if you'll stop," said Dr. Tiraboschi.

"Egg-greed," said Mo.

"So anyway, you're a little way from home, but you can still go home for a weekend, no problem, if you want," said Dr. Tiraboschi.

"Right."

"Good. It's nice to get away from home and sort of cut the apron strings, but still be able to get home when you want. So, tell me what made you decide to switch from majoring in biology to majoring in religion?"

"Well, it's kind of a long story. I grew up in the Presbyterian church, going to Sunday school, and worship, and all that, but I also always loved nature. And whenever I've really looked more closely at nature, I've been amazed at how intricate it is, the numbers of species on the planet, how plants and animals fit together as part of an ecological system, and how this does not seem to be random. There's some sort of thought that has made it happen and continue to happen. And it fills me with, I'm looking for the right word, I guess, the word is awe. I look at it and I'm filled with awe. And I suppose that has led me to wonder about the meaning behind it all. Why is it here and why are we here and what's the purpose of it all? And I guess that has made me want to know more about the one who made it all. I'm still interested in biology. I'm minoring in it. But I really want to think about the bigger picture. I want to see how God fits in all this."

"Hmm," said Dr. Tiraboschi. "What an interesting story you have. You're doing some deep thinking. I wonder if there's anything else that may have prompted this change?"

Mo's mouth opened slightly, and he paused about three seconds, his mind racing. Then he said, "Um, probably not."

"Probably not?" Dr. Tiraboschi's eyes danced, as he gave Mo a sideways glance, and then he threw his head back and laughed. "Okay. I'll let that go for now. But I better at least sanitize the area." He opened a drawer of his desk and pulled out an aerosol can covered in white paper and labelled with large black letters, "Bullshit Repellant." He began waving it in a giant S as he sprayed it around the room, laughing as he went.

This was how Mo first met his mentor.

<h1 style="text-align:center">Chapter 19</h1>

Mo and Annie both plunged into their studies. Annie was taking a beginning class on Russian literature, tackling Dostoevsky's *Crime and Punishment* in one semester which seemed a ridiculous amount of work for an intro class. But the teacher, Professor Erin Murphy, explained, "We're easing our way into Russian literature. Before you finish your senior year, you'll be reading what many people consider to be the greatest novel ever written, Tolstoy's *Anna Karenina*. But we'll start with something a bit shorter, yet still rich for exploring the human condition and the great questions about goodness, evil, God, and redemption."

Mo, meanwhile, was dealing with the switch from the mainly technical subjects of biology to the universal speculations and declarations about God (and whether God exists), creation, the nature and purpose of humanity, differences and similarities between the various major religions, and the meaning of truth. Mo felt like a kid given $100 and turned loose in a toy store so he could run from one interesting possibility to the next. It was exhilarating and fun, and his curiosity about the intersection of theology and biology was just one more play area in the store.

With Mo's switch to being a religion major and Annie's own reading, there also was a new kind of overlap for their discussion as a couple. One evening as they sat in Annie's room, she on her bed and Mo on the chair at her desk, turned around to face her, Mo asked, "So, are you reading anything interesting in any of your classes?"

Annie said, "Actually, I am. Dr. Murphy has us reading Dostoyevsky's *Crime and Punishment.*"

"Ooh. Russian literature--that sounds hard," said Mo.

"Well, yes, and no," said Annie. "Once you get used to the Russian names and nicknames--I actually drew a small chart of them to keep them all straight in my head--then it's not so bad."

"I'll take your word for it," said Mo, shaking his head and rolling his eyes a little.

"If you'll just listen a second, I want to tell you a little about it," Annie said, as she reached for the book on the floor beside her bed.

"Okay," said Mo, moving his thumb and forefinger across his mouth, the zipper motion, "I'm listening."

"Thank you, sir," said Annie. Mo started to make a comment about the word "sir," but Annie squinched her eyes at him, and he put his hand over his mouth. Annie continued, "Now I haven't finished the book, but I keep thinking of a scene near the beginning. There's this character, a man named Marmeladov. He's a drunk, and even worse he is a pimp, prostituting his own teenage daughter for money."

"Oh, my God, what a sleaze!" said Mo.

"Yes. At any rate," said Annie, her voice serious. "As I was saying, there's a scene at the beginning of the book, only about 30 pages in, when Marmeladov is talking to Raskolnikov, who's the main character of the book, the character who is going to become a murderer. And Marmeladov is being very honest about who he is, the scum of a person he has become. But he says nobody needs to feel sorry for him. He says, "I need to be crucified, not pitied! Crucified!" And then he starts talking about Christ and the final judgment. And he lists all these people that Christ will forgive, including Marmeladov's poor prostitute daughter Sonia, who I don't think needs to be forgiven.

"At any rate, then he comes to the part I like best. Marmeladov says, "And He will judge and forgive all, the good and the evil, the wise and the humble….And when He has finished judging all, He will summon us, too: 'You, too, come forth,' He will say, 'Come forth, you drunkards; come forth, you weaklings; come forth, you shameless ones!' And we will all come forth unashamed. And we will stand before Him, and He will say: 'You are swine, made in the image of the Beast, with his seal upon you: but you, too, come unto me!' And the wise and the clever will cry out: 'Lord! Why dost thou receive these men?' And He will say: 'I receive them, O wise and clever ones, because not one among them considered himself worthy of this….' And He will stretch out His hands unto us, and we will fall before Him and weep…and we will understand everything…"

Annie looked up from the book, and Mo's cheeks were wet. His eyes met hers.

"That is so beautiful," he said.

"Yes, it is," she answered, "And it made me think of our talk about who might be going to heaven and who might not, and how you and I were puzzling about that. It's still early in the book, but Dostoyevsky is at least hinting he thinks that everybody finally makes it."

"True," said Mo. "And it's interesting what he uses as his rationale for that universal acceptance. Basically, it all seems to come down to God's judgment followed by our confession of sin followed by God's infinite mercy."

Annie said, "I know. There's nothing about being good enough or saying the right things, even though I know that's important. But in the end, it just seems to come down to God's mercy. And just think, Dostoyevsky wrote this in 1866. I'll bet some of the church people didn't agree with what he wrote."

"Yep, I'm sure some of the church members weren't pleased with the idea that everybody might make it into heaven," said Mo. "But I like that last line you read. How did it go? "And we will understand everything…"

"Yeah, that's it," said Annie. "And we will understand everything."

<h1 style="text-align:center">Chapter 20</h1>

As the year unfolded Mo and Annie did not understand everything yet, but they began to understand some things at least. Mo saw more and more that his decision to switch majors was the right choice, a better matching of his intellectual gifts and his relentless interest in the existence of God, who God was, and what that meant not just for his life but for all life. He never lost his curiosity and love for nature. It just blended into the mix that was his priorities—God, family, nature, and Annie. And not necessarily in that order.

Meanwhile, the relationship between Mo and Annie was deepening. Mo had been there for Annie in facing down the bullies. He had accepted her not as "damaged goods" as some people of that conservative time and place might have but simply as a person who had made the choice that seemed right to her. Over the summer of dates and long conversations, Annie and Mo had gotten to know each other better as they talked, and laughed, and risked sharing some of their imperfections with each other. They had comforted each other after Regina's death. And now even their two college majors brought them closer as they discussed eternal questions from the vantage points of literature and religion. Each morning they couldn't wait to see each other at breakfast and each evening they hated to leave each other when they said goodnight. But often since their successful encounter with the bullies, their goodnights ended with a kiss, and "Good night. See you in the morning."

One evening they walked around the campus. It was fall in Charleston. The palmetto trees stayed green, but the stifling summer heat had given way to cool but comfortable temperatures. Mo wore a hooded sweatshirt and faded blue jeans, and Annie wore a wool sweater and blue jeans against the chill. They held hands as they walked, nodding, and saying hello as other students passed.

Mo said, "So tell me about your day."

Annie said, "Oh, it was a day. Nothing all that unusual. We're still making our way through *Crime and Punishment.*"

"Anybody get punished yet or are they still just committing crimes?" asked Mo, giving Annie a sideways glance and the hint of a smirk.

"I'm getting ready to punish somebody," said Annie giving Mo a light backhand to the stomach, as he bent forward pretending she had knocked the breath out of him. As he was straightening back up, he suddenly put one arm around Annie's waist and the other arm behind her knees and swooped her up, as she shrieked with laughter. Then he began to spin around with her in his arms as Annie yelled, "Put me down! Put me down!" Mo made two complete rotations before getting dizzy, mis-stepping, and falling to the ground with Annie on top of him.

"You idiot! Are you okay?" asked Annie laughing.

"I was just following instructions," he said. "You told me to put you down."

Both breathing hard, Annie sat up, straddling Mo's waist. Then she leaned down, her hair splashing across his face, and she put her mouth next to his ear.

"I love you, you dumbhead," she whispered.

"You do?" he answered, his eyes wide.

"Yes, silly," she said.

"I love you too," he said, kissing her hard on the mouth as students walked by applauding and commenting. "Very graceful." "Nice landing." "Y'all just gonna go ahead and make out right here in the grass?"

But Mo and Annie didn't care. They were in love.

Chapter 21

Like Annie, Mo's religion professors were feeding him a variety of undergraduate bite-sized portions of great religious thinking.

In his Christianity 101 lecture one bright sunny morning Dr. Tiraboschi explained, "The Christian theologian Paul Tillich wrote, 'Faith is the state of being ultimately concerned.' In other words, whatever or whoever is most important to a person, that person's 'ultimate concern' is his or her God. So, country or family or success or money or power or pleasure or something else might become the 'ultimate concern' in a person's life. But only God is truly deserving of ultimate concern, ultimate devotion. All other devotions should be secondary, or they are idols.

"Tillich also argued that faith required 'courage' and 'risk,' because it involves trust, the investment of the self, rather than mere head knowledge 'belief.' Because faith involves courage and risk, it also leaves the possibility of failure. So, with so much at stake, it's okay for people of faith to doubt. And, as Tillich wrote, 'Doubt isn't the opposite of faith; it is an element of faith.'"

Mo raised his hand and asked, "So, Dr. T, if faith is a matter of being 'ultimately concerned,' what's to prevent us from misunderstanding who God is and what God wants, and then having that 'ultimate concern' turn into something awful, like, say, the Spanish Inquisition, or the Salem Witch Hunts, or something like that? How do we know we're really believing and doing what God wants, instead of just what we convince ourselves God wants or just what we want?"

"Hmm. A very fine question, Grasshopper," said Dr. T, imitating the accent of the Showlin Kung Fu master from the 1970s TV show "Kung Fu." "Anybody in the class want to take a *swing* at an answer?"

There were three full seconds of silence as Dr. T scanned the room, his eyes resting on some of the especially strong students, as well as a few others who looked down and tried to hide in the back of the classroom to avoid being called on. Finally, Suzanne Sanders, a pale, thin, female student with short brown hair, oval-shaped glasses, and hoop earrings, raised her hand and spoke.

"Well, I think we just need to do what the Bible says. Like it says on the bumper sticker, 'God said it. I believe it. That settles it.'" she answered, her voice school marm loud and confident.

"Hmm. Alright," said Dr. T. "Thank you. Others?" Reggie Smith, a tall, Black student wearing an "Earth, Wind, and Fire" long-sleeved t-shirt, and blue jeans raised his hand.

"Yeah, but the Bible says a lot of things, you know. The Apostle Paul says, 'Slaves be obedient to your masters.' And 'women be silent in church.' Only crazy people still believe that."

Dr. T. said, "Hmm, good points, Reggie," and with a faint smile he added, "Subtle too. The evangelist Billy Graham likes to hold up a Bible and announce to the crowds at his crusades, 'The Bible says…' But, as we'll learn, the Bible says many things, some of them helpful, some of them not, some of them contradictory, some of them poetic, some of them literal. The Bible is a symphony of voices, sometimes voices of dissonance, sometimes of harmony, sometimes comforting, other times challenging. Whenever you hear somebody announce, 'The Bible says…' I encourage you to perk up your ears and be ready to think about the grand sweep of the scriptures, not just an isolated verse or passage.

"So, we're still addressing Mo's question. With Tillich's definition of faith as 'ultimate concern,' and with his insistence that faith requires 'courage,' and 'risk,' how do we know we are doing God's will and not just our own? Anybody else want to jump in?" A soft, rarely heard voice belonging to Amy Yamato, a petite, long-haired, Asian student, came from the back of the classroom.

"Maybe we don't," she said. "We don't know for certain. We read the Bible, pray, and talk to other people, but we still might be wrong. Sometimes the great majority of people are wrong about something, like protecting slavery, and only a few people are right. Other times the larger group gets it right, and the individual or small group gets it wrong. But if one person or a small group of people feel that they are right, it takes a lot of courage to keep speaking out."

Amy's voice rose, "I've talked to my grandfather many times. He and our family were sent to the U.S. relocation camps for Japanese Americans during World War II. Even though about 33,000 Japanese Americans served in the U.S. military during the war and earned incredible numbers of military decorations for service, our people were treated like dirt by the U.S. government. My grandfather said our family lost almost everything, and we were handled as though we were the enemy of the United States, even though we loved this country and had done nothing wrong. Disease and overcrowding were awful in the camp, and people died. And all along, my grandfather knew what our country's leaders were doing to our family and other Japanese Americans was wrong. So, he spoke out and he was punished by the relocation camp officers for it. But he just kept speaking out and getting into trouble for speaking out. And he's still waiting for an apology from the U.S. government, just an apology. I don't think he will ever get one. But he was right, and he was willing to stand up and speak out. It was a risk, and it took courage, but he was right."

For a moment, no one in the class talked, whispered, or moved.

Then Dr. T spoke in a slow quiet voice, "Thank you for sharing your story, Amy. Your grandfather showed you, and now he shows us, what faith looks like, an investment of himself in the truth, taking a risk, and being courageous for what is right, even if it's costly. That's what Tillich says faith is daily, and usually it's demonstrated in less dramatic ways. But maybe one day each of us will have the occasion to test our faith with greater risk that will also require deeper courage. That day may come for each of us."

The bell rang, breaking the spell, and the class members began gathering their belongings and they began standing to leave, Dr. T. raised his voice a little, without shouting and said, "Don't forget your reading assignment and your five-page papers on Tillich are due on Monday. Have a good weekend!"

Chapter 22

As Mo and Annie continued to spend time together over the semester, they began to trust each other even more and to discover that they had many of the same values and interests. But, of course, beyond all that they were physically attracted to each other too. Annie's beauty was luminous with her flame red hair and blue eyes set against almost translucent skin. And Mo was still amazed that she was even dating him, much less his girlfriend. But he also knew that he loved her for more than her looks. He admired how smart she was, her brave spirit, her hard work, and her concern for other people. He also enjoyed the way she still picked on him and how she could dance.

Annie meanwhile appreciated Mo's looks too, his strong arms, chest, and legs. The way he looked at people straight-on without pretense. Mo's face was rugged, especially with the half-moon scar under his eye, but after a while it was as though the scar disappeared from Annie's vision. "Besides," she said, "It's macho as hell. I wouldn't want to date a pretty boy." And what first attracted Annie to Mo continued to attract her—his honesty, kindness, intelligence, and humor, and a little bit of shyness around women.

After her freshmen year dating and pregnancy experience, Annie had decided not to be sexually active again until she knew there was deeper commitment in her relationship. Now she and Mo knew that greater commitment to each other was real. They had a frank conversation about mutual responsibility and combining methods of contraception to be extra careful trying to avoid another pregnancy.

And one Friday night in January, when Mo's roommate had gone home for the weekend, Annie and Mo went up to his dorm room. They turned on some romantic music and made love for the first time. Afterwards, both marveled not only at how much pleasure they had felt but also how close they felt as a couple.

Chapter 23

Of course, all was not bliss. Each lover had ways of irritating the other. Thanks to the strictness of her parents, as well as her own attention to detail, Annie had developed a habit of silently correcting the grammar of other people. This was not particularly irritating to Mo if Annie simply complained to him later in private. But sometimes, especially if she had been drinking or was tired or had had too much coffee, a grammatical correction might pop out of her mouth before she could stop it.

Once, Annie asked Mo if he had seen her friend, Suzanne. Mo said, "I saw her about an hour ago. She was laying on the couch in the student life center."

"Unless Suzanne transformed into a hen laying eggs, she wasn't laying on the couch," said Annie.

Mo just sighed and shook his head.

A local TV news anchor praised the opening of a new Charleston restaurant as "very unique." And Annie announced to the students sitting in the dorm common area watching TV with her, "I don't understand why he gets that wrong. He's being paid to get it right. Unique means one of a kind. There's no such thing as *very unique*. You're either one of a kind or you're not."

"Annie!" shouted a couple of her exasperated friends.

"I'm going to pick up some burgers for Monica and I. Do you want one?" said her friend Sally one day in the student life center.

"You mean 'for Monica *and me*,' said Annie. "For is a preposition and it takes the objective not subjective case."

"Oh. My. God. I cannot believe you are correcting my grammar. What in the hell is wrong with you, Annie? Did you suddenly become an English professor and I missed the big news?" asked Sally holding her hands palms up in front of her in beseeching angry bewilderment.

One friend scratched from the friend list.

When they walked outside and they were alone, Mo exploded. "Damn it, Annie! Can't you just let it go?"

"No," she said. "I'm trying to help people speak correctly, because when language becomes sloppy, so does thinking. And when thinking becomes sloppy eventually ignorance, suffering, and cruelty follow."

"Wow! All that because somebody used the wrong pronoun?" asked Mo.

"Yes," said Annie as she gave Mo a kiss on the cheek and turned the other direction to head to her next class. Over her shoulder she called out, "You're kind of slow on the uptake, but you're cute."

Mo had his own exasperating habits. For one thing, he was usually late. This became such a bad habit that Annie finally sat down and talked with him over lunch, a lunch he was ten minutes late for.

"Mo, your being late most of the time is very frustrating to me, and it's going to get you in trouble sometime in life," said Annie.

"I know. I'm sorry, Annie. I just get so busy with something, so immersed in it that I lose track of time," said Mo.

"Well," said Annie, "It's disrespectful to others. It says to them that you don't value their time, and that means you also don't value them."

"Really? I'm being disrespectful because I'm a little bit late sometimes? And this comes from the grammar correction queen," said Mo rolling his eyes.

"Okay, fine. Be an ass about it. I'm just trying to help you. And you're not 'a little bit late sometimes,' you're a little bit late almost all the time," said Annie, her eyes blazing.

The other bad habit for Mo involved his room. If you entered the dorm room he shared with his roommate, Kyle Pettigrew, initially you might think all was well. There before you was a bed that had been made up, complete with hospital corners. You couldn't bounce a quarter on it military style, but it was tight and neat. The bookcase/dresser/partition shelves beside the bed contained framed family photos, textbooks, and a small stereo system with turntable and speakers, and a few record albums stacked on their sides, name labels facing out in the same direction. There was a dirty clothes basket in the small closet. At the foot of the bed was the standard school-issued chair and desk. The papers on the desk were neatly arranged, as were any books, and a metal cup held several pens, pencils, and highlighters. Onto a small corkboard were tacked reminder notes such as "Chem study group Wed. at 2:00," "Dr. Shelton meeting Friday at 10:00 a.m.—don't forget!" and "Date, Saturday at 5:00—pick up flowers." Kyle's father was a mortician, and his mother was a typing instructor at a high school. "A place for everything and everything in its place," was the old saying drilled into Kyle. And his side of the room was a perfect example of the saying in action.

But if you continued to walk farther into the room, you passed by Kyle's bed and the bookcase/dresser/partition shelves and you found yourself in another universe. The bed before you was not made, unless Annie might be coming over, and then fresh sheets and covers might be arranged in some semblance of order to impress her. Books, bags of Doritos and barbequed potato chips (closed with clothespins), salted Planter's Peanuts in cans, containers of Gatorade (some opened and some not), various papers, unframed photos of family, but especially of Annie, running shoes and running clothes, all were arranged on the shelves as though thrown there at the whims of an angry toddler. There was a dirty clothes basket in the closet, but dirty clothes also found their way into other areas of the room. The desk featured several stacks of papers, some of them notes from classes, some photocopied articles that Mo had read or meant to read, nature photos, especially photos of snakes in the wild, and various books covered the entire surface. Pens and pencils could be found by foraging for a while. Strips of scrap paper littered the desk, but some of the reminder items were for dates that had already passed. The overall impression you got was that Mo was a packrat on steroids.

One day Annie made a surprise visit. As she walked past the partition to Mo's section of the room, her mouth dropped open, and she began to laugh.

"Oh my God! What happened in here? Is this a murder scene or what? I shouldn't insult murder scenes," she said.

"Shut up," said Mo, laughing a little bit himself. "I didn't know you were coming, or I would have straightened up a little bit."

"A little bit? Sir, may I suggest you begin by bringing in a backhoe and a dump truck? Mo, don't you ever throw anything away?"

"Yes, I do, but I keep a lot of stuff, because you never know when you might need it."

"Yeah. Okay, but when do you think you're going to need these bottle caps on the desk or this potato chip bag with two potato chips in it? And do you think these dirty socks on the floor might be happier in the laundry basket in your closet?"

"All right. I get it," said Mo. "I'll clean up a little bit."

"Good," said Annie. "It would be a shame for an anonymous individual to contact the health department."

"Give it a rest."

Chapter 24

As he had in high school, Mo continued with his long-distance running. His freshman year at Garden College, he had run with the cross-country team. Though he trained hard and raced even harder, Mo was strictly a middle-of-the-pack runner. He enjoyed the discipline of training and the friendships he made, but by his sophomore year in college he was trying to balance time for his studies, a part-time job at the library, and especially time with Annie. His life had become hectic, and Mo decided to leave the team and just run for fun and enter the occasional local road race on his own. He enjoyed running on the Charleston sideroads early in the morning or sometimes even at night while wearing a reflective vest so that car drivers might see him and give him space. Mo joked to his friends, "I'm giving the drivers something to aim at."

He usually ran alone, and he found that this was holy time for him, minutes, and hours when he might mull over problems he was facing or things that were happening in the world. Sometimes he thought he heard God speaking to him during the run, sometimes afterwards as he cooled down, stretched, and showered. Either way, this time alone concentrating on something else was charged with holy possibility, because he did not know when God might take the opportunity to break in past the barriers of his busyness.

One crisp winter morning, Mo had headed out on a six-mile run that took him down city streets and then finally to run along the beach. Because of the chill and the early hour, there was only a scattering of people on the beach, and Mo felt himself moving into a comfortable rhythm. As he ran with the ocean to his right, waves gently crashing onto the beach, he felt again the immensity of the creation, and a sense of time beyond time. And within him welled up an unexpected gratitude for all that he had received from God's hand, appreciation for the immeasurable diversity of plants, animals, weather, and landscape in the world, and thankfulness finally that, like the endless ocean, he trusted his own life would one day be merged into the universe's own boundless gratitude, peace, and love.

"Mo," said the voice, "Do you love me?"

"I do," he said, "But I know I'm not the best follower."

"Never mind that," said the voice, "I am going to ask you to do something difficult with your life."

"What?" asked Mo.

"You'll see," said the voice.

"Are you ready?" asked the voice.

"I don't know," said Mo.

"I will help you," said the voice.

"Okay."

Chapter 25

Over time, Dr. T and Mo developed a friendship. Mo would stop by his office with questions about something he was reading or a theological question he was puzzling about. And unless he was swamped with work, Dr. T was happy to talk. After a few months had gone by, Mo asked, "Would you tell me a little bit about yourself, your life, please?

"Sure," Dr. T said, "I grew up in the Mid-West and went to the College of Wooster, one of the small, strong liberal arts colleges up there in Ohio. After completing my bachelor's (a dual degree in sociology and religion), I spent a couple of years working with the Peace Corps in Africa teaching English. After that I returned to the states, and knocked out a master's degree, and immediately after that a doctorate from the University of Chicago Divinity School.

"I don't have children and I've never married. But I have several friends in the area, and, of course, Sylvester, to keep me company. Like you, I run to keep in shape, but I don't run nearly as far or as fast as you do. I also play a little bit of tennis. I have eclectic taste in music. I love the symphony and I drive to Charlotte several times a year to hear it live. My favorite composers are Beethoven and Brahms with all their musical storms and drama. On the other hand, I also like Fleetwood Mac, Eagles, Chicago, Eric Clapton, and Earth Wind and Fire. I go to a few concerts most years. That's pretty much my life. Not that exciting. My parents are still living near Columbus, Ohio, and I have a brother in Pittsburgh, Pennsylvania."

"You graduated from divinity school. Did you get ordained and serve as a minister for a while?" asked Mo.

"No," said Dr. T looking down, and for an instant his normally cheerful face flashed something. Pain? Anger? Mo wasn't sure. And then it was gone, and Dr. T was back to his cheerful self. "That just wasn't in the cards," he continued. "I never pursued it. And I probably never will. Now, what about you? You told me when I first met you that you changed from majoring in biology to majoring in religion and minoring in biology, because you wanted to explore 'the big picture.' I think that's how you put it. But then when I asked you if there were any other reason, you waffled like a kid trying to explain how the cookies had gone missing from the kitchen cabinet. It was so bad, I had to whip out the bullshit repellant, remember?"

"How could I ever forget?" asked Mo, a trace of smile threatening to cross his face.

"So," said Dr. T, "We know each other a little better now. Do you feel more comfortable telling me what the other reason was or is? I'll keep it in confidence if you wish."

Mo took a deep breath and sighed.

"Okay. I guess so," he said. "But I'd appreciate it if you would keep this in confidence."

"I will," said Dr. T, his voice serious.

"Sometimes God talks to me," said Mo. "I don't mean that I hear a voice out loud. I'm not crazy. Of course, my girlfriend Annie tells me, 'If you were crazy, would you know you're crazy?' At any rate, sometimes God talks to me and says things. Like when I was at the funeral angry and grieving my friend Regina's death, I swear I heard God say, 'Take that anger of yours and use it for something good. Take me on, (like I'm Jacob wrestling God or something). Take me on if you dare. Come and wrestle with what it means to be a human being serving as my instrument of justice and love in this broken world.'

"When I complained that God was supposed to be comforting, God said, 'I am. But comfort comes in different forms. And sometimes the best comfort is a challenge. Are you ready?' When I told God that I'm not good enough, (and I'm not trying to be fake modest here) God made fun of me, asked whether I had been paying attention in Sunday school and church, and mentioned all the flawed people in the Bible that God used. And then I told God, 'But you'll have to help me.' And God just said, 'Of course.' Not 'Behold, I will come and prepareth thee!' Not 'I will send an Aaron to do the talking for you.' No, just, 'Of course,' all matter of fact, like God does this sort of thing all the time."

"Maybe God does," said Dr. T.

"Well, not with me," said Mo.

"Did God or the voice give you any more details?" asked Dr. T.

"Not really," said Mo. "But I do find myself sort of constructing sermons in my head during worship sometimes."

"Well, all twenty-year-old college students do that, right?" said Dr. T holding back a grin.

"Shut up," said Mo, starting to smile, and then immediately apologized. "I'm sorry. I shouldn't have said that to you. I guess it *is* kind of strange."

"Well, that's one word for it, but maybe another word for it would be 'confirmation,'" said Dr. T.

"Confirmation? You mean like when I joined the church" asked Mo, his mind flashing years back to his confirmation class.

"No. I'm thinking it might be more confirmation about what your next step could be after you graduate from Garden College. Have you ever thought about going to seminary to become a minister?"

"Yeah, but I'm not good enough for that. I really do commit a lot of sins. You should hear me cuss," said Mo.

"What about that conversation with God, and God telling you about all those sinners in the Bible that God used? What about that?" asked Dr. T.

"I know. That's what I'm struggling with," said Mo.

"Well, you don't have to figure it out today, but I'd be honored to help you go through a discernment process about how God might be calling you," said Dr. T.

"Thanks," said Mo. "I'd appreciate that."

Chapter 26

Over the next few months, Mo undertook a spiritual discernment process. Dr. T. had him focus more on his prayers, including spending part of his daily devotional time asking God for clarity about what he should be doing with his life. Mo began journaling, noting the people, activities, and interests in his spiritual journey that made him feel closer to God and the things that made him feel farther away. He explored various "call stories" in the Bible, in which different individuals received "a call" from God to do something. There was Abraham who was told, at age 75, to leave behind his country, family, possessions, his secure and settled existence to go to a land yet unseen based on a promise that could not be proved in advance. The Prophet Jeremiah was told to preach a word of judgment to Judah's political and religious leaders who had failed to protect the poor and weak in their society. The Apostle Paul went from being "Saul" an accessory to murder of Christians, to being renamed "Paul," the foremost spokesperson of this newly formed Christian faith.

"Mo, you've covered quite a few 'call stories' from the Bible," said Dr T. "But go back. There's another obvious one. What about your namesake? What was his calling?"

"I guess it was to speak on behalf of God to the Egyptian Pharaoh, saying, 'Let my people go.' So, his calling was to be God's instrument for freeing Israel from slavery," said Mo.

"And what do you remember about who Moses was as a person?" asked Dr. T.

"He was scared a little. Not eloquent," said Mo.

"Yes. What else? Think about earlier in his life. What did he do?" asked Dr. T.

"Well," said Mo, "The Pharaoh had made a decree that all male Hebrew babies were to be killed. So, after his birth, Moses' Hebrew mother hid him and then put him in a waterproof basket and sent him floating down the Nile River where she hoped he'd be rescued. Moses' sister was watching from a safe distance to see what would happen. And the Pharaoh's daughter found him. Moses' sister walked up and (without giving away the secret) suggested that Moses' natural mother just might be a good nurse for him. So, Moses' natural mother ended up rearing him in the Pharaoh's household for a while, and then eventually giving him back to the Pharaoh's daughter who named him Moses', which means 'to draw' or something like that, because he was 'drawn' from the water."

"Well done! Good memory," said Dr. T., "And what else? Think about when Moses was a grown man."

"Well, he did murder an Egyptian who was beating an Israelite," said Mo.

"Exactly. Gosh, do you think he was 'good enough' for his calling?" asked Dr. T. a little bit of playful sarcasm slipping out.

"All right. You've made your point," said Mo. "But do you think all this stuff in the Bible is really true?"

"You mean is it historically true? That I do not know. But I believe some of it is historically true and some of it is symbolically and eternally true," said Dr. T. "But it's not all literally true. You already learned that in your confirmation class, and you've heard it again here in college."

"But which parts do you think are historically true?" asked Mo.

"I'm not sure. I guess I'm more certain about the parts that I think are *not* historically true. You know, people living to be hundreds of years old. A flood that covered the entire world. The earth having four corners (as in a flat earth). There are numerous passages that are scientifically false.

"There are also passages in which God is depicted as cruel and God is said to command others to be cruel. I think those passages are untrue. You know, God commanding Israel to stone disobedient sons, adulterers, or people engaged in homosexual acts. The list goes on. And despite what the Bible says, I don't believe God ever commanded Israel to kill every man, woman, child, and beast in some of the lands it conquered. I think that people *claimed* this as God's command, but their listening was distorted by their sinful self-interest. At best, God may have said, 'You need to maintain your distinctive and faithful lives and not get sucked into the destructive idolatries (such as temple prostitution) of this conquered culture.' I just don't accept God as cruel and demanding cruelty from the faithful as historically true. What finally matters to me is love. Which passages in the Bible teach us about love? That's what is important to me," said Dr. T.

"So, the Bible is simple then. Just love each other, right?" said Mo.

"Oh, no," said Dr. T. laughing. "The Bible is very complicated, because love is very complicated too. It's not just warm feelings. It's action. It's working for equal rights. Making sure everybody has a decent place to live, enough food to eat, fair treatment in the courts, freedom to speak and worship as they choose, and much more. It's very complicated," said Dr. T. "And maybe that's what you'll spend much of your life struggling with. Can you imagine what a rich and rewarding life that might be?"

Chapter 27

Their sophomore and junior years at Garden College passed in a blur of studies, parties and dances with friends, long-distance running for Mo, intramural tennis for Annie, and ever-deepening love between the two young people. Summers continued the pattern of part-time jobs. Mo cut yards and worked with the SC Wildlife Commission, especially studying snakes but also other reptiles. Annie continued lifeguarding. During non-work hours the couple went to the movies, ate out, talked, and when they had the chance, made love. Sometimes it seemed as though life could not get any better.

By their senior year, Mo had worked through his spiritual discernment process with Dr. T. And he discerned what Presbyterians described as "a sense of call," in his case, a feeling that God wished for him to become a minister. As Mo reflected on what this meant for him, he realized that, yes, he had had the strange experience of hearing a voice in his head that he identified with God (though this was certainly not something he could prove). At the same time there were more down to earth sorts of signs that he might be "called" to the ministry. He had discovered fulfillment, even fun, in theological reflection. He had gifts for ministry—intelligence, compassion, creativity, persistence, and a sense of humor. And it seemed as though he might be able to help others with what he would learn to do if he continued his theological education and training.

With Dr. T.'s support, Mo decided to apply to graduate school to enter a Master of Divinity program designed for future ministers. He asked Dr. T. for his suggestions.

He said, "Well, there are divinity schools. Typically, they are professional schools, like medical schools and law schools, that are part of universities. And there are seminaries, usually free-standing graduate schools for religious education, often connected to and supported by a particular denomination or denominations. I think a divinity school education, such as the divinity school at Harvard or Yale or the University of Chicago, might be especially exciting for your ever-questioning mind. But a Presbyterian-affiliated seminary might be a better fit if you truly feel you might become the pastor of a Presbyterian church one day. I'd suggest doing some research about the possibilities."

Mo weighed the options for months, visited a couple of the seminary campuses, as well as a divinity school. He applied to two Presbyterian seminaries and was accepted at both. He finally decided to attend Covenant

Presbyterian Seminary in Nashville, Tennessee. Covenant was well-known as a small, academically challenging seminary, especially noted for its homiletics (preaching) faculty.

Meanwhile, Annie was also weighing her options. Did she want to teach English in secondary schools, or should she consider graduate school herself? Would she make a better teacher or a better writer, or should she try to do both? And if she were accepted in a graduate school a long distance from Mo, what then?

She and Mo talked about the possibilities and challenges for some time, as well as what their future might look like. Without telling Annie, Mo knew the answer as clearly as anything he had ever known. After Annie had begun to date him, even pretend dating, he had never considered dating anyone else. He knew the love he felt for Annie was beyond her physical beauty. It was also their deep friendship, how they respected each other, enjoyed learning from and about each other, how they laughed and played and had fun together, and their shared faith and values.

But there was also this peculiar attraction that she had felt for him starting all the way back in junior high school, maybe even before that, an attraction she had acted upon first, because, heaven knows, he might never have gotten the courage to approach her otherwise. She had many potential suitors in high school and college, but for some inexplicable reason she was attracted to him, the guy with the giant scar on his face, the one who was tongue-tied around girls, the weirdo who liked church. Mo often said to God in his prayers, "I know I don't deserve her, but thank you!"

Then how should he ask her to marry him? Mo wanted to do something memorable and romantic, and he wanted to do it soon before their graduate school and job prospects became even more complicated. So, he planned.

Chapter 28

On an upcoming weekend, Mo, and Annie rode home to Dover together and went to church. After worship was over, they went out to Michael's for lunch. Mo got the Cherry Bomb burger and Annie got the Hocus Pocus. They talked about the service, especially the music and the sermon. They liked how Dr. McIntyre had used some humor to ease into a more serious subject—how the gospel challenged us to protect the environment and how the world did not belong to us. It was merely lent to us, placed temporarily into our stewardship. And God expected it to be cared for, not polluted with smog, acid rain, strip-mining, sewage in the waters, and plants and animals dying.

On their way out of the church after the service, Mo and Annie had noticed several appreciative church members thanking the pastor for talking so clearly and "biblically" about such a crucial subject. But then they also noticed a couple of angry parishioners who met Dr. McIntyre at the door and complained about what a downer of a sermon he had given. "Didn't you ever read in the Bible that we are supposed to have 'dominion' over the creation?" said one angry, balding older man with dyed black hair.

The angry reactions were amazing to Mo and Annie. Annie said, "What were they expecting? Did they think he was going to say, 'Sure. Go right ahead and pollute all you want. God wants the planet to be destroyed.'"? As astonished as they were by the furious church members, Mo and Annie were pleased that the pastor had not apologized or backed down when confronted. He had simply said, "I'd be happy to talk with you further about this, if you would like to schedule an appointment this week." But the older man had said nothing, and just stomped away.

Mo and Annie finished their lunch and drove back to campus together. As they drove, Mo sang to Annie. His voice wasn't great, but she loved it when he sang. So, he popped in a cassette tape of Billy Vera and the Beaters singing "At This Moment." He turned it down low, and then sang along so that he could find the right pitches. While he sang and drove, he threw in some silly schmaltz and goofy faces and occasionally looked over at Annie, who laughed and smiled.

When they got back to campus, still slightly full of lunch, they had a light dinner of salad in the cafeteria. And then as evening was coming on, Mo smiled and said, "Let's go for a walk."

"Okay," said Annie smiling back.

The temperature was a little cool. So, they zipped their jackets and held hands as they walked. At one point on their walk, Mo stopped, and reached into the pocket of his jacket. He pulled out a small cassette player and pushed the button. It was Kenny Rogers singing "Lady." Annie looked at him and laughed. Then he took her left hand in his left hand, and he put his right hand around her waist, and he led her in a simple dance, just a box-step really. But it was better dancing than Mo had ever done before. Annie giggled and said, "Oh, my God. When did you learn to do this? And who taught you?"

"My mother. And I've been practicing on my own for a few weeks too," he said.

"I love it," she said.

When the song ended, Mo grinned and gave a small, stiff bow. "Thank you for the honor of the dance, madam," he said. And then he took three steps back, reached into his other jacket pocket, pulled out a small box that he opened. It was a ring with a small diamond in the center surrounded by green emeralds, because he remembered Annie had said once that emeralds were her favorite gemstone. As Annie's hands covered her mouth and her eyes welled with tears, Mo knelt on one knee and with a shaky voice he said, "Annie, I love you, and I want your face to be the first one I see every morning and the last one I see every night. I want to have a family with you, and travel with you, and laugh and cry with you, and grow old with you, and watch you become a grumpy old woman who corrects people's grammar. I love you. Will you marry me?"

With the last sentences the tears slipped down Annie's cheeks even as she laughed, and shook her head, and stared down at Mo, she said, "You idiot. Yes. I'll marry you."

So, with their marriage plans made, the couple decided they would be moving to Nashville for Mo to attend seminary, and Annie would search for a teaching position in the city to get some experience teaching and to pay the bills. After Mo finished his seminary master's degree (a three-year program), Annie would get her own master's degree once they moved to Mo's first church. Mo would become the beloved pastor of a vibrant, healthy, growing congregation where he and Annie would enjoy decades of happy, dedicated service. Annie, herself, would complete her master's degree and maybe even a doctorate and begin writing and perhaps become a professor. Along the way, the couple would have a child or even children. They would grow old together, spoil grandchildren, and retire somewhere warm. This was their plan.

Chapter 29

As Mo and Annie began their last semester at Garden College, there was a certain familiarity not only in their relationship with each other but with their friends and with the school itself. They had some confidence about what people might say and do, because, after all, they had spent time together and seen patterns develop. Mo trusted his small group of friends would continue to have his back. He also had come to see Dr. T. not only as a mentor and professor but a friend he hoped to keep in touch with after graduation.

One morning as he was walking down the hall of his dorm, Mo was greeted by Harold Childress, another religion major. Herald had always impressed Mo as yet another fundamentalist pursuing a college degree not so much to broaden his horizons and grapple with the great questions of the age but simply to continue holding his same narrow and ridiculous beliefs. A college degree would serve as "evidence" that he was "open-minded," a believer in the Christian faith and in science, when, in fact, with grim resolve he rejected much of the most basic well-established scientific knowledge. But today the normally sour Harold seemed positively giddy.

"Did you hear the news?" Harold asked Mo with breathless excitement.

"What?" asked Mo, wary to encounter Harold in such a happy mood.

"Yesterday, late in the afternoon, Dr. T. was caught in, let's say, a *compromising* position with philosophy professor Dr. Tim Atkins, at Dr. T's office. It seems the office door wasn't locked, and a student knocked, thought she heard Dr. T say, 'come in,' and then walked in and there they were. So gross! Rumor has it that the board will be asking for his resignation ASAP. Thank God!"

Stunned, Mo shouted, "Harold, get away from me, now!"

"What? I'm just telling you what happened," said Harold suppressing a smile.

"Get the hell away from me, now!" shouted Mo, as he stormed out of the dorm, and walked to Dr. T's office.

The office door was closed, and Mo knocked. No answer. He knocked again and this time added, "Dr. T., it's Mo. Can I talk with you, please?"

"Mo," said Dr. T. from behind the closed door, "I'm really not the best company right now."

"I heard the news," said Mo. "Or at least I heard one version of the news. I just want to talk with you and get the truth. Will you let me in, please? I won't stay long. I promise."

Silence. Then the door opened halfway. Dr. T., his face unshaven, eyes with dark circles underneath, his shirt more wrinkled than normal, stood with one hand on the doorknob as he looked at Mo, trying to figure out the attitude of the person before him.

Finally, he said, "Come on in, Mo." Motioning toward the couch he said, "Have a seat. May I pour you some leftover coffee?"

"No, thanks," said Mo, as he sat down. "I'm just going to say it. Harold Childress told me that you and Dr. Atkins were found in a compromising position in your office yesterday, and that the board would be asking for your resignation immediately. That's not true, is it?"

Dr. T. sighed, crossed his arms, stared at a row of books on the bookshelf, and then said, "Yes, it is true."

"You're a homosexual?" asked Mo, genuinely puzzled, his hands held open in front of him.

"Yes," said Dr. T., "Though men in our sexual community prefer to be called 'gay' and women prefer to be called 'lesbian,' rather than homosexual, which is more of a psychological term, than a self-affirming one."

"Self-affirming?" asked Mo. "According to the Bible, homosexuality is a sin. It doesn't sound like something that needs to be 'self-affirmed' to me."

Dr. T. sighed again. "Yes, the Bible does mention same-sex acts in just a few scattered verses, and it sometimes calls them a sin. But remember we've talked about how we must interpret the Bible in new ways for new times with the new knowledge that we have? You know, the way we've re-interpreted the role of women and deemphasized the passages that subjugate women and emphasized the passages that affirm their equality. And, of course, we've rejected the biblical passages that condone slavery or even that tell slaves, as Paul says, 'to be obedient to your masters.'"

"Yeah," said, Mo.

"Well," said Dr. T. "The passages about same-sex acts also can and should be re-interpreted too because biblical scholars and church historians know that the few passages about same-sex acts are concerned with purity laws that we no longer observe, or abusive kinds of behavior, not constructive, loving relationships. Gay and lesbian people today just want the same rights as heterosexual people, what we call 'straight' people. Does that make sense to you?"

"I don't know, sort of, I guess," said Mo, as he touched his face and looked at the floor. "I mean I've never been one of those people who picks on homosexuals, um, I mean gay and lesbian people. I don't go around calling them names or trying to keep them out of the fraternities, that sort of thing. But I'm going to have to think about the idea of 'self-affirming.' And that it's not a sin. That's new to me. I'm not saying you're wrong. I'm just saying I need to think and pray about this."

"Okay," said Dr. T. "And you can do what I still cannot do, at least I cannot do openly. You can work to change people's understanding."

"But I just don't know if it's right. And I don't know if I can do it," said Mo, his voice suddenly starting to break.

"You're going to know. You'll be learning more about this issue when you get to seminary. And you can do it; you can help change people's understanding," said Dr. T.— his voice now quiet and resolved.

After Mo left Dr. T.'s office his mind was swirling. Of all the professors at Garden College, Dr. T. was the one he respected most, and now he would probably be fired for "immorality." And were his actions immoral? Maybe. That's what he'd always heard and believed. And maybe Dr. T.'s explanation was just some clever attempt to escape responsibility for his behavior. And maybe it was a convenient dismissal of the Bible's clear message on the subject.

But when Mo thought about it more, he saw that the signs were there all along. Never married. No girlfriend or even talk about women. Sort of an artsy guy. But Dr. T. had never made a pass at him, and as far as Mo knew there were no complaints that he had made advances on any of the other male students either.

Mo found Annie at lunch, and he shared the story with her, along with his worries that maybe it was a sin. And why hadn't he noticed the signs of Dr. T's homosexuality all along?

Annie listened, her face looking more and more grave as she said, "Uh huh," between bites of salad. Finally, after Mo had spent about five minutes getting everything out, he stopped and looked at Annie. She set her fork down, looked him directly in the face, and said, "You really should hear yourself, Mo. Here's this man who has been one of the best friends you've ever had. He's been a mentor for you, someone who has stood up for you. And here you are worried about 'homosexuality' being a sin, and if it is a sin, acting as though it worse than any of the others. What about the stuff you and I do, and we're not married yet? That's fornication."

"Well," said Mo, turning red and starting to say more.

"I'm not finished," said Annie, her eyes flashing. "And you come up with all these 'signs' about Dr. T. that you 'should have' caught, you say. Do you have any idea about your ridiculous stereotypes and prejudices? Did you think he was going to wear a pink triangle that said, 'Watch out! I'm gay!'? He needs your support right now, not your stereotypes, and certainly not your judgment. What if you organized a group of students and had them send a signed letter to the administration asking for Dr. T. to be kept on? Or what if you set up a rally to support him?"

Mo was dumbfounded and angry and said nothing for a few seconds.

"I don't appreciate your comparing what we do to what he did," he said. "And how many students do you think would sign a damn letter supporting him? Three or four? And how many would come to a rally to support him? About the same. I'd be the laughingstock of the college. People would assume that I'm gay too. I'd be getting picked on for the rest of my life."

Annie stood and picked up her tray. Her face flushed and her eyes filled with tears as she glared down at Mo who just sat angry and confused.

She said, "Mo, I've never been ashamed of you, but I'm ashamed of you today. If you don't stand up for your friend, you'll regret it the rest of your life. Think about that. Right now, I just need a break from you." Annie turned and walked over to dump the rest of her lunch contents in the trashcans and to place her tray on the conveyer belt to go back to be washed.

A few people at the tables near Mo snickered and murmured. "Ooh. Looks like some trouble with those two." "Looks like trouble in paradise."

Mo ate the rest of his lunch, put his tray away, and left the cafeteria his mind still raging. Part of him knew that Annie was right, and that made Mo even more angry. Why did he have to get involved? Wasn't this something for the faculty and administration to deal with, not a damn student, especially not one just a few months away from graduating. And this was a small college where people loved to gossip and the whole episode had the potential for causing rumors about Mo already. He imagined the comments. "You know, Mo Campbell was the teacher's pet, so to speak." "Mo Campbell spent a lot of time with Dr. T. I'll bet there were penetrating insights." "Did Mo Campbell get 'special attention'?"

Yet Mo knew he should stand up for his friend and mentor against what ultimately amounted to a bunch of bullies with official titles. He knew what he should do.

The week passed. Dr. T. met with the administration and faculty team assigned to his case. He told the team, "I've done nothing wrong. If this had happened with a straight professor, you would have had no concerns, but because of my sexual orientation you treat me with a double standard."

He was given the "opportunity" to resign and receive a small severance or be fired and receive nothing. As a matter of principle, he chose to be fired, and by a vote of 6 to 1 was terminated. He cleaned out his office and was gone before Monday morning. Over the next few months, word circulated that he was unable to find another teaching position, and that he had gone into non-profit work as the director of a homeless shelter in the Atlanta area. Mo never organized anything to protest what happened, and he did not even come and say goodbye. He regretted it the rest of his life.

And once again, Mo was furious at the bullies he viewed as a self-righteous little band of "intellectuals" who enjoyed destroying a decent human being. But, even more, Mo was angry with himself, because he had had the chance to show at least a little bit of courage, but he'd been a coward, again. And he had been given the opportunity to demonstrate his gratitude for Dr. T's mentoring of him over the years. But instead, he had chosen the easy way and the lazy way of avoiding Dr. T. altogether. A biblical image came into Mo's thoughts—the disciples abandoning Jesus when the authorities came to arrest him before his trial and crucifixion. One of them, Peter, even denied knowing who Jesus three times was. Mo thought, "Maybe my name should be Peter. I screwed up. Dear God, I've been such a hypocrite and a coward. Help me never abandon a friend or a right cause again."

Chapter 30

Of course, with Dr. T.'s departure, Mo was given a new faculty advisor for his final semester of study--Dr. Snelling, a stiff, 60-something-year-old, white-haired professor who had developed the annoying habit of speaking very slowly and marking practically every pause in his speech with "um." "Um, we will be comparing Judaism, Christianity, and Islam, um, in this course. On the final exam, you will, um, be expected to provide some, um, detail about the similarities and differences between the religions." The more Mo listened to the man, the more it seemed to him that the extra slow cadence and the use of "um" was not just a verbal tic or something that flowed from nervousness. Instead, he thought it was a way of lending a false gravity to everything he said. It was a method of exercising control because it took so damned long for him to say anything that by the time he had finished saying something you had to give serious consideration as to whether it was worth arguing with him and risk another ten minutes of listening. Mo usually just bit his tongue, and counted the weeks left in the semester.

The semester finally did end. On their last night as students, Mo and Annie spent a few minutes walking around the campus. They looked at classroom buildings where they had taken notes until their hands were sore, and they had had their minds expanded like balloons ready to pop. They walked by the library and recalled all the time they'd spent in study groups there, the hours devoted to digging through card files and microfilm, how many times they had endured stern looks from librarians who were weary of their too loud voices and their necking in between the book racks. "This is not a brothel. Take it outside, please."

Then they drove down to the ocean, held hands, and walked along the beach in the dark.

Mo said, "Hey, English major, how would you describe this scene?"

Annie thought for a moment and then said, "The ocean breezes smell like salt water and possibility, the beginning of life. And the sound of waves crashing is peaceful, but also a reminder that life comes crashing in on us in waves, waves unending, waves we must stand against."

Mo said, "I love you, Annie. Let's stand together."

"Yes," and she kissed him.

The next day Annie graduated Magna Cum Laude and received the William Carrillo Award for promise in English Literature. Mo, meanwhile, was just pleased that he had managed to graduate Cum Laude. For years afterwards, Annie mainly resisted the temptation to tease him about her superior academic achievements.

As they walked from the graduation to their cars, Mo turned, his eyes scanning the campus, drinking it all in one last time. He'd found the love of his life, what he thought was the calling of his life, and the weakness and challenge of his life, all during his time at this place. This was sacred ground and this chapter in his life was closing. He stopped and turned slowly in a full circle trying to take it all in, and to hold the image in his mind like a photo he could pull out of his wallet and look at whenever he wanted. Then he turned and walked to his car.

Chapter 31

Their small early summer wedding was officiated by Dr. McIntyre and attended by their friends and family. Annie was pleased that Mo managed to arrive at the church more than an hour early. What she didn't know was that Mo's dad not only served as his best man for the service but also made sure he wasn't late. Mo's dad had even made sure he got the wedding rings from Mo the night before and placed them beside his car keys and wallet. Though he knew Mo could be a little scatter-brained when he was under pressure, he and his wife were also intensely proud of the young man their son had turned out to be.

Denise was Annie's maid of honor. In typical Denise fashion, while assisting in the women's dressing room she remained cool and calm during the flurry of last-minute details and strong emotions. At one point, the professional wedding photographer, a twenty-something-year-old named Bob Troutman, demanded that Annie and the bridesmaids pose for "one more candid shot." Annie, who just wanted to catch her breath, sit in silence for ten seconds, and then make one last bathroom stop said, "No. We're not posing for one more candid shot. We've already posed for twenty 'candid shots,' and if we posed, then they were not candid shots!"

Bob said, "Oh, my. I just wanted to…"

Denise interrupted him, "Bob, we really appreciate your thorough work. Now, it would be great if you could stop over and take some photos of the guys in their dressing room and the guests as they arrive. Thanks so much."

Bob nodded and left the room.

Denise looked at Annie and said, "Alright now, girl. Breathe. You got this."

"You're right," said Annie, sighing. "You're a good friend."

"I know," said Denise. And the two women laughed.

The service itself was lovely. As Annie, dressed in a flowing white wedding gown and accompanied by her father, made her way down the center aisle of the church, Mo felt his eyes filling with tears. He bit the inside of his mouth to keep from crying. In his wedding sermon, Dr. McIntyre made the congregation laugh when said, "The sermon is for Mo and Annie, but it's okay if the rest of you listen in too." He reminded the couple that they were promising to love each other and to remain married to each other for the rest of their lives. "The Apostle Paul tells us that one of the keys of love," Dr. McIntyre said, "is patience, allowing our beloved partner holy space to be different, to be other, himself or herself, not a clone of ourself." Though the rest of the service passed in a blur, this was the one line from the wedding that Mo remembered for the rest of his life. He and Annie would need to be patient with each other.

After a three-day weekend honeymoon in the mountains near Asheville, North Carolina, Mo, and Annie drove to Nashville where they moved into a small, one-bedroom apartment on campus and Mo began seminary. The place had light green linoleum floors, off-white cinderblock walls, a couple of window unit air conditioners, and all the charm of a U.S. Army barracks. But it was home, and good enough for a young couple just getting started.

New Testament Greek was offered in the summer as a six-week intensive study. The method was like the U.S. military style of teaching languages-- intensive study of a language, maybe eight hours a day, for several weeks with testing weekly. Then once the intensive study was completed, using the language on a regular, less intensive basis. Mo had never been strong with languages (he'd made a D in high school Spanish, for heaven's sake). So, the notion of learning even rudimentary New Testament Greek in such a short time was something he looked forward with the enthusiasm of a housecat anticipating a bath. But fortunately Annie was excellent in languages. So she helped Mo survive those formidable six weeks. Eventually, over time, and with the advent of computerized biblical language programs, Mo became reasonably proficient not only in New Testament Greek, but later in the more difficult biblical language, Hebrew.

As Mo left the apartment to walk to the first class, Annie handed him a brown paper bag lunch with a red smiley face drawn with magic marker on the outside. She flashed him a smile and gave him a kiss, and said, "Now, don't take any shit off those other kids."

"Shut up," said Mo, laughing. "Thanks for the lunch, smart ass. I love you and I'll see you around 5:00."

"I love you too," she said, still laughing. "You can do this."

"We'll see," he said.

"You can do this."

"Okay, I can do this with your help."

 As Mo walked across the campus, he noted the stately old red-brick buildings with ivy climbing up them, 100-year-old oak trees, and manicured lawns that gave quiet voice to a long heritage of faithful scholarship. Men and women, from young adult to seniors, walking, ambling, shuffling, or speed-walking in various directions toward the different buildings. He wondered, "Am I going to be smart enough? What are the other students going to be like? Are they going to be these extremely holy people who never say a bad word, never complain, never gossip, and never lust? And here *he* was. Damn! Maybe this was not a good idea."

But then Mo recalled that voice he'd heard at the funeral and the conversation about "being good enough."

"Okay, God," he thought, "If this is what you want me to do, make it clear. If it's not, make that clear too. But if it's not what you want me to do, it's going to be kind of embarrassing for me, you know."

Mo stepped into the Elijah Springer Building, a Gothic structure with pointed arches and flying buttresses on the outside. Inside, he paused to look at massive stained-glass windows depicting biblical scenes. Underneath were brass nameplates indicating the window donor and whom the window was donated in honor of. As he made his way down the hall to the stairs, he noticed the dark wood banisters smoothed by thousands of hands and rich green carpets worn by thousands of footsteps by students like him, but also by professors, theological giants of the church over the decades. He walked up the stairs to the second floor, located the classroom that had a dot-matrix printer-generated sign taped outside it that read, "Introduction to New Testament Greek." He took a breath and walked in. There were probably twenty people seated at desks, with another ten or so still coming into the room around the same time as Mo, about five minutes before start time. Mo looked around and found a desk in the center of the room, about midway back. He nodded at the person who would be sitting right behind him, a slender, brown-haired woman, probably in her late twenties, with dimpled cheeks. Before he could sit down, she smiled, held out her hand, and said, "Hey, I'm Kathleen Summers. How are you?"

Mo shook her hand, and said, "Um, fine, I'm Mo Campbell. How are you?"

"Good," she said. "You ready for this?" she asked as she opened her hands, palms up, indicating the class itself.

"I don't know," he said. "I hope so."

"Same here, a little nervous," she said, smiling again. "But it's kind of exciting too. We're going to be able to read the Bible in its original languages. How cool is that?"

"It's really cool," he said.

As he sat down, a stocky, middle-aged African American man, with short hair flecked with gray, in a seat to his left, gave his hand a firm shake and introduced himself. "Hi. Samuel Sutton," he said with a nod and a quiet voice.

"Mo Campbell," he answered, "Nice to meet you."

Two people, a thin man, probably in his 40s, a beak nose, and long arms, and a woman, medium build, probably in her 30s, red hair, freckled skin, came into the room and stood facing the class. "Good morning, everybody! I'm Robert Johnson. Beside me is my excellent teaching assistant, Nancy O'Brien. Welcome to New Testament Greek. Let's begin our time together with prayer. O God, You who have flung the galaxies into space, formed the mountains, and filled the seas, You who have grown the mighty sequoias and given life to the hummingbirds, You who have made the ecosystem to work together, and You who have made each one of us, just a little lower than the angels, and precious in your sight, to You be all glory, honor, and praise forever. You have called us to this time and place to study an ancient word, a comforting and troubling word, a human word, and a holy one. Guide our conversations and our learning that we might grow as your people and be faithful interpreters of your word for a world hungry to hear good news. We pray through Christ our Lord. Amen."

"Amen," answered the class. Other than Sunday school or confirmation classes, it was the first time in Mo's life that he had experienced someone leading a prayer to begin a class. Mo decided he liked it, and, as he discovered, this was typically how most of his seminary classes would begin, with a prayer, sometimes brief, sometimes lengthy. He came to realize that his education, like his messy life, was bracketed by prayer, often led by Christians who were more intelligent and faithful than he was. It was inspiring and humbling at the same time.

As he expected, New Testament Greek was difficult for Mo. Though many of the letters in the Greek alphabet looked like English letters, such as an alpha that looked a lot like an a, an epsilon that resembled an e, and an omicron like o, some of the letters were different. And then there were all the grammatical parts of speech he needed to remember from grade school, or in his case, learn for the first time, since he tended to speak English well, not by knowing the rules exactly but simply from hearing and reading it spoken correctly. And thank God for Annie who *did* know the rules and could explain them to him in the evenings.

On their second day of class, Dr. Johnson recommended that the students form small study groups to help them learn the material and to encourage each other. Mo was in a group with Kathleen and Samuel. These two people also became Mo's best friends at the seminary during the three years that it took to complete the Master of Divinity degree program designed primarily for students who would be entering pastoral or chaplaincy ministries. The name of the degree itself seemed a bit arrogant to Mo—a *Master* of Divinity degree? Who in the world was a *master* of God? Apparently, decades earlier students in the graduate schools did earn Bachelor of Divinity degrees, but that was confusing to people who had master's degrees from other graduate schools, such as lawyers. Besides, maybe a *Bachelor* of Divinity was unpretentious to the extreme, and everybody knows if you try too hard to be unpretentious then you are being pretentious. Or so the thinking may have gone.

Thanks to his study group friends, as well as Annie, and his own hard work, Mo managed to pass New Testament Greek the first time. This was a great relief for him, since he assumed if he failed Greek, he would certainly fail Hebrew which was much more difficult, with hardly any letters that looked like English, and confusing grammatical rules. And, of course, just to be even more difficult, Hebrew was read from right to left, instead of from left to right.

Chapter 32

After completing the summer New Testament Greek session, Mo had his first semester of regular classes. He was enrolled in New Testament (Part I), Church History (Part I), Introduction to Preaching, and Christian Ethics. Mo was pleased to notice that Kathleen and Samuel were also in the Christian Ethics class. Professor Norton, a thirty-something-year-old whiz kid graduate of Harvard Divinity School, taught the class. On the first day, after a brief morning prayer, he launched into a mesmerizing, rapid-fire lecture.

At one point he said, "When you graduate from this old school in three years, maybe a few of you will feel that you have not incurred enough debt. So, you will decide to go on to pursue a Ph.D. I am not certain that Christians with such highfalutin degrees are welcomed into heaven, but we we'll trust in God's mercy to overcome our pride."

A couple of students in the class offered a startled giggle at this. Dr. Norton continued. "But most of you will head off to become pastors or chaplains somewhere out in the sticks of Alabama or in the suburbs of DC or in the inner-city of New York. And when you get there, wherever *there* is, you will be the official local Christian ethicist in that place. Oh, rest assured there will be other Christian ethicists there. The fundamentalist preacher down the street who has a long list of people going to hell if they don't repent and make a verbal confession of Jesus is Lord before they die. The church council member who has attended several Billy Graham rallies and says he is 'born again,' and why doesn't the church emphasize being 'born again' more? And maybe add in the church member who never misses a Sunday school class or worship and who reads serious theology.

"There will be other Christian ethicists there. But you will be the official local Christian ethicist for your community. And the question that will come to you in various forms, again and again, sometimes stated explicitly, and sometimes implicitly, will be, 'What is the right thing to do?' And you will need to be prepared to say something deeper than, 'Well, the Bible says…' as if the Bible were so simple that you could easily just a lift a verse here or there to answer any question. And you will need to be ready to deal with the complexity of the Bible and what we now know, especially in various areas of science, that the biblical writers did not know. You will also have the tender task not only have discerning what is right but also discerning how to speak that rightness to people who are struggling with their own brokenness, hurt, and sin, people who live in a world that delights them, but also perplexes and wounds them. 'What is the right thing to do?' Your calling will be to provide answers and paths that are faithful and true, ways attuned with the will of God, God help you. How you will respond to these questioning people, what resources you will rely upon, will be the subject of this class over the next semester."

Once again, Mo felt the weight of the calling before him. People would be depending on him to have learned how Christians can and should make intelligent and faithful ethical decisions. They would expect him to have thought through some of the burning social justice issues of the day, and even to begin anticipating and preparing for future issues.

Dr. Norton was a scholar from the United Methodist tradition and one of the more helpful ideas he shared was what the Methodists called "The Wesleyan Quadrilateral," or "The Methodist Quadrilateral" for making ethical decisions. Instead of just relying on the Bible, ethical choices swung on four hinges "Scripture, Tradition, Reason, and Experience."

"For example," said Dr. Norton. "Remember how most of the church denied women the opportunity to be ordained as ministers for centuries. Church leaders, especially male church leaders in power, argued that the Bible was clear on this issue, and they made sure they pointed to the passages that supported their views. However, the Bible says more than one thing about women and leadership, doesn't it? So, the church began reexamining the Bible and noticing how frequently women were mentioned as being in positions of leadership and how they were even called *diakonos*, which you students of Greek know can be translated as "deacon" or even as "minister." But beyond the Bible, the church examined tradition. Had it always been "tradition" that women were excluded from ordination? Careful research said the answer to that question was 'no.' Women have held high offices in the church over the centuries. It had just been downplayed by church historians. And what of "reason." What did "reason" tell us about women's abilities for ministry? An honest answer, of course, was that women's abilities were equal or superior to men's abilities. Finally, what did our experience, the experience of men and women tell us? Again, our experience told us that women were more than capable of serving as ordained ministers. So, it took a while, and there were lots of arguments and struggles, but finally many of the church denominations changed their policies and began ordaining women. Yet some still have not changed. May they see the light!"

A student in the first row raised her hand and asked, "Are there any issues right now that you think the church may be changing its mind about if it uses the quadrilateral?"

"I'm glad you asked," said Dr. Norton. "I do. I think the church will be rethinking its beliefs about gay and lesbian people, including ordination for them and some sort of marriage or commitment service."

Several students groaned and rolled their eyes. A few made comments barely under their breath. "That'll never happen." "Well, the Bible says it's a sin." "Yeah, that'll be the day they close the church."

"It sounds as though a number of you have already made up your minds about this issue," said Dr. Norton, squinting his eyes. "Just realize that this matter may not be as simple as you imagine. Even now, major Christian theologians, biblical scholars, and ethicists are doing research, writing papers and books, and engaging in vigorous debate. And the good news is that you are also going to have your own opportunity to jump into the fray. For your term paper, due at the end of the semester, you will submit an argument for or against same-sex ordination and same-sex marriage. You may come down on either side of the issue, but you must show me that you have done serious research, and that you adequately address all four areas: scripture, tradition, reason, and experience. I think you are going to be surprised at what you discover."

Once again, there were a few groans and some of Mo's classmates rolled their eyes. One student, a runner-thin middle-aged woman, said, "All I know is they're going to hell."

"Stop! Stop right there!" said Dr. Norton, his right hand held up, fingers spread apart, as if to hold someone back. His voice was raised just below a shout. "Be aware that many of us have gay or lesbian relatives and friends. We also unknowingly work with and encounter gay and lesbian people every day. And there may even be gay or lesbian students in this school or in this classroom. You do not have to agree with me that these are our brothers and sisters who just happen to have a different sexual orientation. But I do expect you to refrain from verbal attacks and wholesale condemnation while you're in my classroom. Is that understood by everyone?" Not wanting to embarrass her, Dr. Norton gave only a quick glance at the woman who had spoken, her face now crimson. But then his eyes panned across the entire class.

There were a few angry faces, and one man sitting in the back whispered to his friend, "I'm going to change my class schedule to something else." But most of the students nodded in agreement with the professor and there were many quiet murmurs of "yes."

Mo was astonished. He'd somehow imagined seminary as a place of gentle, quiet reflection, neatly folded hands, and bowed heads. He had worried about whether he would be able to fit into that saintly, otherworldly mold. But it was dawning on him that that mold did not exist here. And this class was more like a kind of battle, a spiritual battle, a battle of interpretation and understanding, but a battle, nonetheless. And as Dr. T. had promised him, he would be learning about a subject he needed to know more about.

Bring it on.

Chapter 33

As he had before, Mo studied alone, or with his friends Kathleen and Samuel in the library, and occasionally with them over coffee in the student center. One day while the three were sitting in a corner of the student center, Mo said, "You know, we've been studying together since Greek school, several months now. And the odd thing is we've been so busy that we've never really told our stories to each other, at least not much about us. Would y'all be interested in sharing a little bit more? I'm not trying to pressure you, but I'm just curious. I'd be glad to go first."

Kathleen and Samuel looked at each other with faint smiles and raised eyebrows, and then they looked back at Mo.

"Um," said Kathleen, "How much do you want to know? And could we keep our stories just between us?"

"I really don't want to pry," said Mo. "I'd just like to know a bit more, whatever you're comfortable sharing. And I'd certainly keep it in confidence."

"Yeah, same here," said Samuel, his face more serious than usual. "I'll keep things in confidence. I mean, that's what we're going to be doing once we go into the ministry, right?"

"Great, I'll go first," said Mo, who then told the story of his growing up in Dover, how he met Annie, their dating, a bit about his sense of calling, and his time in college.

Kathleen smiled, genuinely pleased, and said, "What an interesting story of your life so far. I enjoyed hearing it, except the part about the snakes."

"Same here," said Samuel nodding his head. "But not a fan of snakes."

They all laughed. There was an awkward pause. Then Kathleen and Samuel looked at each other and laughed again as each asked the other at the same time, "Do you want to go next?"

Samuel said, "That's fine. I'll go next. I grew up in Richmond, Virginia, the firstborn of three children. I have two sisters. My father was a pastor in the American Baptist Church denomination, progressive Christians. Mom worked as a bank teller. My sisters and I were church kids, down at the church several days a week for whatever was going on. The difference was that my sisters did not like it that much, but I adored it. I loved seeing my dad in the pulpit and watching him preach and hearing people in the congregation shout, 'Amen!' or 'Preach on!' or 'Yes!' I loved the sweet old ladies who would grab me and pull me close and whisper encouragement in my ears, and the old men who would shake my hand hard and tease me and say, 'This young fella is growing up *right!*' I loved all that. It just felt like a foretaste of heaven. So, when I began to sense a calling from God, it wasn't like it is for some people who want to run away from it. No. I embraced it. It felt like coming home to me. And here I am."

Mo and Kathleen nodded and smiled. Then Mo said, "May I ask you a personal question?"

"Well, that depends on what the question is," said Samuel with a faint smile and his eyes glancing to the side.

"I just want to know what it was like growing up Black in Richmond, Virginia."

Samuel's mouth dropped open a fraction of an inch. He hesitated, stared at Mo, took a deep breath in, and then blew it out. And at last he spoke, his voice soft and slow. "It was hard, harder than it should have been. Because my ancestors had been abducted and brought to this country as slaves, we had so many disadvantages. We were treated with unspeakable viciousness by White people. We had to fight for the right to be free. The right not to be raped or lynched. Then the right to vote and hold office. To own property. To get a decent education. To marry someone of another race. To drink from the same water fountains as White people. To sit in the same seats as White people. To enjoy the same U.S. Veterans benefits. To be able to live in the same neighborhoods as White people, and to be treated with the same dignity as White people. Not to get beaten up or killed by the police for 'sassing' or looking at them 'the wrong way.' We had to fight for so many things.

"It was hard growing up Black in Richmond where every day I would travel down Monument Avenue and see shrines that were erected many years after the Civil War to honor men who had fought to secede from the Union and to keep my family in slavery. These monuments, along with the rebel flags I often saw, were nothing less than a stick in the eye of Black folks, a way of saying, 'You think you won, but you didn't. You'll never win. We are still in control. So don't you forget who you are and get too uppity.'"

As Samuel looked at them, Mo and Kathleen shook their heads in sadness and said nothing for a moment.

Then Mo said, "I'm so sorry. I already knew some of what you said, but not all of it. Much of it I had never even considered. I'm so sorry this happened to you and your family and probably my relatives were part of the reason why. I'm sorry but thank you for telling us. Now we know."

"Yes," said Kathleen. "I'm sorry too. Thank you for teaching us."

Samuel nodded his head once. He said nothing.

Finally, Samuel said, "So, you know some of my story. Let's hear Kathleen's story."

"Whew! Okay," said Kathleen. "I grew up in New York City, the second of two daughters. My parents are Joe and Connie Lighthouse. My dad was, and still is, a part of the crew on one of the Staten Island ferries and my mom was, and is, a preschool teacher assistant. My sister, Rosemary, is about five years older, and, despite my parents' disapproval, lives with her boyfriend, Mark, in a tiny apartment in the Bay Ridge section of Brooklyn. She's a waitress, and an occasional student at Kingsborough Community College, majoring in liberal arts. Mark is an aspiring artist who's sold a few paintings each year. But he's good at drinking coffee and smoking pot."

Mo and Samuel laughed.

"I was a serious student in high school, usually made the honor roll. I also enjoyed sports, especially competitive swimming. Now, here's the confidential part of my story," she continued as she gave a quick look in the eye to Mo and Samuel. "I dated a little bit in high school, and even had a few sexual experiences with men. But I never really had a long-term relationship. And over time, and with the help of an insightful therapist, I finally figured out why. I realized that I'm attracted to women. I'm a lesbian."

Mo's mouth dropped open, and he said, "But you don't look…" And then he caught himself.

"You were going to say I don't 'look like a lesbian,' right?" asked Kathleen.

Mo's flushed crimson. "Um, that's not what I meant…Actually, it *is* what I meant, and I see my prejudice showing again. I'm sorry."

"That's okay," said Kathleen. "People have these stereotypes. I just don't fit them."

"Well," said Mo, "To borrow your line, thanks for teaching us."

They all laughed.

Then Mo asked, "So, may I also ask you a personal question?"

"Okay. You're on a roll with the personal questions," she said with the hint of a smile.

"I know. Please forgive me if it's too much. But what's it like to be you, to be a lesbian in the late 1980s?"

"Hmm. That is a personal question, but also a good question," she said. "It's not easy. I must hide who I am from most people, especially from my denomination, or I won't get ordained no matter how hard I study and how much I learn. You know, 'self-avowed, unrepentant sinner' and all that. I also must hide it from some other people, especially some straight men, who might do me harm, as in trying to murder me. So, even though I have a woman I'm in love with, I'm very careful about public displays of affection that might get my partner and me attacked or killed. And it's just as dangerous, probably even more so, for gay men, you know."

Mo and Samuel nodded.

"Does your family know?" asked Mo.

"My sister does, and she's cool with it. My parents don't know. They may suspect something since I never come around their house with a boyfriend. Then again, they may just think I'm choosy about who I date. One day I hope I'll be able to tell them the truth."

"But how did you decide to become a lesbian?" asked Mo.

"How did you decide to become straight?" asked Kathleen.

"Okay, I see your point," said Mo, red-faced and sweating again.

"Being a lesbian is not something I chose; it's something I discovered about myself. And it's not just about the sex that happens in the bedroom (though that's part of it). It's really about my sexual orientation, who I am at my core. Imagine trying to make yourself gay. How would that be? Now, imagine your relationship with Annie. How does it feel? It doesn't feel forced, right? It just feels natural. That's the way being a lesbian is for me."

"All right, one last question," said Mo. "If I haven't already asked enough stupid questions for one day." Kathleen smiled. Mo continued, "What about all the stuff in the Bible about same-sex relationships? What do you do with all that?"

"Well, I've done some research, just like we're going to do in our class, and yeah, there are some passages in the Bible that're tricky. But the Bible scholars are now saying that the few same-sex passages in the Bible are about cleanliness laws we don't believe in anymore. Or the Hebrew people's concern about anything that looks 'unnatural.' Or concerns about failure to procreate because people basically wanted to have large families because many of the children died. Or there was a reaction to abusive sexual relationships, including homosexual rape, molestation of children, promiscuity, and finally, Paul's worry that same-sex relationships were signs of idolatry (which, of course, they aren't). So, none of the standard 'biblical' arguments against same-sex relationships hold water. It'll really be interesting as we do more research and look at the other three parts of the quadrilateral—tradition, reason, and experience. Of course, I can speak to experience, but I can't yet speak about it publicly."

Samuel said, "I hope one day soon you'll be able to speak about it publicly without fear."

"So, do I," Kathleen said. "And I hope for the day when I'm not discriminated against because of my sexual orientation. I look forward to the time when my partner and I can get married, own property together, maybe raise children together, and all the other things that straight people take for granted. Oh, and it would be nice not to be told again and again that I'm going to hell. I don't believe it."

Mo and Samuel shook their heads and Mo said, "I don't believe it either." Samuel nodded in agreement.

Chapter 34

As the semester continued, the Christian Ethics class did look at all four hinges of the quadrilateral and discovered strong arguments for same-sex rights based on tradition, reason, and experience. Still, there were several students in the class who were angry about what they called "the total disregard of the clear meaning of the Bible." But then Dr. Norton had the students look up several passages in the Bible, passages from the Old Testament and the New Testament. "Slaves, obey your earthly masters…" Colossians 3:22 "Wives, be subject to your husbands…" Ephesians 5:2 "Happy shall they be who take your little ones and dash them against the rock!" Psalm 137:9 "Women be silent in the churches" 1 Corinthians 14:34 "If someone has a stubborn and rebellious son who will not obey his father and mother…Then all the men of the town shall stone him to death." Deuteronomy 21:18-21 "Yet she [women] shall be saved through childbearing…" 1 Timothy 2:15

"Anybody here want to take the Bible at face value and simply apply everything in it without interpretation?" asked Dr. Norton.

Silence.

Then a man's voice piped up from the back of the class, "No. But I *am* going to show my wife that text about wives being subject to their husbands. It's been nice knowing y'all."

The class exploded into laughter.

Not only did the students receive instruction about using the quadrilateral for making ethical decisions, but they also learned about proper interpretation of the Bible itself. Mo was surprised at how complex the interpretation process was. When it came to responsible reading of the Bible, it wasn't merely a case of lifting a few verses out of context, known as "proof-texting." Instead, there were biblical interpretation criteria that had been developed over the centuries. For instance, the Bible's purpose is to tell about God and God's intention for the world. Scripture isn't a science book and was never meant to be read that way. In fact, the biblical writers thought that the earth is flat, the sun 'rises and sets,' men carry 'a seed' and women are basically just incubators for the seed, and so on.

And there were other criteria that the students learned. All true interpretations of the Bible must be ones that are led by the Spirit and serve to increase love, not hatred. Scripture must be read in the context of the entire Bible, and it must be read acknowledging its historical context. Interpretations of scripture can and should change, as they did when it came to slavery, Civil Rights, women's rights, children's rights, and, as Mo, Samuel, and Kathleen believed, gay rights. After all, though scripture was called holy, it was still written by human beings who were inspired by God. And these human beings were not mere robots with God moving their hands across the parchment. So, the Bible had to be reinterpreted for every age. It was a living word, not a dead one.

During his three years of study at the seminary, Mo completed classes in Old Testament, New Testament, preaching, Greek, Hebrew, church polity, leadership, church history, evangelism, spirituality, Christian education, pastoral care, and other subjects. It was a daunting process, but Mo passed each step on the journey, including the denomination's dreaded five-part ordination exams (like the BAR exam for lawyers). Finally, with a breath of relief, at the beginning of May 1990 Mo was ready to graduate and find a pastoral position somewhere.

Chapter 35

At the graduation ceremony and worship service, Dr. Norton, who had been selected by popular vote of the senior class, preached a sermon he titled "Cross Calling." His text for the sermon came from Mark 8:31-38, a section of the Bible in which Jesus challenged his followers, "If any want to become my followers, let them deny themselves and take up their cross and follow me." After finishing the reading, Dr. Norton began his sermon by admitting that perhaps the biblical text he'd chosen seemed awfully harsh and challenging for such a joyous occasion, but in that harshness and challenge was good news not only for the graduates but for the world. He reminded those in attendance of the world around them full of poverty, hunger, violence, oppression, as well as the beauty, wonder, generosity, and justice. Then he said, "I'm going to speak a word now especially for the graduates, but it's okay if the rest of you listen too." A few people in the congregation smiled or laughed, and he smiled with them. And then he was silent, as if centering himself.

He said, "Let me remind the graduating class of some history they have learned from professors in the church history department. You recall reading about the rise of Hitler and The Third Reich in Nazi Germany, and how most German Christians went along with Hitler and the Nazis and became The German National Church. Photos of church leaders of the time laughing and talking with the Nazis are chilling. Even more chilling is that these were not country bumpkins who were duped into going along with Hitler. These were some of the most sophisticated and educated people on the planet, and some of them were Christian theologians of world renown. How could they go along with the madman Hitler and his murderous machine, and encourage their churches to go along too? This is an evil stain upon the church that no amount of time will make clean.

"But you also remember a small group of German Christians stood against Hitler and the Nazis, and they formed what was called The Confessing Church that confessed Christ as Lord and Savior. They rejected the melding of church and state, and especially they repudiated Hitler's presumption of Lordship. The Confessing Church produced a document called The Theological Declaration of Barmen that declared Christ's Lordship in no uncertain terms and by quiet implication put Hitler in his place. Karl Barth, a German theologian, and pastor, was the primary author of the document. And he had to flee Germany for his life after its publication.

"But there was another German theologian you have also studied about. His name was Dietrich Bonhoeffer. He was a brilliant young professor who wrote several books, deeply influential then and now. In one of those books, *The Cost of Discipleship*, he said, 'When Christ calls [each of us] he bids [each of us] come and die.' And Bonhoeffer warned about what he called 'cheap grace,' 'grace without discipleship,' grace without costly commitment.

"Like Barth, Bonhoeffer was opposed to Hitler and the Nazis. And for a while he lived in the U.S. teaching at Union Theological Seminary in New York City. Then he lived in London, serving as a pastor. He could have stayed there remaining safe during the war that was coming. But he chose to return to Germany, because he felt it was his duty to stand with his country and against tyranny. Though he was a pacifist, he decided to participate in a plot to assassinate Hitler with a bomb. The plot failed. Bonhoeffer and the other conspirators were captured, interrogated, tortured, and killed. In fact, Bonhoeffer was hanged by the Nazis just a month before the end of the war. He was engaged to be married and he was only 39 years old. His final words before being hanged were, 'This is the end—for me the beginning of life.'

Dr. Norton paused, looking out at the graduation congregation. He continued. "And Jesus said, 'Behold I send you out as sheep among wolves. Be wise as serpents and innocent as doves.' The work you are being sent by God to do is joyful and holy, but it is not for the faint of heart. You are being sent out to preach and teach a word of grace and challenge, to lead countless church committee meetings that are sometimes fun, sometimes boring, and sometimes angry, to perform weddings for happy couples, baptisms for weeping adults and laughing babies, to pray and hold the hands of people who are sick, and to speak words of truth and hope over those who have died.

"But moreover, never forget that you are also being sent as sheep among wolves. You will be called by God to speak God's truth in love, and it will not always be appreciated. In fact, if you do what you are called to do, sometimes you will be hated for it, by those you expect, and by those you do not expect. I believe that every era has its own 'wolves,' be they people or policies or situations, that we who minister are called to confront while being wise as serpents and innocent as doves. Sometimes, like Barth, we will survive. Other times, like Bonhoeffer, we will die. And the only way we have the courage to do what we are called to do is to remember who calls us and who we ultimately belong to. We remember who we are and whose we are."

Dr. Norton's voice caught, and he stopped for a moment as he searched the congregation for the face of each of his students who sat in the pews before him. Then he spoke again, his voice measured and gentle. "So, graduates, leave here with gladness and anticipation, but also ready to take up your cross and lay down your life knowing that when that day comes, it is the end, but also the beginning of life. Through Christ our Lord and Savior. Amen." Soft amens sounded throughout the congregation, and then the service continued.

Mo heard no voice in his head, but he felt as if God had spoken to him again. And he made a promise to himself. *I will do my best to speak the truth in love and not be a coward. May God give me the courage.*

Chapter 36

Annie, meanwhile, was facing challenges herself. For three years, she had adored teaching English to elementary school children in one of Nashville's poor, urban neighborhoods, and she was passionate about giving these at-risk students the tools they needed early in life to succeed. Annie also discovered she had natural gifts of patience, a sense of humor, and persistence for working with kids, especially kids who came from difficult circumstances. With Mo's graduation and their departure to his first church, she would have to say goodbye to "her kids" and trust that somehow another fulfilling teaching assignment would come along.

So, now the question for Mo and Annie was: Where would they go that might be a good fit for both?

In some ways, they didn't get to decide this solely on their own. In the Presbyterian denomination, there was a matching process for pastors and church. It was practically a "free market" system with churches writing résumés and potential pastors writing their own résumés that were entered into an initial matching service. If there were enough interest on both sides there were typically phone interviews, sermons, face to face interviews, lots of praying, a congregational vote, and both sides needing to feel "a sense of call." And neither side knew exactly how the Spirit might be at work or the Spirit might be ignored and whether it would end up being a good match. There was a lot of mystery and unpredictability in it all. And who knew where you might end up?

Mo received a call to become the pastor of the First Presbyterian Church of Plainview, North Carolina. The congregation had about 150 members (around 80 of them showed up for worship on a typical Sunday) and the church was in a town of 13,000 people, 75 miles outside of Charlotte. The area was mainly blue collar and conservative. Industries included a small freight company, a frozen foods packaging and distribution center, and a furniture manufacturing site.

The church itself was more politically diverse than the town. There were a few flaming liberals scattered throughout the congregation, folks who not only believed in the ordination of women (something the denomination had approved in the 1950s) but who would be just fine actually having a female pastor serve their own church. These same people were just beginning to be more open about gay and lesbian rights (the notion of full LGBTQ+ rights would come later) and some of them, especially some of the women were pro-choice. They were also committed to racial justice, though there was certainly debate about what that truly meant.

On the other hand, most of the congregation was conservative in almost any way you could imagine. Politically—fans of Jesse Helms and quietly accepting of his race-baiting election strategy. Theologically verbal confession of Jesus as Lord gets you into heaven. Unbelievers are heading for hell. "Social justice"? Those were suspicious words, communist sounding, even. Gay and lesbian rights? They had the right to repent or at least have the decency to keep what they did private. Abortion? No way. This was murder. Racial justice? Okay. If it didn't mean any real changes to society or who was allowed to live in the neighborhood or belong to the country club.

This was the church Mo was called to serve.

Chapter 37

In mid-June 1990, Mo and Annie moved their belongings, including a few pieces of furniture, into the simple, two-story, brick manse located near the church. Several members of the congregation's Pastor Nominating Committee met them at the manse. They held a posterboard sign that read "Welcome!" and they gave a little cheer as the moving van pulled in. Though professional movers did most of the work, some of the younger members of the committee helped carry things into the house and assisted in unpacking. They provided a delicious lunch of fried chicken, mashed potatoes and gravy, green beans, biscuits, and peach pie for dessert. The whole day was an enthusiastic and promising beginning.

Annie soon set about putting the place into some semblance of a logical order and Mo served as the muscle for her various house projects. As the young couple settled in over the next few weeks, the main thing they felt was gratitude--for their new little town to live in, for this faith community to serve, for each other as a couple--gratitude to God for all of it.

As was typical, much of the congregation was comprised of retirees, but there were also some young people, (pretty much anybody under the age of 50 was considered young), as well as about five "young families" who had children under the age of 18. Mo was the church's only full-time employee. Occasionally, he was referred to as "the senior pastor," but there were no other pastors on the staff for him to be senior to. There was a part-time secretary, Melinda Russell, who worked Monday-Thursday, 9:00 a.m.-1:00 p.m., a part-time organist/choir director, Susan Callahan, and a part-time custodian (sometimes referred to with the old church language as a sexton— someone who cares for a church's property), Ed Jones.

The church held Sunday school for all ages at 10:00 a.m. and worship at 11:00 a.m. Youth group met on Sunday evening at 6:00. Committees and the church's session met on Wednesday evenings. The church's chancel choir rehearsed on Thursday nights at 7:00.

Mo's job was to preach and lead worship almost every Sunday, except his yearly four vacation Sundays, as well as two Sundays for study leave, and the occasional Sunday for a guest speaker. The old unofficial guideline for sermon preparation was that the preacher would be likely to spend "one hour of preparation for each minute in the pulpit." Mo didn't know if that were true or not, but his sermons were usually around 15 minutes long. And between translating the Hebrew or Greek, examining the historical and biblical context, reading biblical commentaries, brainstorming sermon illustrations and ways of connecting the sermon with the congregation, he figured he did, indeed, spend about 15 hours a week preparing sermons, and another several hours preparing the Sunday morning prayers and liturgy.

His responsibilities also included teaching a Sunday school class, and maybe another class or two at other times during the week. Taking care of the church's administration, (including working with and supervising the staff). Leading the youth group (sometimes with Annie's help or the help of a couple of church members). Visiting people who were in the hospital or in nursing homes, or simply lonely in their own homes. Providing pastoral care (a shortened and less formal version of counseling) for people who were troubled or facing a crisis. Attending and helping equip the church committees. Officiating at weddings and funerals. Assisting needy persons who came to the church looking for money or food. Representing the church in the community. Taking part in the presbytery's ministries (including serving on a presbytery committee or task force). And taking care of whatever else might come up during the week.

Theoretically, this was all to be completed in around 40 hours a week, and Mo was to take Friday as his sabbath day. He also was supposed to have Saturdays off. He usually rested on Fridays, unless an emergency pastoral visit arose or there happened to be a wedding rehearsal or a funeral, and on Saturdays he often finished his sermon and/or other Sunday preparation. It was a full life, and sometimes a hectic one too, moving from one task and one deadline to the next.

Annie, meanwhile, settled into their new life too. She found a position teaching English at Plainview High School (home of the Screaming Eagles). In some ways, it was not going to provide the same emotional rewards as her work in Nashville had. But there was the thrill of being able to tackle *Wuthering Heights* with a class, instead of *See Spot Run*. There were also still plenty of challenges and satisfactions of working with older youth whose parents, in many cases, were not particularly well-educated.

But the biggest challenge Annie faced was a provincialism that hung like a pall over the town, and the high school especially. There was sort of a perverse pride in being backwards, "rednecks," as some of the townspeople described themselves. An aggressive and willful ignorance was cultivated by some. This led to suspicion about outsiders and resistance to meaningful change that was sweeping through society. The U.S. raced to embrace cultural change in the 1990s, but Plainview ambled decades behind in happy obliviousness.

Chapter 38

Mo's first order of business as a new pastor was to build relationships with the church members. Building relationships was something he naturally enjoyed. It seemed to him that there was a mystery about other human beings, an unfolding like a flower, as you got to know their history and who they were. This was one of the great privileges of being a pastor—the opportunity to get to know so many people on a deeper level. But rather than approaching this in a haphazard way, Mo developed a plan. Working with the Presbyterian Women's Circle, he set up a series of lunches with small groups of members at the church so that he might get to know them, and they might get to know him. On the chalkboard he wrote three questions. 1. Tell me something unusual about yourself, something memorable. 2. Tell me about a time you really felt proud of First Presbyterian Church. 3. Tell me about when you really felt God's presence here.

Gladys Norfleet, an 80-something-year old with short white hair and a twinkle in her eye said, "Welcome to our church, Rev. Campbell. Something unusual about me? My senior year in high school, I won the 'Best Dancer' award at the prom. Want to give it a whirl?" she asked as she winked and extended her hand toward him. Mo and the people around the table, smiled and chuckled.

"Good to know," said Mo. "I'm not much of a dancer, but my wife is. I'd have to practice a lot before I could dance with you."

Each of the other participants answered the first question as well. Aaron Spencer, a gentle old man with a quivery voice and shaky hands, said he learned to milk his first cow when he was six. Meredith Howe, a slender middle-aged woman wearing a dark-green business suit, mentioned that she had been a model for a local clothing company in her younger days. And Alex Shillow, a pudgy guy in his 40s said, "I played defensive lineman on a state championship football team in Rhode Island."

All the answers to the second question about when folks felt proud about First Presbyterian had something to do with service or giving. This encouraged Mo.

"I was very proud of our church when we came together after the tornado three years ago and helped several families in our area."

"I remember when we had a surprise baby shower for a young woman and her fiancée who had been worshiping with us for a while. Nobody complained that they weren't married yet. We still see them in church a couple of times a year, usually Christmas and Easter."

"It really made me proud of First Presbyterian when we raised all the money we needed for the stained-glass window repair in just six months."

Then they came to the third question, asking when people had felt God's presence at the church. Here the answers were more varied.

"At the funeral for my mother. People took time out of their busy lives to attend. The service itself was so meaningful, and I appreciated what our pastor then had to say. The church also prepared us a delicious meal, and everyone was so kind."

"Definitely the Christmas Eve Candlelight Service three years ago. The Lord caused everything to come together—the sermon, the music, the candles, the children, and then the fellowship afterwards. It was perfect, just perfect. I cried a little when we sang 'Silent Night' by candlelight."

"Youth Sunday, that's when I felt God's presence. Looking up there and seeing those young people, the future of the church, leading the service. It made me feel so hopeful."

Mo repeated the listening process five times, and with each group he recorded his own brief notes about what was said and who said it. This helped him learn names and faces, what mattered to people, where the church had felt God's presence.

Eventually, Mo helped lead the congregation through a second process, this time seeking to discern how God might be leading the church into the future. Looking at the church's particular strengths and weaknesses, values, interests, and passions, and the needs of the community around them, how might God be leading the church? What were some possible emphases? How would the church need to be staffed to meet the goals? What were the challenges and threats to reaching the goals? What were the resources and guides? How long would it all take and how much would it cost?

Though it might have looked simple enough to persons who had no church connections, Mo knew there were countless details and moving parts to this organization. And because the members were not simply paid employees who could be supervised, hired, directed, or even fired liked workers in a company, this added another level of complexity to pastoral ministry.

Chapter 39

Mo learned early on that one of the interesting things about being a pastor was the sheer variety of tasks that came with the job, the different ages he worked with, and the unpredictability of what might happen each day and night. One time he met with a small group of college students. They had returned to the church for an annual social gathering over the Christmas break. Gathered in the church's youth room where they had spent many fun hours, upon their return, each sought out their own distinctive painted contribution to the walls—initials, sports identifiers, nicknames, and so on festooning the room.

Of course, former youth now came back not only happy to see each other and to pick on each other but to challenge the orthodoxy of their upbringing. At one point the conversation shifted from talk about who was dating whom, and what school was like, and how hard the classes were. The discussion turned to theology.

Sally McGee, a thin, intense, blond-haired student wearing a baggy outfit said, "I don't have a problem with Christmas and the baby Jesus. I can accept the idea that God would come in an innocent baby. I mean a newborn baby is super-pure, the ultimate in purity, like God." The others nodded, shrugged, and agreed. "But" she continued her voice rising, "I can no longer accept the proposition of Jesus being sacrificed on the cross for my sins. That makes no sense to me. That's not love. That's just child abuse."

One of the students gave a nervous laugh and said, "Whoa! That's a new way of looking at things." Several of the students looked surprised and uncomfortable, shaking their heads. Sally's best friend, Marie Lambert, crossed her arms and nodded in agreement with her. And everyone turned and looked toward Mo. He glanced at their young faces, and then he spoke, his voice calm and quiet. "I hear you, Sally. The crucifixion is an awful mystery, isn't it? How can such brutality in any way be part of God's so-called plan? *That* I do not know, and I don't want to be glib. But stay with me for a minute. If we think about the nature of love itself, we may begin to see some hints, not perfect answers but hints of how to make some sense of the crucifixion. Try thinking about it this way. When each of us is born, we come into the world as babies--helpless, utterly dependent upon our parents to care for us, right? And *how* do they care for us? When we're hungry, they feed us. When we need to be held, they hold us. When our diaper needs to be changed, they change it. We cry and our parents give us whatever we need

134

when we need it. It doesn't matter if it's 9:00 p.m., 1:00 a.m., 2:00 a.m., all day, all night, exhausting. Is it always easy? No. Is it always fun? Of course not. But is it loving in a sacrificial way? Yes. Our parents make sacrifices for us throughout our lives. And eventually we hope we learn to make sacrifices for others. Because that's the very nature of love. You see there really is no such thing as love without sacrifice."

Mo noticed a couple of the students, nodding, hands to their faces, puzzling and pondering. But after a moment, Sally said with a firm but not harsh voice, "Well, you make some good points, but I still don't see why Jesus had to die. Couldn't God be loving without Jesus dying?"

"I guess we'll leave it as a mystery," said Mo. "I'll be interested to hear how your own interpretations develop over the years."

Chapter 40

Mo knew that being a pastor was more than merely providing theological insight for various ages, and more than teaching, as important as that was. A ministry of presence was also required. That meant his going to the people, not just expecting them to come to him. And hospital and home visitation were ways that Mo thought God was especially present to people in their need. And it was an important way for pastors to build stronger relationships with his parishioners.

So, Mo made sure he often visited people who were in the hospital. He typically went several times a week, something he really enjoyed. Mo would drive to the hospital, walk to the patient's room, knock on the door, and usually enter with a smile. Early on, he sometimes might have to introduce himself. "Hi, I'm Mo Campbell, the new pastor at First Presbyterian. It's good to meet you, but I'm sorry you're in here. What's going on?" And at this point, Mo was very good about keeping his mouth shut, and listening, instead of just waiting, as some pastors did, for a chance to jump in and talk non-stop, or worse yet, jump in and talk about himself or give unsolicited advice. Mo was good about listening and confining his remarks to quick interjections. "Oh." "I'm sorry." "That sounds terrible." "Wow. That sounds painful."

Mo discovered that hospital patients often liked to talk about their medical condition for a while, sometimes for a long while. It was as if they needed to share with someone else the burden of a terrible weight they had been carrying all by themselves. But, after unloading that weight by explaining, sometimes with tears, sadness, or anger what they were going through, the patients might suddenly switch to other subjects. Maybe a basketball game. "How 'bout them Heels? They gonna beat Duke this year?" Or "So, Mo, how are you and Annie liking our church?" Or "What do you think of our town?" Or "Well, I may be sick, but I know there are other people worse off than I am."

Whenever patients steered the conversation away from whatever medical need had brought them to the hospital, Mo learned simply to let the patient take the conversation down whatever curvy road he or she wanted to travel. Eventually, Mo might bring the discussion back around to whatever the malady was if that's where the patient wanted to go. He almost always ended the visit with a prayer. And he usually asked God for physical healing, except when it seemed the best healing for a terminally ill person might be to die and move on to the next world—the final healing. In that case, Mo even might say something such as, "Loving God, we pray for an end to this suffering, that it might not be overwhelming, that the pain relievers might be effective and suffering relieved. And when it is time, we ask that this precious child of yours be received safely into the arms of your mercy."

Mo sometimes pondered how prayer really worked. There were, of course, plenty of ministers and other Christians who acted as though they had prayer itself all figured out. Some were certain that prayer affected the person who prayed, but it had no influence on God. This was an appealing theory, especially when prayers weren't answered as Mo had hoped. For example, the person he'd prayed for who had been slightly ill, instead became gravely ill, and died. "Well, that's because the prayer was for the person doing the praying, and it didn't affect God," could say people who were so "rational" about prayer. But then what could you say about prayers that were answered as requested? What did you say about the time when a miracle just seemed to drop down out of a heaven, and the deathly ill, seemingly hopeless person got better, went home, and lived to a ripe old age? What did you say then? "Thanks for nothing, God. You had nothing to do with it." Really?

On the other side, were the Christians who were certain that prayers would be "effective" if they were just offered with enough fervor or the person doing the praying were "worthy enough," or the prayer were "God's will," basically whatever God already wanted to happen. Then the prayers would get answered as requested. The problem with this approach was that Mo knew there were plenty of times when he and other people prayed for something, say, the healing of a child, and the child got worse and died. How in the hell was that the will of God? And how awful to believe that you had to be fervent enough or worthy enough for healing to take place or it was your fault that things got worse. And what kind of a cruel God were we dealing with? Damn!

So, Mo really wasn't sure how prayer worked. He just held onto the belief that God is good and loving and wants what's best for us. According to the Bible God wants us to ask for what we need. Yet sometimes our prayers don't get answered as we request. Why? Maybe God's power is temporarily limited as we live in this messy world, filled with evil, and brokenness, and human choices. Maybe, figured Mo, everything gets made right in the world to come, and for now we struggle along doing the best we can. But this explanation seemed awfully thin when somebody was really suffering or facing an early death.

One morning Mo was phoned at the church office by the weeping daughter of a church member. Her 83-year-old mother who lived alone was in the hospital. The night before, her house had been broken into. The perpetrator had beaten her, and then covered her head with a pillowcase, and raped her before he left with her money, credit cards, and jewelry. She had been taken to the hospital by ambulance and was in a regular room recovering from the attack.

Mo drove to the hospital, entered the room, and there lay this dear woman, her face, and arms red and purple with bruises, her lips split, and her broken nose pushed back into place. When she saw Mo, she said nothing, but just gave a slight shake of her head side to side, her eyes filling with tears. Mo was not sure what to say. He hesitated, but then knelt by her bed, took one of her bruised hands and kissed the back of it. "I'm so sorry," he said, as tears rolled down his own cheeks. Later, Mo could never recall what he said for a prayer that day or even if he said a prayer at all. "Maybe," he thought, "My tears and her tears were the prayer."

Chapter 41

Besides hospital visitation, Mo also concentrated on visiting people in their homes. One afternoon, early in his ministry at First Presbyterian Church, Mo went to deliver home communion to a "shut-in." Mo thought the term itself was a dreary, but sometimes accurate description of someone, usually an elderly person, who lived alone, unable to get out by himself or herself anymore, dependent upon others to bring necessities and provide some companionship.

As usual, Mo was running a bit late for his pastoral visit. He had some handwritten directions and an address for a widower, Charlie Hayes, who lived on a dirt road in the country about 10 miles outside Plainview. Tires squealing as he left the church's driveway, Mo figured if he drove about 5 miles an hour over the speed limit, he'd only be about 5 or 10 minutes late. Quietly cursing his own procrastination, and remembering Annie's comments about his habitual lateness, he sped down country lanes, over rolling hills, past farms, dilapidated barns, and fields dotted with cows and sheep. Finally, one of the directions was "Turn right at the second dirt road, after Poteet Road, and the house is on the right." Skidding to a stop, Mo realized he'd just missed the dirt road. Cursing again, louder, and slamming his hand against the dashboard, he executed a three-point turn on the asphalt, headed back, turned onto the dirt road, and then immediately pulled into the driveway of a small light blue house with peeling paint, some rotted boards along the base, a place that had seen better days.

Communion kit and the *Supplemental Liturgical Resource* liturgy for the Lord's Supper in hand, Mo strode through an overgrown yard, up the front steps, and rang the doorbell. No answer. He tried again. No answer. He glanced through the dirty door window and thought he saw someone inside. Finally, he gave the door a strong knock. A weak voice from inside called, "Come in!" Mo pushed, the door stuck, then creaked open and Mo took in the scene. He was entering a small living room—old, stained carpet, dingy off-white walls, and faded curtains. And ahead of him sat an elderly man in a wheelchair. He gave Mo a smile and yelled, "I have a little trouble hearing! Nice to see you, young man!"

"Yes!" yelled Mo, "Nice to see you too! I'm Mo Campbell!" He offered a handshake and the man in the wheelchair responded with a talon-like grip.

"Pleased to meet you!" yelled the man.

"I just came to get acquainted and bring you communion, okay?!"

"Yes. That'll be fine!"

"Tell me about yourself, please!"

And the man began to speak about his life. He told about being a young man, and getting married to his wife, Violet. He said, "She was prettier than the first rose blooming in springtime. Of course, we were as poor as stray dogs, but we didn't know it. We were in love, and doing exactly what we wanted to do, farming. Like my daddy before me, I always had dairy farming in my blood, and I loved the cows and the rhythm of life tending to 'em. Violet and I were never able to have children and that made us sad. And it hurt me to get old and have my body all broke down and must retire from farming when I was only 75." The man continued to talk and spoke of his deep, grinding sorrow at Violet's death, three years before his retirement. He spoke for about 20 minutes straight and said all this with barely a pause, hardly enough space for Mo to throw in an empathetic "Oh," "I'm sorry," "That sounds hard."

At last Mo said, "You've had a wonderful life, but also a difficult one, especially lately! I'm so sorry about Violet's death. I'm going to pray for you!" And Mo did pray. Then he asked, "May I go into your kitchen and get the communion elements ready?!"

"Certainly, it's right through there!" and he pointed to the room to the left of the living room.

With his portable communion set in hand, Mo walked into the kitchen. He noticed dirty dishes in the sink, and a black and white cat slinking around, considering jumping up on the kitchen counter. He set the communion set on the kitchen table. And just as he opened the black communion set to pour the grape juice from the container into the clear miniature plastic cups, he glanced over at a stack of mail also on the table, various bills, and junk mail. After a few seconds he noticed that the mail was addressed to James Holton. All of it was addressed to James Holton. And then he slowly realized his mistake.

He went back into the living room, and said, "I think I may be at the wrong house! You're not Charlies Hayes, are you?!"

"No, I'm James Holton!"

His face reddening, Mo said, "I'm so sorry. I'm new to the church and the area and I've gone to the wrong house! I was supposed to be visiting Charlie Hayes!"

"Oh, he lives at the next house down, at the bottom of the dirt road! I'm James Holton!"

"Yes, I understand now! I apologize for the mix-up! I'll get my things and get out of your way!"

"Wait, can you just stay and have communion with me?!"

Mo was surprised and thought for a moment. Though he didn't know anything about this man's faith and his understanding of Holy Communion, it seems stupid and rude to hold some sort of theological examination just then. So, Mo simply said, "Of course!" And the two of them celebrated communion together, James's eyes glistening as Mo spoke the ancient words of institution: "The Body of Christ given for you. The blood of Christ shed for you." They ate and drank together. Then Mo offered a closing communion prayer and added an additional prayer for his new friend, James.

As Mo prepared to leave, James said, "Do you have to go?!"

"I do," said Mo. "Charlie Hayes is going to be wondering why I'm so late!"

"Well, please come back!"

"I will!" said Mo.

So, Mo did visit with him on a regular basis. Whenever he would schedule a communion visit with Charlie, he would also phone and set up a visit with James on the same day.

When James died two years later, Mo received a phone call from his niece Michelle Hanahan to inform him. She said, "My Uncle James didn't have many friends or relatives, and his heart was absolutely broken when Violet died. And then his heart broke again when he couldn't farm any more. Especially he missed the cows, having them to tend to, and I guess in a way, love, the way you or I might love a good dog or cat. He had so much heartbreak. But you were one of the good things in his life. He really looked forward to your visits." Mo thought to himself, *Dear God, I think I visited this man maybe three times a year, talked a few minutes, and brought him communion. It didn't seem like much. But I guess you never know. Lord, you promised to be at work, even in our paltry efforts. And so you have been. Thank you.*

Mo conducted the funeral in the church sanctuary on a Wednesday afternoon. There were maybe twenty people in attendance, including the family. And then at the gravesite service, there were five people counting the funeral director, three family members, and Mo. Mo spoke the traditional five-minute "ashes to ashes, dust to dust" service, and then the funeral home and cemetery workers were ready to lower the casket into the grave. Mo usually didn't stay for that part of the process, but this day he walked over and put his hand on the casket and imagined James inside. Silently he said, *Goodbye, old friend.* Then they lowered the casket into the red clay ground. And Mo drove back to the church.

Chapter 42

During Mo's first year at the church, worship attendance had increased from an average of 80 people per Sunday to 95 people per Sunday. There were a few more young families who had gotten involved. Giving to the church's budget was up slightly as well. Positive stories about the congregation's response to poverty locally through food and housing assistance, and job training were sometimes appearing in the local newspaper. Mo sensed excitement about how things were going. The congregation laughed easily and often.

But in the summer of 1991, at its then annual national meeting (known as the General Assembly) the Presbyterian Church (USA) took up yet another study of human sexuality. This study suggested a "justice/love" ethic for several sexual issues, including the ordination of gay and lesbian persons to the Ministry of Word and Sacrament, and even the possibility of some sort of blessing of a same-sex union. Predictably, conservatives in the denomination were incensed, and the study paper's majority and minority report suggestions were voted down. But as part of the process the denomination adopted "Guidelines for Presbyterians During Times of Disagreement" (a set of rules for how groups within the church could deal with conflict fairly and constructively).

Mo felt it was important for the congregation to understand the complexity of the sexual issues at hand. So, he led a series of Sunday school classes, as well as evening studies, on the subject. The liberal members of First Presbyterian were thrilled. In many areas of the U.S., changes in sexual mores were rocketing towards the 21st century, while their little town was trotting along pulled by a horse and buggy. Now, they were finally going to have long overdue discussion about new understandings about human sexuality and their faith.

On the other hand, the moderates and conservatives were much more concerned about protecting "the unity of the church." This was a phrase Mo would hear invoked repeatedly over the years whenever he or someone else in the church wanted to talk about controversial issues of justice and peacemaking. Mo learned to be suspicious of the language. And he came to see it yet another excuse for not talking about difficult, but important ethical issues, because such talk might challenge members and make them feel "uncomfortable."

Ten people attended the first Sunday school class titled "Justice and Love—A Reexamination of Human Sexuality and our Christian Faith." Mo had given copies of the 129-page General Assembly report to each member of the class in advance. The assignment was to read the first 29 pages before the first class that met in what was known as The Sadie McCutchen classroom, a small room with weathered gray carpet, white-painted cinderblock walls, named after one of the charter members, an unofficial saint of the church who was known for her winsome personality. A color portrait of "Miss Sadie's" smiling face hung in a prominent place on the wall as you entered the room.

As the bell rang for class to begin, Mo got up and closed the classroom door, and then took his seat at a large round table with the others. He flashed a nervous smile as he scanned the group and made a mental note of where he thought each person might land on the precarious terrain of the issues before them. Liberal, moderate, or conservative—the labels were slippery, yet still a starting point as Mo imagined how he might approach the class.

Straight across from him sat a couple in their early 70s, Nathan and Eloise Hays, already well-known to Mo, via the church grapevine, as extremely conservative members. They scowled back at Mo's smile. Beside them on one side were the Mitchells, Tom and Susan, a couple in their fifties, also known to be quite conservative, and not looking too pleased. To Mo's right sat Maureen Reynolds, a fifty-something year-old, with long brown hair flecked with gray. She was one of the church's liberals. She gave Mo a broad smile, and he got the impression that she would back him up if things got heated. Beside her was her friend, Agnes Davidson, seventy years old, a widow, and another liberal. On Mo's left, was George McKay, a forty-five-year-old man whose wife was not attending the classes. Mo thought he might be a liberal, but he was rather quiet, and it was hard to tell. And then rounding out the rest of the group were the Bennetts, a young couple in their 30s, and the Ashtons, a couple in their 80s. In both cases, Mo was unable to figure out where they might place themselves on the liberal-moderate-conservative scale. He took a breath and began.

"Welcome, everybody. It's great to see you. Thanks for coming. Let's start with a prayer. Holy One, as we gather again as your children, help us to listen to you, listen to each other, and listen to ourselves that we might hear your truth, new insights, and fresh possibilities breaking forth, through Christ our Lord. Amen." Mo continued his introduction.

He said, "Again, welcome. Let's go around the room and introduce ourselves, please. Say your name and what you're hoping to get from this class. I'll begin. I'm Mo, and I'm hoping to read this report together and have some respectful dialogue to see what we might learn together. I know the topics are controversial. So, we might have some vigorous dialogue, but I'm trusting it will be respectful. Along with the report, I sent you a resource from the denomination 'Guidelines for Presbyterians During Times of Disagreement.' I'd like to adopt the guidelines as rules for our class conversations. Would that be acceptable with everyone?"

Nobody objected. A few people nodded yes.

Mo said, "Great. We'll plan to use these guidelines for our conversations. Let's continue with introductions and hopes."

Maureen Reynolds said, "I'm just glad that Mo is having us discuss this report, because this is a very important subject for us to talk about as Christians."

Agnes Davidson added, "I feel the same. Each of us needs to be informed and so does the whole church."

When they got to Nathan and Eloise Hays the tone shifted. Nathan looked at Mo and then scanned the class as he said, "I'll speak for both of us and say we are very disappointed by what we have read in this report so far, and we are even more disappointed that our pastor is leading a study of it, instead of standing up for biblical truth." He glared at Mo, who was surprised but not shocked. He continued, "Frankly, Eloise and I, and many other families in this church, will be deciding how much we're going to pledge financially based on whether our denomination and our church return to biblical standards of behavior. And some families may not even remain in the membership if we don't see such a return."

"Hmm. Thank you for sharing your thoughts. This is a critical issue for you and some other church members," said Mo, his face grave. "I'd like to know who these other families are so that we could all sit down and talk face to face over a cup of coffee or lunch."

"I'm not at liberty to say," said Nathan as if he were a middle school principal scolding a misbehaving student. "But I can tell you I speak for a number of our well-respected members."

"I hear you," said Mo, "But if you'll look at the 'Guidelines for Presbyterians During Times of Disagreement' that we're using as our rules for discussion, we really need to speak to each other face to face, just as Jesus commanded in Matthew 18. That way we can be clear about what the issues are and do our best to honor each other and try to understand each other."

"Well, I can tell you, that's not going to happen," said Nathan. "These people *know* what the Bible says about homosexuality, and they don't need somebody who goes off to seminary for three years to come in here and tell them differently." The other members of the class looked very uncomfortable, but no one spoke.

"Okay," said Mo, taking a deep breath, "I hope they will change their minds and be willing to talk face to face." He had the other people introduce themselves. The Mitchells shared similar complaints and threats of withholding pledges or leaving the church, but the other couples basically said, "We know the issues in this report matter to many people. We just want to learn more before we make up our minds."

Finally, Mo came to the last class member, George McKay. He paused, looked down, blinked a couple of times, then spoke in a dignified and nearly inaudible voice. "These issues are explosive, and they have the potential to split the entire denomination and to divide our congregation. I'm worried about that, and I'm worried about members withholding their pledges or quitting the church over this. But you know what worries me more? People blackmailing the church with threats to silence our even discussing these issues. That worries me more. Jesus said, 'You will know the truth and the truth will set you free.' But how can we know the truth if we don't even talk? And how can we talk, if people hide in the shadows and make threats, but refuse to come and talk face to face as Christians? The issues in this report are not just theoretical. They are issues that affect other human beings made in the image of God. And I am so disappointed to hear the judgmental attitudes some people in our church are adopting."

Mo noticed that as George spoke, he was careful not to look directly at Nathan and Eloise or Tom and Sue, but the four of them looked down, red-faced, and furious at his words. Mo suspected that he did not make eye contact not because he was afraid of them but simply because he didn't want to seem aggressive.

Over the next six weeks, Mo moved into the class materials that addressed the changing interpretation of biblical passages, evolving scientific knowledge about human sexuality, the church's varied history on the subject, human experience, and so on. Conversations around the table were sometimes difficult, but Nathan and Eloise and Tom and Sue did not return after the first week. In fact, he learned they had begun searching for another congregation to join, and there were several other families who left around then as well.

But at the same time, word got out in the Plainview community that this was a church in which gay and lesbian people and their families might be more welcome than in some of the other churches in town, especially the conservative and fundamentalist churches. A few new people visited the church, and some even joined.

So, Mo decided to preach a sermon about the issues in the report. He warned the church in advance that he would speak frankly, but not graphically about issues of human sexuality in his sermon. And that Sunday the church would have an alternate activity for children and youth whose parents were concerned that this might be "too adult" for them to hear.

Despite all the preparation and the warnings, several people got up and stormed out during the sermon. And then, a few months later, the session of the church became concerned when the stewardship campaign came up short thanks to the departure of some of the church's big givers.

<h1 style="text-align:center">Chapter 43</h1>

Members of the church's Personnel Committee, five people, scheduled a meeting with Mo in one of the church classrooms on a Wednesday at 7:00 p.m. Millie Simpson, chairperson, called the meeting to order with a prayer and then she said, "So, we're officially called to order. I'm going to go ahead and get us going and we have one item on the agenda—the relationship between Mo and First Presbyterian Church." Mo raised his eyebrows and his mouth dropped open slightly, but he said nothing.

She continued while looking mainly at Mo, but occasionally glancing at other members of the committee. "I'll start by saying that many people in the church are thankful for the ministry you've done during your time here. It's certainly a challenge to be the pastor of a church, and we can tell you've really learned a lot and grown since you've been with us. Several our members speak highly of you and your ministry. But that said, there are some serious problems. Financial giving to the church is down ten percent. Worship attendance has dropped by fifteen percent. Though we have taken in some new members from the Plainview area, we haven't gotten as many new members as we've lost, and I'm not sure how to say this, but the new members aren't the same *quality* of the members we've lost." Mo felt a mixture of sadness and anger rising in him like an old-fashioned outdoor thermometer, but he still said nothing. After all, she had the floor.

"I think I speak for the committee," Millie said, receiving slight head nods from the other members, "but things just aren't working out. I imagine you already know this, Mo. So, we suggest that you go ahead and get your résumé together and find a new church as soon as possible. Several of us are willing to serve as positive references if you leave quietly."

There was silence for a moment.

Then Mo spoke, his voice soft and anguished, "I'm surprised. I thought things were going well. I mean most of the churches are struggling a little bit with giving and attendance, but I thought we were typical in those areas. And what do you mean that the new members are not of the same *quality* as the longtime members?"

"I think you know what we mean," said Don Meyer, a paunchy, balding, middle-aged man, and president of the Plainview National Bank. "I see no reason to belabor this."

"Well, I don't know what you mean," said Mo. "But if you feel I should leave, then I will leave."

Irma Pine, a member in her early seventies jumped in, "It's really been all this sex stuff that you've insisted on discussing all the time. The congregation isn't ready for it, but you've refused to back off. If I could offer you a suggestion, (and I'm certain I echo the opinions of quite a few members in our church), you really need to learn how to listen better. You need to meet people where they are, instead of trying to force them to believe what you believe, and what those 'theological experts' believe. First Presbyterian has always been 'a family church,' not an 'issues church.' You should have known that. But you're still young. Now I guess you know."

After the meeting ended, Mo drove home and gave Annie the news. She was tearful and angry as they sat at the kitchen table. "They don't appreciate what they have," she said. "You've worked so hard and given people a chance to learn about something important that's going to have a great impact on their lives. You've given them a framework for tackling all sorts of ethical issues besides these sexual issues. But instead of being willing to learn and be challenged and be a little bit uncomfortable, they've just rejected you. And some of them won't even talk to you face to face. So 'Christian' of them! And I cared about these people, and if we move, I'll have to say goodbye to my teaching position and my kids. I'm so damn angry at these people."

"I am too," said Mo, meeting her gaze, then shaking his head, and taking a deep breath.

Mo did update his résumé, what was called a Personal Information Form, or PIF, in the Presbyterian system and began a search for a new congregation. As the Personnel Committee members had promised, they gave Mo positive references, as did the leadership of the presbytery. When asked, they all tended to share the same vague message about what had happened, "It was just a difference in vision. And he's a young pastor, still learning."

Mo was able to find another position in just a few months. It was the Memorial Drive Presbyterian Church in Sidwell, North Carolina, close to where he had grown up. So, he and Annie prepared to move after only two years in Plainview.

Chapter 44

The week before their move, Mo got a phone call at the church from George McKay. He said, "Mo, I know your schedule must be hectic as you prepare to move, but I'm wondering if I could schedule an hour, or even less, to come by your office and talk with you privately before you leave town." Mo penciled the meeting on his calendar for Wednesday afternoon at 1:00.

At one o'clock sharp that day, the church secretary buzzed Mo's office phone and said, "Mo, George McKay is here to see you."

"Send him in, please," said Mo.

As George entered the room, Mo stood and gave him a firm handshake. He said, "May I get you a cup of coffee or tea, or a glass of water?"

"No, thank you," he said, noting the unusual spaces on the office bookshelves, bookshelves normally crammed with books that were now packed into moving boxes stacked around on the carpeted floor. "I know you're very busy. So, I'll try not to take too much of your time."

"That's okay. There's no need to rush. I want to hear what you have to say," said Mo, who noticed that George dried his hands on his pants and fidgeted a bit in his chair. "Let's begin with a prayer." Mo prayed, "God of our lives, be with us now as we have conversation. Send your peace and understanding. Through Christ our Lord. Amen." Then Mo offered a small smile, looked at George, and said, "So, what brings you here today?"

George looked down at the floor, and then looked up and met Mo's eyes, clearly uncomfortable about something. Finally, he said, "I should have talked to you sooner. I *wish* I had talked to you sooner. Whatever I tell you in here is confidential, right?"

"Yes," said Mo, "with only two exceptions. If you are hurting a child or planning to hurt yourself, I will not keep that in confidence."

"Okay. Good. Neither of those apply to what I'm going to tell you," said George, his face and body relaxing a little. "You remember when you taught the class on the sexuality report a few months ago, and I said it was more than a theoretical issue, it was something that affected real people?"

Mo nodded and said, "Uh huh. I remember."

George took a breath and then said, "What I need to tell you is that my younger son, Tim, is gay. I'm not sure if anybody in this church knows. Hardly anybody in my family even knows. But he came out of the closet to his mother and me about two years ago. He'd moved to California, and met someone who is now his partner, Sam.

"At Christmas Tim came home by himself and sat down with my wife and me and told us the truth. Of course, we'd already noticed that he hadn't dated any girls since early in high school. But still we were oblivious about his sexuality, or maybe we were just in denial. And when he told us, I'm ashamed to say we were hurt and angry. We said some things we shouldn't have said, some hurtful things. So, Tim went back to California and our relationship was very strained. We hardly spoke to each other at all. It was horrible.

"Eventually, his mother and I started to do a little bit of research on homosexuality, and we learned some of what we later talked about in the class you taught. Being gay is an orientation that people discover, not a choice they make as 'a lifestyle.' It's not a sin. It's a variation that occurs in other animals in nature, just as it occurs for human beings. The main thing is that it can and should be loving, just as we expect from straight people, no more, no less.

"And that's what it is for Tim. We learned this firsthand last year by getting his permission and flying out to California to see Tim and his partner, Sam, who is delightful, by the way. We apologized for the hurtful things we'd said, and thank God, Tim forgave us."

George's voice caught, and he paused as he looked at the floor again, his eyes filling with tears. Finally, half-sobbing he said, "It was like a miracle. We got our son back, and he got his parents back."

Mo's own eyes were brimming, and he reached up to wipe a tear away. Then he said quietly, "Thank God."

No one said anything for a few seconds. Then George looked at Mo and spoke again. "I just want you to know that I'm grateful for you and Annie and what you've brought to our church. It took courage to do what you've done, and I'm sorry you've been pushed out by people who would not listen. But even more I'm sorry I let you down by not speaking up. My wife and I will miss you."

"I'll miss you too," said Mo, who meant it, but who also thought, *I do wish you had spoken up before. But now it's too late.*

There was a final Sunday lunch reception at First Presbyterian with cake and a going away envelope containing $300. One of the church's middle-aged elders, Roger Street, stood in front of a mic in the church's fellowship hall, and looking at Mo and Annie he said, "We hate to see you two leave us so soon, but you've certainly stirred things up and made your mark here, haven't you?" he said with a sweet smile. Several parishioners coughed or looked down at the linoleum. "We certainly thought that you and beautiful Annie would be around and have some children to add to the church rolls." More people looking at the floor and now a few folks clearing their throats. "But all good things must come to an end, and we hope the next church will be a better fit for you. On behalf of the church, here's a going away gift in this envelope. We wish you God's blessings." Mo took the envelope and said, "Thank you. We're grateful for our time with you, and we will miss you. We'll keep you in our prayers." He stepped away from the mic, and the people in attendance applauded as he and Annie made their way back to their seats at their table and ate lunch.

A few supportive members stopped by and gave Mo and Annie hugs and said kind things. The dissatisfied members attended the reception but did not stop by to speak or they simply skipped the reception entirely. The church's intentions were good, but the whole affair was awkward and uncomfortable. To Mo it felt kind of like the times in his junior high school days when he had asked a pretty girl to dance with him at a party, but she had said no.

Chapter 45

So, Mo and Annie moved on to the next church, Memorial Drive Presbyterian in Sidwell, SC. Sidwell, population 20,106, was known for being a bedroom community of Charlotte, NC. A bit more progressive than Plainview, (the mayor was a Democrat, though quiet about that affiliation) it was still a conservative community dominated by conservative Protestant churches and the Republican Party. The main industries were the county hospital, a small private college, several peach orchards that employed locals as well as migrant workers, and an electronics company plant that had moved down to the area from Ohio so that the owners could enjoy warmer weather, and pay lower wages and lower taxes.

Mo and Annie bought an old farmhouse, a fixer-upper, rustic and cozy on a couple of acres in the country just outside town. Not long after they moved in, they stopped by the county animal shelter and got a dog, a one-year-old Labrador retriever mix they named "Jürgen" (for the theologian Jürgen Moltmann) and a golden-brown housecat they called "Fee-lion." The two pets got along well, because Fee-lion immediately asserted her benevolent dominance over Jürgen at their first meeting by nonchalantly walking up to rub her head and body against him and purr. Her meaning seemed clear. "You and I are not going to have any problems, are we? You belong to me."

The land on which Mo's and Annie's farmhouse was situated was a kind of nature sanctuary that enveloped the couple with the songs of birds, crickets, and frogs, the splendor and fragrance of the flowers burst into bloom in the spring and the spectacular tree leaves turning into blazes of color in the fall. They both enjoyed sledding and playing in the rare snowstorms that came, and they tolerated the interminable oven heat of summer.

The congregation where Mo was called as pastor was like First Presbyterian, but a little bit larger—215 members with around a 100 showing up on a typical Sunday. Like First Presbyterian, the church was a mixture of liberals, moderates, and conservatives with moderates and conservatives still most of the church. There were a few more young families. So, the church employed a part-time Director of Christian Education/Youth Director, Amy Hutchins. Amy had grown up in the church and been an active member whose participation in the Christian Education program had gradually led to a paid position for her.

Mo did some asking around about Amy and he got varied reports. On the one hand, she was well-liked by several members and their children. She had been in the paid position for almost ten years, and had formed close relationships with the kids, especially because she emphasized, above all else, making the program "fun." On the other hand, the former pastor told Mo in confidence that Amy's programing sometimes lacked theological substance and she liked to be a repository for gossip and discontent in the church, including gossip and discontent about the pastor or other staff members. She had a sharp tongue and a tendency to behave in a passive-aggressive way when told by the pastor to do something that she didn't want to do.

The organist/choir director, Gerald Offenbacher, was also a mixed bag, according to the people Mo contacted. His nickname was GO. He'd graduated from the large and well-respected Indiana University School of Music, and he was a strong musician who played the organ well and set high standards for the choir. But he also sometimes ran his rehearsals with a volcanic temper, shouting at choir members who were not professionals but simply volunteering their time. And according to the previous pastor, his prima donna attitude occasionally led to angry and public disagreements with the pastor, as well as private sniping about the pastor to choir members. He hated the stereotype, but Mo knew there were reasons why some choirs were known as "the war department of the church." He made a mental note about Amy and Gerald and thought, *Well, they both have gifts to share, but I may have my work cut out for me as far as getting them to work together as part of a team. We'll see if what I've been told turns out to be true.*

Annie was surprised to find a new job right away teaching English at Sidwell High School. Another teacher had gone on maternity leave and she would be out for at least several months. So, Annie was able to continue her career without a break. As it turned out, after a few months the teacher decided not to return to the classroom and Annie kept the position for the entire year.

The high school where she taught was not only larger than Plainview, but also more racially diverse—about 40% of the students Black and 60% White. It made for an interesting dynamic. There was an assumption by many, (but not all) of the White students, their parents, and the largely White faculty that Whites were superior. The N-word was usually not spoken in public, but was used a lot in private, especially in the case of Blacks who might be viewed as "uppity," and forgetful of who they were and their station in life.

There were occasional "race riots" between large groups of White and Black students fighting each other with fists or sometimes with knives. Blame for the riots was typically placed upon Black students, though usually the instigators of the fights were White students enraged about interracial dating at the school, especially when a Black male and a White female student were involved. Sometimes a fight might also break out because a Black male student simply was flirtatious or merely friendly towards a White female student. White males and Black females might be friends, even to the point of teasing one another, but it was understood that no serious relationship would develop. The sexual boundaries between the races were practically biblical, as though there were an "abomination" listed and hidden away somewhere in scripture demanding racial separation, like an electric fence with a switch that could be turned off and on, as needed, but only by Whites, and only in certain situations.

A few White male students also enjoyed driving around town in pick-up trucks with huge Confederate battle flags flapping out of the windows or from the cab of the trucks. This was deemed by the truck drivers and their passengers to be a celebration of their "Southern heritage." Oddly enough, their celebration often found them driving through predominantly Black sections of town while they whooped and hollered and played "Dixie" over and over with electronic car horns.

For the most part, faculty members would not actually speak their racist assumptions aloud, but Black students nonetheless discovered that they were much more likely to be paddled or suspended for school rule violations that merely got the White students a stern look and a lecture from the teacher or principal or even a wink. "Now, don't do that again. I'd hate to have to talk to your mom or dad when I see 'em at the country club."

Remarkably, Black kids who happened to excel at sports were lauded if they helped bring home the state championships that the town was known for. Likewise, Black kids who showed superior achievement in music, art, or academics received recognition as well, but not nearly what the top Black athletes received. And mysteriously, in each case their elevated personhood status ended as soon as high school was over, unless, of course, they could earn an athletic scholarship to a major university and continue to bring reflected glory to the high school and the town.

Even the high school yearbook was designed to protect what later generations would call White Privilege. The selection of homecoming queen was made by majority vote of all the students in the high school. But several years earlier, several White females and one Black female had vied for the title. The vote-counting had been conducted in private by the principal and one of the White staff members who quickly disposed of the actual results via a sneaky trip to the school's dumpster. The Black student had won the vote, but the principal announced one of the White students as the winner.

Realizing that this voting "problem" would return, the next year the principal announced that the school would henceforth elect a Miss White Sidwell High

School and a Miss Black Sidwell High school as a way of being "respectful" to both races. This was viewed by many White folks as a magnanimous gesture on his part, "allowing Black students to have a chance to be recognized too." But the Black community, of course, suspected otherwise.

The gross, as well as subtle racial injustices mystified Annie and Mo who had both grown up in more progressive Christian households where racial epithets were considered disgraceful and racial injustice was meant to be rooted out, just as the gospel and the Civil Rights Movement demanded. In fact, Presbyterians had been heavily involved in the Civil Rights Movement, marching along with Civil Rights leaders, and drafting statements and confessions of faith that attacked the sin of racism and reaffirmed the equality of human beings made in the image of God.

Yet, Annie and Mo had grown up in the South and they knew that racism was as entrenched and pervasive as the dripping humidity of a mid-July morning. What they did not yet know was how they were unaware of their own buried and more subtle racism. They had some learning to do.

Chapter 46

After Annie got off the phone with her friend, Susan, she said to Mo, "Susan says 'hello' and sends her love."

"Of course. You know all your friends are in love with me," Mo said.

Annie rolled her eyes so hard he thought she might pull a muscle. "Yes, I know," she said with a sigh. "It must be a terrible burden for you."

"Yes," he answered, his voice solemn, "I'm so tired of being objectified, treated as a mere sex object. But, of course, I also possess such a steely commitment to you that I never let those shameless friends of yours get anywhere with me. My chaste reputation remained intact, thank goodness."

"Thank goodness," laughed Annie. "Whatever happened to that shy tongue-tied boy who sat in Sunday school class with me and turned red when I teased him?"

"You have created a monster," he said. "So, are you going to our high school class reunion with me or not? You know I want to show you off as my trophy wife," he said.

"I've already told you that that's the same weekend as our annual girls' getaway."

"Damn!"

"You should have planned better," she said.

"Planned better? It's a high school class reunion, for heaven's sake. I didn't get to pick the date!" he said.

"I'm surprised you didn't use some of the clout from your sexual chemistry to arrange a different date," she said.

"Alas, I've saved all that for you, dear" he said.

And this is how Mo ended up attending his 10-year class reunion alone, while Annie went away for her annual girls' getaway. And this is how things got so messy.

On that Friday, Mo dropped Annie off at the Charlotte International Airport, making sure to lift her bag out of the trunk and set it on the sidewalk, before giving Annie a hug and a quick kiss on the lips. He watched her swinging hips for just a moment as she walked toward the terminal glass doors, and he thought she was still a beauty. Too bad she wasn't going to the reunion with him, because, all teasing aside, he did enjoy her company. And she sometimes helped him extricate his foot from his mouth when he got too talkative, and it didn't hurt if he could show her off a bit.

Before the airport police could get too antsy about his car loitering at the drop-off curb, Mo got back in and headed home. Once home, he was struck again by how quiet the place was without Annie's comments and questions and general puttering around. No one to ask how his day was going and what he wanted for dinner, and did he have anything he wanted to watch on TV. The only sound was Fee-lion demanding her food about two hours early. This was a fight not worth waging. Mo decided to go ahead and feed her, and he might as well feed Jürgen early while he was at it.

He then settled in with a frozen Digorneo's pepperoni pizza (thin crust) and a couple of Guinness Stout beers while he watched *The Shawshank Redemption* for the 3rd time. "Get busy living or get busy dying." Mo went to bed around 11:00.

Saturday morning, he woke up and after eating a light breakfast and going for a three-mile run, he decided he better make sure he had the right clothes for the reunion that evening. He didn't want to go too formal and look like a pretentious jerk. On the other hand, he didn't want to be too casual and look like he was either poverty-stricken or just lazy and dumb. Crap! If he'd only asked Annie to pick out something before she left. He finally settled on some khaki dress slacks, brown semi-casual dress shoes, and a sky-blue long-sleeved shirt.

Mo tried to imagine the reunion in advance. What would the hall look like? Would there be decorations screaming "Welcome back, class of 1983!" Would there be a band or just a DJ playing oldies? How about some snacks, something including stuff not on his low cholesterol diet? Some alcohol to loosen tense people up? Who would be there and what they'd be wearing? But he had never been to one of the reunions before, and his graduating class had about three hundred students. So, it was hard to conjure up an image of what to expect. He figured at least a few people he knew would be there. David, his best friend who now lived in Fort Lauderdale and worked as a gerontologist. Melinda, who was now a high school guidance counselor in Des Moines, Iowa. Bill, who taught English at North Carolina A&T in Greensboro. And Tonya who was a lawyer in Atlanta. Other than those people, he had no idea.

But the big question Mo and his classmates wondered about was whether their classmate and now famous actress Sharon Lyn Russell would show up. And if she did show up, how would she treat her classmates? Mo figured she wouldn't show, and if she did, she would act like a snob, and her bodyguard would stalk around acting like an MMA fighter looking for the tiniest excuse to body slam anybody who got too close.

Mo and Sharon Lyn had some history together. They'd been on one, and exactly one date back in the eighth grade. It was a first date for both and ended with a quick and fumbling kiss (Mo's first ever kiss, Sharon Lyn's second). Not long after their date, Sharon Lyn had begun dating other boys. By the time she was in high school (especially by her senior year) she had begun to develop into the world-class beauty she would eventually become. By their senior year in high school, though they would still say hello in the hallways, Mo and Sharon Lyn travelled in different circles—Mo in the nerdy, good grades crowd and Sharon Lyn in the popular, slightly wild bunch. All these years later, despite the wonders of Facebook and Google, they'd had no contact with each other. Sure, Mo had Googled Sharon Lyn's name a few times, just to see what she'd been up to—lots of acting gigs, three beautiful weddings, and three ugly divorces. He'd also gone to see some of her movies. But he wasn't exactly a huge fan. He just viewed her as a distant friend. Still, he was curious. Would she show up? And, if she did, what would she be like?

Finally, Saturday night arrived. Mo called Annie on her cell but got her voicemail. He figured she was probably out to dinner with the girls ordering appetizers and a pitcher of margaritas to share. Or maybe she was back at the hotel, she, and her buddies, sharing stories, cackling over the dumb stuff their husbands had done over the previous year. Mo left a message. "Hey, baby. Hope you're having fun, but not too much fun. I'm getting dressed and heading over to the reunion. I wish you were going with me. Talk to you later or maybe tomorrow morning. Stay out of trouble. Love you." He brushed his teeth first (didn't want to get any toothpaste on his outfit) then put on his clothes for the reunion. Mo took a last look in the hall mirror, noted the alarming expansion of the bald spot on the top of his head, sighed, grabbed his car keys from the bowl on the kitchen counter, and headed out the door.

Driving to the town about an hour away, he finally pulled up to the meeting hall of VFW #609, parked in the dimly lit gravel lot, checked his face in the rearview mirror to make sure his hair looked okay, and nothing was hanging out of his nose. All good. He took a deep breath and got out. All he wanted from the evening was to have a good time, and not to embarrass himself. Mo noticed a few other people, familiar, mostly couples and mostly a bit heavier, heading into the hall, and for a second it puzzled him, but then "Oh, yeah," he thought, "We're all a decade older."

Mo crunched across the lot and before he opened the hall's outer door, he could hear and feel thumping music from a DJ playing 80s and 90s tunes—Culture Club singing, "Do You Really Want to Hurt Me." Yikes! At least without Annie accompanying him, he wouldn't have to dance in public.

He stepped inside, eyes adjusting to the subdued light. Ahead of him was a short line of people inching toward a sign-in table where some of his classmates sat with bright red papier Mache decorations above them that shouted "WELCOME BACK CLASS OF 1983! WE *STILL* ROCK!" As people got to the table, they were being welcomed by the greeters. Then they were signing in, paying the $25.00 entrance fee (there better be some decent snacks and alcohol), and picking up programs that listed the order of activities for the evening, "Opening remarks by the class president," "A word from the class reunion committee." "The singing of the alma mater." Ugh.

As Mo got near the table, he heard a voice behind him yell, "Mo! What's up, baby!?" And at the same moment, a biceps locked around his neck from behind and a fist thudded on his right shoulder.

"Ow! Damn it, David! I'm going to have bruise tomorrow."

"Waah! Quit whining, ya baby! Bring it in!"

He turned around and was lifted from the floor courtesy of a bear hug from his best friend from high school, David. He had stayed in shape and looked like he could still play center on the football team. David shouted above the music, "Son, you have turned into such a wuss! What happened to you? Annie must've worn you down. Boy, you are *whipped*. Speaking of Annie, where *is* that beautiful woman? I know she's dying to give me a kiss."

"She didn't come," Mo said.

"Didn't come? Are y'all having problems?"

"No. No. Nothing like that. She had a girls' weekend already scheduled."

"Uh huh," he said. "A likely story."

"Shut up."

"I'm just saying. You know you married up."

"Yeah, I know."

"All right then. No worries. I'll be your wingman in reverse. I'll make sure you don't do anything stupid with these lovely young women classmates. And

I'll make sure, being the currently unattached guy that I am, that *I* do stupid things with them. Deal?"

"Shut up."

Mo and David wandered over to the food and drinks. Mo got a paper plate emblazoned with "1983" on it and began loading up with potato chips and onion dip, country ham biscuits, and miniature hot dogs cooking in barbeque sauce in crock pots. David watched, shaking his head in mock disbelief.

"Son, you are frickin' going to *die* eating that shit. It's a damn good thing you're married, 'cause I know good and well, Annie doesn't let you eat like that, or you'd be dead by now."

"Mind your own business, old people doctor!" said Mo. But every time Mo added another item of junk food, David would reach over and drop a carrot, or a cherry tomato or a slice of bell pepper onto his plate beside it.

"Man, you are *so* irritating," said Mo.

"Just trying to keep your dumb butt out of the hospital," said David.

"Okay, mama."

"That's alright, son."

They were interrupted by a classmate tapping on a microphone. It was the class president, a tall, still reasonably fit man, with just a hint of gray along his temples. He flashed a toothy grin and shouted, "What's up, class of 83?!" A mild cheer arose from the crowd. "Welcome back. Where did the years go? Those of us who live in states where weed is legal are asking that very question. Just kidding, y'all! But the rest of us are saying, school, jobs, spouses, kids, that's where. At any rate, great to see everybody. Now, we'll hear from the reunion committee—Betsy Stephens, Monica Walker, Tyler Thorton, and Bill Pendergrass."

There was scattered polite applause as the group made its way up on stage, with Betsy coming to the microphone, and the others just standing around her. Betsy, blonde hair (and dyed to keep it that way) stood about five feet tall, had put on about twenty pounds since high school, still attractive, and still perky (also her nickname). She bounced on the balls of her feet as she put emphasis on odd syllables as she spoke.

"83, are you *rea*dy to party? Look at your program for the *or*der for the evening. After we sing the *al*ma mater, we're going to turn the DJ loose to play your favorite hits from back in the *day*."

"Dear God, are these people ever going to shut up?" said Mo under his breath.

"Simmer down, there, cowboy," said David.

Then it was time to sing the alma mater. And Mo, who sang like a drunk man who'd just received a shot of Novocain and had teeth pulled, thought, "Oh, great, another opportunity to look awful."

He tried to lip sync, but David started laughing and said, "Wait. What? You don't know the alma mater?"

"Be quiet," he hissed.

"Come on, man! Give us some volume. Show some school spirit." And by this point people were smiling and laughing, Mo turning red-faced. And all he wanted to do was to have a good time and to get through the reunion without being embarrassed.

And then finally the singing was over, except there was a commotion coming from backstage, the sound of excited voices, and then, walking up to the mic, glowering bodyguard trailing discreetly behind her, was Sharon Lyn Russell herself, in a form-fitting red, sequined dress, gorgeous, radiant. Her classmates cheered. But as Sharon Lyn walked, something seemed a bit off to Mo. Obviously, she was ten years older than he remembered her, a few bulges, and wrinkles that even Hollywood's best plastic surgeons hadn't completely suctioned, filled, and erased. But there was also something different, something about her stride. She looked unsteady on her feet, like a newborn colt trying to take its first steps.

She reached the mic, grinned, gave a silly teeter-totter beauty queen wave, and before the cheers subsided, started to speak. "Hey, y'all! Remember little ole me? I got out of this hick town, and now, now, I'm, I'm a damn movie star." There were some nervous giggles coming from the crowd. "But hey, it's good to see my 83*rs*." 83*ers*—it occurred to Mo that she had created a new word. And as Sharon Lyn continued to talk, her words sometimes slurring, something else also occurred to Mo—she was drunk or high or both. So distracted by her condition, it took a moment for Mo to register that Sharon Lyn had finished her impromptu speech with a whoop and a "Go, 83ers!" Then with her bodyguard walking just behind her, looking as surly as ever, Sharon Lyn walked off the stage, began making her way down the back steps, and then walking toward her happy classmates. She was enveloped by hugs that made her bodyguard look even more menacing, but he simply watched each person who met her, the placement of hands, the angle of a cellphone camera, whether a hug might be too tight or held too long. Nothing seemed amiss.

Sharon Lyn spent the next hour drinking, talking, and laughing with her old high school friends, the popular crowd. Mo settled into conversation with his own old friends, but never venturing too far from the tables with snacks and drinks. By gosh, he was going to get his twenty-five dollars' worth. His friends, Ann, and Bill, were comparing the differences in weather between Iowa and South Carolina, and arguing about which age of students, high school, or college, was more satisfying and irritating to work with. South Carolina was the unanimous winner for weather, but there was a lot of disagreement about whether high school or college students were more satisfying and irritating. But then suddenly the conversation stopped as Ann and Bill looked past and behind Mo who turned around and saw none other than Sharon Lynn heading his way. She was flashing her Hollywood smile, a grin that seemed to expose more teeth than a human mouth might contain. But Mo noticed that her gait seemed even more unsteady, and when she spoke, gesturing with her arms, some of the drink she held in her hand sloshed onto the floor.

"Mo-says!" she wagged her finger, laughing at the same time she walked and staggered toward him. "Why are you trying to avoid your first love and your first kiss? Don't you love me anymore?"

All eyes and lots of cellphone cameras turned Mo's way and his face turned the color of a red delicious apple. His mouth dropped open. And then she was upon him as she tripped over her feet, stumbling forward. And he caught her about the waist, and he slipped on the drink that she slopped onto the floor, and he was falling backward, Sharon Lyn landing on top of him, planting a kiss on his mouth while a dozen cellphone cameras clicked. Sharon Lyn let out a shriek of laughter which her bodyguard took as a cry for help, and Mo was dimly aware of an immense and very angry man lifting Sharon Lyn off him and simultaneously kneeling, pulling back his fist to punch him. And just as the punch was thrown at Mo's face, there was a tremendous guttural roar, "Aaaaaah!" as David took several running steps, flying into the man, blindsiding him, hitting him low, leading with his shoulder, wrapping him up, and not only knocking him several feet across the floor but in the process causing him to bang his head on the floor, leaving him dazed, moaning.

By now, the DJ had stopped playing songs, and the room was quiet except a few sounds. Stunned classmates. "Oh, my God!" "Did you see that?" "Holy shit!"

Sharon Lyn held her hand out to help Mo up, but he was wise enough not to take it. "You, okay?" she asked.

"Yeah."

"You really know how to welcome a girl home."

"Yeah."

"I'm going to go check on my guy. He's a little high strung" she said and walked over to her bodyguard who lay on the floor rubbing his head, groaning. "Son of a bitch, blindsided me. He *blind*sided me."

Somebody in the crowd said, "Is there a doctor here?"

"Um, I'm a doctor," said David, a little out of breath, but happy and none the worse for the wear.

Two uniformed police officers showed up, handcuffed Mo, David, and the bodyguard, before asking what happened, taking statements, and letting all three go with a warning. Cellphones, of course, captured every glorious moment. An ambulance arrived, but the bodyguard refused to be taken to the hospital for observation. He just kept saying, "He blindsided me. You saw it. He blindsided me!"

Mo's phone began to vibrate in his pocket. He looked and saw that it was a FaceTime call, Annie. Uh oh. He sighed and answered the call. "Hey, babe."

"I just got photos from ten of our classmates and I just want to know what in the hell is going on. Are you okay? What happened?"

"Sweetie, it's a long story, a long story. But don't worry, I'm fine."

And just then, a hand came from behind him, David, turning the camera toward his own smirking face. "Annie, we missed you here. It's been a *great* party, but kinda quiet, and you owe me a kiss. Mo will tell you all about it, but don't you worry, he's being good."

David slapped Mo on the shoulder. "See? I told you I had your back."

"Shut up."

Chapter 47

After they had been at Memorial Drive a few years, family members, as well as church members, began to make comments about Mo and Annie having children. These remarks from family were offered at large family gatherings, such as Thanksgiving, Christmas, and Easter. After the Thanksgiving meal at her home (and a couple of glasses of White Zinfandel wine), Annie's mother stood with Annie and Mo in her small kitchen, nibbling leftovers, and cleaning up. Without warning, she patted Annie's belly and smiled at Mo and Annie.

"So, when are you two going to get busy and give us some grandchildren? We're not getting any younger, you know? We'd like to have some before you cart us off to the nursing home."

Mo, speechless, blushed.

"Mom!" yelled Annie as she rolled her eyes, "Could you please not talk about this? We'll have children when we have children."

"But are you even trying?"

"Mom, I can't believe you! Stop asking. It's private." And so it went.

Church members meanwhile had their own methods of communication.

Camile Daughtry, a thin, 80-something-year-old volunteer in the church's infant/toddler nursery room on Sunday mornings, caught Annie as she was walking down the hall past the nursery one Sunday.

"Annie, you're as pretty as a peach! Would you look in this nursery for a second?" she called from the doorway.

"Thank you. Yes, ma'am," said Annie, stopping and peering into the room that contained three toddlers playing with toys and wandering around.

"What do you notice?" asked Camile.

"Uh, three kids and you? Did your assistant have to miss today?"

"No, she'll be here shortly. That's not what's missing. Do you notice what's missing?"

Annie gazed around again. "Um, no ma'am, I guess I don't."

"Babies. There are no babies in here, and this is supposed to be a Sunday school room for infants and toddlers. You know you and Mo could do something about that." She grinned, raised her shoulders, dropped them, and glanced at Annie's face and then at her stomach.

For a moment Annie felt real anger flare inside her, but then sighed, let it go, and said, "It's always good to see you, Camile. Have a blessed Sunday." And she turned and walked down the hallway.

That day Mo taught an adult Sunday school class, led worship, and preached a sermon, and then had meetings until late afternoon. He arrived home tired and a bit frazzled. He and Annie finally relaxed with burgers cooked on their grill and washed down with Budweiser.

"So, what did you think of worship this morning?" asked Mo.

"I thought it was great. I'm still laughing about the children's sermon and little Betsy Roth deciding that was the perfect time to lift her dress up so that the congregation could really see her shiny new shoes," said Annie, laughing.

Mo also laughed, and then asked, "What did you think of the adult sermon?"

"It was really good," said Annie. "I liked the opening story. It caught my attention and made me smile, but it also made a good point.

"Anything else?"

"Yeah, you had one grammatical error. You said, 'This is good news for you and I.' You should have said, 'This is good news for you and me.'"

"Damn," said Mo. "And I know that one. I think I just got distracted in mid-sentence."

"Right," said Annie, raising one eyebrow.

"Shut up, grammar girl."

"You asked for my feedback," she said.

"I know," said Mo. "I'm just kidding. I do appreciate your help. How was the delivery?"

"Good," she said. "You didn't look down at the manuscript that much. How many times did you read it through aloud before service?"

"Six."

"Well, it showed," said Annie. "You didn't have the manuscript memorized, but you seemed to have the gist of it, and you weren't hemming and hawing and searching for words."

"Do I ever?"

"Not very often," she said. "There was that one Sunday last month."

"I was sick as a dog, and taking that cold and flu medicine that made me spacy and a little bit emotional," said Mo.

"Yes, I remember. You got a little weepy at the end of the sermon and it's not as though you were reading 'Old Yeller.' But I'm not really being fair, just having a little fun with you. I'll stop," she said.

"Thanks, smartass.

"You're welcome, dear. By the way, on another topic, Camile Daughtry was volunteering in the nursery/toddler room this morning, and she caught me as I walked by the room."

"Okay. And?"

"She shared the happy news that you and I need to start having some babies to replenish the church nursery's supply."

Mo laughed. "Seriously?"

"Seriously," said Annie.

"What did you say back to her?" asked Mo.

"Well, I managed not to yell at her and tell her that our decision about children is none of her damn business. Instead, I just said, 'Nice to see you. Have a blessed Sunday,' and I left."

"Wow! I'm sorry," said Mo. "Her boundaries need a little work."

"Ya think?"

"Yes. I wonder if maybe some family systems theory responses would work with her. Maybe try giving her a playful response. 'Camile, Mo, and I have been hoping that someone in the congregation would go ahead and give us the green light to start a family. Thanks for assuming the role.'"

Annie threw her head back and giggled. "Okay. Good one, but you know that's just going to be perceived as a smarty-pants answer, and disrespectful."

"Maybe," said Mo. "You could also try paradox. 'Camile, I'm glad you're on the ball with this. How often would you like me to check in with you on the pregnancy progress? Once a week? Daily? Hourly? We may need pointers on process too."

Annie snickered and shook her head. "So bad. You know this family systems mumbo jumbo sounds great in theory, but in practice it doesn't work that well, especially when the person you're dealing with is easily angered and has some control over your salary."

"I know," said Mo. "It's hard. I'm sorry. Maybe you and I could think of some things to say that don't sound disrespectful and aggressive, but also don't leave us stuck having to deal with people refusing to maintain boundaries and who keep trying to control our lives."

"Okay," said Annie. "I'm willing to work on it with you."

Chapter 48

Over the next few years, Mo and Annie did try to respond to some of the most over-the-top parishioner comments with playful or paradoxical answers as a way of continuing to set boundaries with people who sometimes wanted to be controlling or overly critical or both. Sometimes it worked and the offenders recognized their need to back off a little. Sometimes it didn't, and the offenders just attempted to be more controlling or critical. They became angry and complained to other church members. It was a difficult part of the ministry for Mo and Annie.

But the question of whether to have a baby was answered early one spring morning when Annie walked from the master bathroom into the bedroom. She lay down beside Mo, who was half-awake, gave him a light punch on the shoulder, and announced, "Wake up, stud boy! I'm pregnant." The pregnancy was celebrated not only by Mo and Annie, and their family but by the church members with many lovely comments and even a surprise baby shower that brought Annie to tears.

Camile Daughtry's reaction to the news was, "Well, it's about time."

"Yes," said Annie with a sweet smile. "Once I realized we had your permission to give birth, things really moved along."

There were, as there are in many congregations, women and men who insisted on making comments about Annie's appearance during the pregnancy. Nice: "You positively glow." Not so nice: "We'll see how long it takes you to lose the baby-weight after this is over and get back to that figure you had before."

As the pregnancy progressed, several women and a few children asked if they could touch Annie's stomach. She bit her tongue and said, "Okay." On a Sunday morning after worship, one late-middle-aged male parishioner, Sheldon Davidson, known unofficially as the congregation's creep, decided to give Annie one of his well-known and despised overly tight and lengthy hugs (always given in the name of Christian love and fellowship). And he followed it by reaching down to put his hand on her abdomen with a smile.

Annie reacted in an instant without even thinking, just jerking his hand away, and saying, "Oh no, you don't."

Sheldon's mouth half-opened in shock, and he said, "I was just being friendly and rejoicing in this blessed new life."

"Of course, you were," said Annie, her voice icy, as she whirled around and walked away.

Sheldon decided that day that he would wait for an opportunity to get revenge.

Chapter 49

The pregnancy was uneventful, and after eight and half months Annie delivered a healthy baby girl, Sarah Rachel Campbell, seven pounds and six ounces, with red hair and blue eyes. She looked like a vintage porcelain doll. But as she grew up, it became clear that she was like both her parents in some ways—intelligent, outspoken, justice-oriented, feisty, and kind.

Of course, Sarah was reared in the church, but her relationship with it was complicated. As early as elementary school she was impatient with the answers her Sunday school teachers tried to provide for her ceaseless questions. "If God has always been here, then who made God?" "If God can do anything, then why did my friend's dog, Barney, die this week? I loved Barney." "If God is everywhere, why do we have to come to church? And does God see me in the bathroom too? That's so weird." At some point, her exasperated Sunday school teacher said, "Sarah, your father is the pastor. Why don't you ask him these questions?"

Sarah answered, "I did, but I didn't think his answers made sense. So, he told me to ask you."

Junior high and senior high, did not improve Sarah's opinion of Presbyterian religious instruction. Eventually, she asked if she might skip Sunday school altogether if she promised to read the Bible on her own. Mo and Annie were disappointed, but they agreed. Then one day a few months later, Sarah asked Annie in private if she could also skip worship. Annie fixed her with a sad gaze and said, "Sarah, I know you're not fond of worship. It's boring to you, and you don't agree with everything you hear. But it would break your father's heart if you stopped attending, especially with as much time and effort as he puts into his sermons trying to help people. I hope you will be willing to take one hour a week and come worship with us as a family. Once you've graduated and left to be on your own, you can do as you please. I don't want to fight with you, but it would mean a lot if you would continue this one part of being a Christian with us."

Sarah had indeed been prepared for a battle with her mom, but Annie's reminder of how her actions would hurt her father changed her mind. She continued to worship with the family until she graduated from high school.

Sarah was close to both her parents when she was growing up, but for whatever mysterious reason, she was especially close to her dad whom she adored. As a baby, her first word was "Dah," followed a few days later by

"Maw." During early childhood, she remembered dancing with her father, having him push her on the swing, teaching her to ride a bike, and reading to her. Her mom did these things with her as well, but inexplicably her dad was her favorite.

As an adult, some of her cherished memories of her father were the years that he would go out on Thanksgiving or Christmas mornings after breakfast for a visit with one of the shut-ins or nursing home residents whom he was certain would be spending the holiday alone. Her dad and Sarah didn't get dressed up, and the visits were always short, just a quick check-in and prayer, but they meant a lot to the parishioners they visited. And bringing Sarah along was an added treat for some elderly people who rarely got to see children in person. The drive out to see the shut-in was also a chance for Sarah and her father to talk a little bit about whatever was on Sarah's mind--friends, school, and later, boys, and life itself, or even to think some about the meaning of the day.

But, of course, it was practically inevitable that Sarah's feelings would change, and she would grow closer to her mother as she aged. As she got older, more and more Sarah confided in her mom, engaged in "girl talk" about clothes, make-up, dating, career possibilities, and so on. And the Christmas after Sarah turned fifteen years old, she grumbled for the first time about going along with her dad on the shut-in visits. Her father said in a calm voice, "It's okay, sweetie. You don't have to go if you don't want to." But inside his heart began to break like a car windshield hit by a tiny flying pebble on the highway.

"Thanks, dad," she said. "I'm just tired. I'm going to eat something and go back to bed."

So, her father made the trips alone after that. They still felt like holy time to him, but with a little less joy. As Sarah continued as a student at Sidwell High School, like her mother, she became editor of the school newspaper. Sarah was also an athlete like mom and dad, but her sport wasn't tennis or long-distance running; it was soccer. She excelled as a mid-fielder. And like her father, she became known for speaking out about issues of social justice, especially racism, gay rights, and the rights of women. Upon her graduation from high school with honors she headed off to Guilford College in Greensboro, NC where she majored in Peace and Conflict studies.

During her time at Guilford, she dated several guys, and for a brief time experimented with a same-sex relationship, but then realized she was attracted to men. She just had not quite found "the" guy, and did not, in fact, find him until after she graduated and she moved to Washington, D.C. where she began work with Amnesty International. While at Amnesty, she met

Terrence Jackson, a Black lawyer originally from Atlanta (the son of an American Baptist pastor and his elementary school teacher wife). He worked in her department that focused especially on protecting and expanding women's rights in other countries. Sarah and Terrence tackled some projects together, and then she asked him out on a date. Within three months, they were living together. And in six months they married with Mo and Terrance's dad officiating the service at Memorial Drive Presbyterian Church.

Most of the congregation was happy and supportive, but there were a few members who disapproved. Some were already grumbling over the fact that they had heard that the couple had lived together before marriage. "Fornication is a sin," they said, though almost no women or men in the church were virgins on their wedding day.

Other disgruntled members, who would not say so to Mo and Annie, were angry about their pastor's daughter "marrying outside her race." After all, "If God had not wanted the races to be separate, then God wouldn't have made the different colors of skin. And, besides, the pastor's daughter should be setting an example for the other young people." But none of the complaining made its way to the ears of Mo and Annie who were both thrilled that Sarah had found true love.

 Sarah and Terrence settled in Washington, D.C. where they spent many years moving their way up the ladder at Amnesty International. But one sadness for Mo and Annie was that Sarah became more and more frustrated at the slow pace of most of the congregations to lead on issues of justice. They talked and prayed about justice, but leading change in society was such a plodding chore with much of the church complaining and backbiting every step of the way. Gradually Sarah drifted away, attending worship mainly when she was back home with her parents in North Carolina for the holidays.

Chapter 50

The years passed with Mo and Annie living in Sidwell, Mo serving as pastor at Memorial Drive Presbyterian and Annie continuing to teach English at Sidwell High School. Their work was challenging and interesting.

By taking evening and weekend classes, as well as some online work, Annie was able to complete her Master of Fine Arts degree from nearby Granite University in three years. Afterwards, she occasionally submitted essays to magazines and newspapers, and had several pieces that were published. Eventually, she became a part-time adjunct professor at the local community college. With a blend of teaching high school and college, and doing her own writing, Annie felt she had discovered her own calling.

Mo enrolled in the Doctor of Ministry program at Pittsburgh Theological Seminary (the alma mater of "Mr. Rogers"). Attending classes a few weeks a year, he was able to finish the program and receive his doctorate in five years. His final doctoral project was titled, "Believing and Doing: Christian Ethics in the Local Church."

At home, Mo and Annie certainly had their occasional angry disagreement. Both could be stubborn and thoughtless, but they also were quick to apologize and to forgive. And they were happy as a couple, their love deepening over the years as they entered middle-age with a comfortable rhythm about their busy lives. Mo and Annie made sure to carve out time to be together. They loved hiking the nearby Blue Ridge Mountains, biking around their neighborhood, and driving to the beaches in North Carolina and South Carolina. Annie liked to dance, and she coaxed Mo into a dance class which he tolerated. The couple kept in touch with Sarah and Terrance by phone, and relished when they visited them in North Carolina, as well as when Mo and Sarah had the opportunity to travel to "the big city" of DC and take in the National Art Gallery, the Smithsonian, concerts by the National Symphony, and food from all sorts of cool ethnic restaurants. Life was good.

Of course, with Mo's work, church also remained at the center of their lives. Memorial Drive itself never really experienced explosive numerical growth. A few new members joined, some of them younger people attracted not only by the church's programming but by some of the sermons they heard from Mo who was known as an intellectually engaging preacher whose sermons included humor, comfort, and challenge.

Yet there were also losses at the church, not only from the death of older members but also over anger at what Mo had to say in his personal blog "The Middle Lane." He had started writing it in 2014 and settled on its name because Mo considered himself to be a middle-of-the-road moderate, even though many in their conservative community considered him to be forest-fire-blazing liberal. The blog's readership had grown over the years as Mo addressed how the Christian faith might speak to issues of social justice. But during his decades as pastor, Mo had come to realize that there was a long, unwritten list of topics that some church members considered to be off-limits for discussion, writing, or sermons.

Gun control, despite multiple mass shootings, including shootings in schools and even murders of preschool children in Newtown, Connecticut.

Climate change, because according to some parishioners it was just a theory, a lot of nonsense and political garbage. Besides they knew some smart people, not climate scientists, of course, but smart people who said it was all just a natural variation in the earth's temperature. And you notice that it got cold and snowed three times this past winter.

Israel and Palestine were not to be discussed, because the Bible clearly said that Israel was given the land by God and Israel is U.S.'s closest ally in the Middle East. And the Palestinians were all lumped together as terrorists.

Capital punishment could not be discussed because the Bible says, "An eye for an eye, limb for limb, and life for life."

Racism was off limits except to say that there used to be racism in the country a long time ago, but it no longer exists, and people just need to pick themselves up by their bootstraps and quit whining and blaming others.

LGBTQ rights were something that had been forced upon the church "by liberals" and especially by that liberal President Obama. Most church members had come to grudging acceptance, but they didn't want to have the subject "rammed down their throats" by being mentioned over and over in sermons.

Though the denomination that Memorial Drive belonged to, the Presbyterian Church (USA), had long backed reproductive rights for women, many of the members of the congregation wanted to hear nothing about such support. In fact, they acted as though they were part of one of the fundamentalist denominations that forbid abortions, even in cases of rape or incest.

The U.S.'s broken immigration system and the need for comprehensive immigration reform were off the table because those "illegals" were breaking the law by trying to sneak their way into our country. So, they got whatever unpleasantness came their way, and they just needed to wait their turn, even if that might take twenty years.

Poverty could be discussed if it was understood to be something to be addressed solely by individual efforts. Exploding CEO pay was not for conversation, nor was raising the minimum wage. Poor people needed to work harder and the rest of us could contribute to the local food bank or give a donation to the Salvation Army or the Sidwell Community Ministry. But discussions about how important it was not to cut SNAP, free school lunches, and other hunger programs funded for poor U.S. citizens and citizens in developing nations were not to be topics for Sunday school or for Mo's writing and sermons.

These were just a few of the topics Mo realized a significant percentage of his congregation expected him to be silent about, or perhaps to address only in the most vague, non-challenging ways. As he reflected upon his studies of the Bible, especially Jesus and the Old Testament Prophets, it amazed and saddened him that there was so much resistance to addressing such topics central to the Christian faith. He recalled how the Old Testament Prophets and Jesus thundered against social injustice and called out corrupt political leaders who were harming the people, especially the most vulnerable people. So, Mo was motivated to speak out more, but he was also frustrated for having to try to pacify angry church members who threatened to withhold their financial pledges or to leave the church entirely, unless they could control what Mo said.

"Dear God," thought Mo as he considered the unofficial list he had jotted down on a piece of paper. "What's left that we're 'allowed' to talk about in Sunday school or in sermons or in other writing? 'Being nice' and eventually going to heaven? Is that all?" With the world in such dire straits, the church's silence had turned into a dangerous and disgraceful complicity with evil. And Mo knew he would not and could not be silent.

So, over the years, he had addressed all the "forbidden" topics in sermons or Sunday school or dialogues or in his personal blog. And, as threatened, he saw some church members become enraged, withhold their financial pledges, or even leave the church as a form of blackmail. But Mo was fortunate that over the years, the church also took in a sizable number of new members who understood that being Christian meant addressing every issue with faith. This group of church members not only understood this, but they also liked Mo and Annie. And they stood behind them when there were the inevitable furious and coercive parishioners.

Chapter 51

Things might have continued to be manageable at Memorial Drive, not great, but manageable if not for the rise of Donald J. Trump. Starting around 2015, his presidential candidacy created an unimaginable danger to the country and the world. Almost immediately, Mo and many other people recognized who he was. And for Mo and many clergy steeped in the study of the Old Testament Prophets and Jesus, there was a palpable sense of evil emanating from this man and his cronies even before he took office.

In some ways, of course, Trump was merely a clown, a shrill con man, always looking for his next mark. But Mo knew that he was much more sinister than that. Trump specialized in manipulating and bullying people, fanning and creating hatred, dishonesty, intimidation, racism, misogyny, xenophobia, and homophobia on an entirely new scale for a U.S. president.

Mo had heard Trump speak in New York City decades earlier and, even back then, he was amazed at how vacuous and narcissistic he was as he boasted about himself at an event where he was supposed to be honoring others. Then Trump was caught on tape bragging about his treatment of women he found physically attractive, "You know…I just start kissing them. It's like a magnet. Just kiss. I don't even wait. And when you're a star, they let you do it. You can do anything…Grab 'em by the pussy. You can do anything." Trump sloughed his behavior off as "locker room talk." Later, Mo was disgusted when Trump mimicked and mocked a reporter who had a physical disability. And then he lied about it, claiming that he had not made fun of the reporter, even though his contemptible ridicule was captured on videotape for all to see.

Years before, he had called for the death penalty for some Black teenagers convicted of rape and attempted murder of a woman in Central Park. When the boys were later exonerated, Trump refused to acknowledge their innocence or apologize for what he had written and spoken.

In similar fashion, he had been one of the main proponents of the so-called "birther" allegations that President Barack Obama had been born in Kenya, not the U.S. Despite the clear racism in these allegations, and the fact that Obama produced a birth certificate from Hawaii, Trump never formally retracted his claims and said he was sorry. As was his way of life, he was a wannabe tyrant and a pathological liar who loved to cause chaos, and never apologize.

Chapter 52

Mo had started "The Middle Lane" to address how the Christian faith spoke to the great issues of the day. And by 2015, when Trump came on the scene, Mo began to comment on what he observed.

"Today, Donald J. Trump, attacked the physical appearance of Carly Fiorina, one of his GOP Presidential Nominee opponents. 'Look at that face. Would anyone vote for that?' he said. Of course, running for public office requires thick skin and candidates must be prepared for the 'sharp elbows' that come with the process, but this childish, misogynistic bullying is beyond the pale. We're witnessing despicable behavior from someone who says he wants to represent our country on the world stage as the President of the United States. Heaven forbid! Scripture tells us that leaders will be held to a higher standard. It reminds us that we must speak the truth in love. It demands, as Jesus said, that we 'Do unto others as we would have others do unto us.' God help us if this man gets the nomination."

Yet Trump did get nominated, and his behavior only worsened. He threatened to have his opponent, Hillary Clinton, jailed. He encouraged followers at his rallies to chant "Lock her up!" He called her "a nasty woman," and made comments about her needing to go to the restroom during a break in the presidential debates. He claimed that she had covered up thousands of missing emails from her server.

Trump promised that if elected he would build a wall along the entire U.S./Mexico border and that Mexico would pay for it—another ridiculous lie.

With each abominable speech, Mo responded in his blog that now saw its audience expanding to more than 10,000 readers. And as the blog expanded, it began to attract the attention of far-right Trump supporters and White supremacists and so-called "militias" that were nothing more than domestic terrorist groups given a name more dignified than they deserved.

Mo began to receive angry blog posts. At first, he tried to have a discussion with the writers. "So, WhtPowr#1 help me understand why you find Trump to be such an attractive presidential candidate." "Own@thlibs, what makes you think Trump will be such a supporter of the military when he managed to avoid the draft with bone spurs that did not keep him from other activities? And how do you feel about hearing Trump on tape saying that avoiding catching STDs was his 'personal Vietnam'?"

But it was nearly impossible to have a meaningful conversation with the blog posters who just complained, with no evidence, about "socialism," "Marxism," or "communism" from the Democrats. Or they talked about "Hitlery" and "Hillary's missing emails," or "Benghazi" (even though Hillary had sat and answered questions from The House Select Committee for 11 hours, concerning the deaths of 4 Americans there, and she was never charged with any crime).

Eventually, the angry posts degenerated into personal attacks. "What's a so-called pastor doing talking about politics and defending Hillary?" "You're not a preacher. You're the leader of a demonic cult!" And then the personal attacks finally turned into threats. "Don't forget, Mosey Along, we know where you live." "Mo, I've seen pictures of your wife and daughter. Very nice. Delicious."

Mo shared the threatening messages with the police, but the Internet provided some anonymity, and the messages were not threatening enough for charges to be filed.

Trump was elected in 2016. Mo and Annie were astonished and horrified at his election and disturbed by how he may have inadvertently received assistance from Attorney General James Comey's public announcement, just days before Election Day, of his reopening an investigation into Hillary Clinton's emails. But after his election, Mo, and Annie both prayed for Trump to lead with wisdom and compassion. In fact, on Sunday mornings when he led worship, Mo regularly prayed for Trump and other elected leaders by name, asking God to grant them wisdom and compassion. Like other Americans, Mo and Annie hoped that Trump would "grow into the job" once he recognized the enormity of the work before him and the immense responsibility he and his administration now bore.

But Trump never grew into the job at all. Instead, during his time in office he accumulated more than 30,000 lies or misleading statements. Using the language of dictators, again and again he referred to the press as "the enemy of the people," thus endangering their very lives. As he had before, Trump continued to behave as a bully. Using crude insults and threats, he attacked anyone who challenged him or even disagreed with him. In particular, he showed contempt for women, for people of other races, and for people in other countries. His words and behavior emboldened White Supremacist groups who responded with violence.

Misusing his presidential office Trump tried to get officials in Ukraine to provide dirt on a potential future presidential challenger, Joe Biden. The attempt was caught by a decorated U.S. Army officer who reported what he heard. Eventually, Trump was impeached by the House, but in the impeachment trial in the Senate, GOP Senators refused even to call witnesses or listen to testimony. They acquitted Trump of misusing his power and of attempting to obstruct justice, even though it was clear to most observers that he was guilty of both charges. After his acquittal, Trump crowed about his innocence and the "witch hunt," and took revenge on the dedicated public servants who had dared to call him to account.

Meanwhile, Trump's treatment of the environment was suicidal. Almost every publishing climate scientist in the world affirmed that climate change was real, largely caused by human actions, and an existential threat to the world that must be dealt with immediately. But Trump claimed climate change was just another "hoax." So, he pulled the U.S. out of the Paris Climate Accords. He rolled back more than a hundred environmental regulations that were meant to kept the air, soil, and water safer and cleaner.

One of the more disgusting aspects of Trump's policies was his hatred of immigrants. Early on, he made an executive order to ban travel and immigration from several majority Muslim countries. But he reserved a special contempt for immigrants who came from what he called "shithole countries" with mainly Black and Brown populations. His anti-immigration policies at the U.S./Mexico border led to children being separated from their parents and kept in cages. Hundreds of the children were permanently separated from their parents due to failure of officials to keep careful records. It was a disgraceful human rights violation.

When the COVID-19 pandemic hit the U.S. in 2020, Trump again lied to the American people by claiming it was nothing to be concerned about, that it was a hoax perpetrated by the Democrats to make him look bad, and that it would soon disappear "like magic." He made fun of people who wore masks, and he suggested preposterous "cures" such as drinking chlorine or bringing UV light into the human body. Trump refused to formulate a coherent and comprehensive national program for fighting the coronavirus and he called top infectious disease expert Dr. Anthony Fauci "a disaster" and "an idiot" when he disagreed with him. Rather than accept Fauci's advice, he held massive rallies in which few participants wore masks, and these became "super-spreader events" that led to terrible rates of infection, sickness, and death. Experts later calculated that Trump's irresponsibility toward the virus resulted in hundreds of thousands of unnecessary American deaths.

Because it was so vast, it was hard to capture the true depth of Trump's destructiveness and depravity then. But Mo responded to most of the outrages with comments on "The Middle Lane," and the occasional usually subtle reference in a Sunday sermon or pastoral prayer. Blogposts were met by attacks from Trump supporters. But they were outnumbered by positive comments from other people who discerned the charlatan abusing his office for personal gain and feeding his ravenous narcissistic personality disorder. Sermon and prayer references received immediate comments of condemnation or praise from parishioners at the door of the sanctuary after services were over. Most congregants, displeased or pleased, said nothing to Mo. Occasionally, a church member might schedule a meeting to talk about his or her concerns that Mo was speaking about what Trump was doing. But in most cases, he found that these disgruntled congregants had been practically brain-washed by right-wing media and had no real interest in honest discussion of what was clearly happening. They just wanted to vent their anger and claim that Mo was not allowed to name the evil, because that meant he was "being political." It seemed tragic to Mo that politics had become the unspeakable word in church.

Chapter 53

As Mo wrote in his blog and read the responses, he tried to understand the thinking of the Trump supporters. It seemed that they returned to several themes again and again.

"We didn't elect a pastor or a Sunday school teacher. I voted for somebody who would not be a politician, somebody who would speak his mind, even if he has a sharp tongue sometimes. If a firefighter shows up and puts out the fire at your house, you don't care if he/she has a salty tongue." But this argument made no sense to Mo because Trump functioned more like a firefighter who was the arsonist who set the fire and who, when called to help, threw gasoline on the fire.

"I don't agree with all his tweets, but his policies are great. I have more money in my pocket and in my 401K thanks to him." It seemed to Mo this argument minimized whatever insulting or lying, or crazy talk Trump delivered via tweet, and it excused it because of temporary tax cuts, that mainly helped the wealthy, ran up the federal deficit, and eventually would have to be repaid by all Americans through higher taxes.

"Trump loves our country and is trying to make it great again. He's a businessman who believes in capitalism and the rule of law. If you get your way, we'll just have socialism and lawlessness. Why don't you give him a chance?!" Mo was amazed that people seemed not to understand the definition of socialism and that they were so easily duped by the strategy of saying that Democrats were going to force socialism upon the country. And how could Trump supporters entrust the U.S. economy to Trump, with his multiple bankruptcies and unpaid bills, who loved tariffs, cozied up to authoritarians, hid his taxes and falsely claimed they could not be released because they were under IRS audit, and who had broken as many laws as he had?

But finally, the last theme was the one that Mo heard the most, "You Democrats, and you, Mo, so-called preacher, are in favor of baby-killing. But Trump is a pro-life president who is appointing pro-life judges who will get rid of abortion. He is also protecting our religious freedom, instead of kowtowing to the LGBTQ agenda." This theme was especially disappointing to Mo. He knew it often came from a hardened "evangelical" Christian perspective that refused to examine the church's varying stance on abortion and to consider why new knowledge made LGBTQ rights an essential part of following Jesus. Instead, the evangelicals quoted Bible verses out of context and adopted Billy Graham's strategy of holding up the Bible and saying, "The Bible says…" as if such a simplistic approach settled every issue.

It occurred to Mo that the tragic irony was that the greatest enabler of Donald J. Trump was the church in the United States. On the right-wing side of the church were Trump supporters who heard anti-abortion and anti-LGBTQ rights sermons on a regular basis. They pointed to those issues ostensibly as their reason for backing Trump no matter what he did. What went unsaid was their willingness to overlook Trump's misogyny, racism, constant lying, bragging, and whining, and his failure to show even the faintest traces of "do unto others as you would have others do unto you" love and compassion for other human beings.

This was all supported by right-wing clergy who claimed that despite all his disgusting outward appearances, Trump was sent by God to support the Christian faith and be a beacon of light to the nation. Prominent evangelicals such as Franklin Graham, and Robert Jeffries, and kooks such as Paula White and Pat Robertson helped to lead the charge and give energy and additional clout to local preachers who parroted their thinking. It was a huge blot on the entire church, and one more reason that young adults and educated Americans were fleeing the church in droves.

But sadly enough, the rest of the church also unintentionally supported Trump, in a different way. In far too many of the more moderate, progressive, or liberal churches, pastors and members talked about needing to keep unity in "the purple church." By this they did not mean simply acknowledging that within those congregations there were (red) Republicans and (blue) Democrats. What they meant was that instead of simply trying to grapple with whether public policies and political leaders were aligned with the justice and love of God seen in the Old Testament Prophets and in Jesus, the pastors and other leaders in those churches had an obligation to attempt to placate both political parties in their churches.

So, with this "purple church" understanding, pastors especially needed to be careful never to be too specific about the terrible injustices they saw oozing every day from the Trump administration. So, what if Trump separated children from their parents at the border and put them in cages? This was not to be mentioned in sermons or in pastoral prayers. They had to protect "the purple church," and the church budget and the pastor's job which would be threatened if members, especially Trump supporters, got angry and withheld their financial pledges or even quit the church. The church, which was supposed to be a Christian community, became more of a business instead. A false unity mattered more than God's truth, justice, and love.

Mo was disgusted by the silence and complicity of his fellow clergy who said nothing of substance about the wannabe dictator. With the brave example of spiritual forebears, Presbyterians in the American Colonies, how could his fellow pastors remain so quiet in the face of an obvious attempt by Trump to become an autocrat?

But Mo accepted that angry bloggers and enraged church members were just part of the difficulty of speaking the truth in love. He recalled that Jesus said, "Love your enemies and pray for those who persecute you." But Jesus never said, "Don't make any enemies." So, Mo said a silent prayer that blind Trump supporters would one day see the truth, and that where there was blindness in his own understanding, he would also see the truth. Ultimately, he entrusted all people to God's care.

Chapter 54

But then one blog posting sent a shockwave into Mo's and Annie's world. The writer, GdHtsLbs, said, "I know someone who went to Garden College with Mo's wife, Annie. And she says it was common knowledge that Annie had an abortion while she was in college. The preacher's wife is a baby killer!"

This comment released a torrent of hatred on the blog. "Baby murderer!" "Infant butcher!" and "Whore!" were just a few of the labels applied to Annie. Some posters also attacked Mo. "This so-called minister doesn't seem to have any problem with what his wife has done!! I want to hear him at least say that she has repented of her sin and that she has joined in kneeling before God and begging for God's forgiveness." "This guy thinks he can be a preacher and be pro-abortion! He is nothing but a heathen who brings shame on the church! He should be fired!" There were even a few thinly veiled (and often misspelled) death threats. But rather than being cowed, Annie and Mo were enraged at the original poster and at the other people who posted insults.

Of course, there were also empathetic comments posted on the blog. A woman said, "I also had an abortion a long time ago. I was a young mother barely getting by as it was, and when I found out I was pregnant again I decided to abort in the first trimester. It was my decision, not something the government or a bunch of foul-mouthed crazies like you people got to decide for me. I don't regret it." Another writer, a man, said, "My wife and I faced a pregnancy in which the doctors determined that the fetus had massive brain damage and would not live long or enjoy any decent quality of life. So, it was very painful, but we chose the path of the least amount of suffering. These evangelicals don't know what they are talking about. It's not their life. I'm sorry you and Annie are going through this, Mo."

Word spread like an oil spill to the members and the session of Memorial Drive Presbyterian Church. The Personnel Committee called a special meeting to talk with Mo immediately following worship that Sunday. After calling the meeting to order with prayer, the chairperson of the committee, Mildred Owens, a middle-aged conservative woman who worked as a paralegal in a local law firm said, "I think we all know why we're here. Word about Annie's, um, past is all over the church and all over town. And, Mo, your blog and recent sermons dealing with political issues are really getting quite a few of our members upset. People come to church to be comforted.

It's supposed to be a *sanctuary* from the harsh world. They don't come here to be made upset by the pastor and his wife."

The others on the committee nodded and murmured their agreement.

Mo felt sweat dripping under his t-shirt and dress shirt, and his face reddened as he fought to hold back his anger. Finally, he took a deep breath and spoke as calmly as he was able which was not very calmly. "I do not know a subtle way to say this to you all. So, I will just be blunt about it. Annie's past is none of your damned business. It's none of the church's or the town's damned business either. I love my wife and I am proud of her, and I make no apologies for anything she has done."

The committee was stunned into a moment of silence.

Then Mildred spoke again, "Mo, there's no need for you to be cursing here. You, of all people, should be setting an example. We're just trying to be *helpful*, because we're concerned about you and Annie, and we want what's best for you and the church. Several of us have talked before the meeting and we wonder if maybe a letter of apology from you to the church might be appropriate now, a way to bring the temperature down with some of our valuable, longtime members."

Mo felt lightheaded, a sign that his blood pressure was rising. So, he took a couple slow, deep breaths before answering. "I certainly appreciate your concern, but you are not understanding me. There will be no letter of apology because there is nothing to apologize for. And, by the way, who are these 'upset members'? I need to talk with them face to face rather than hearing about their frustrations through the grapevine. That's an unhealthy way of communicating."

Bill Bradford, a retired business owner cleared his throat and spoke as if delivering a lecture to a miscreant high school student employee, "Well, I'm not at liberty to say who they are. I'll just say they are influential people in this church and this community. And I'm not sure if you understand the gravity of the situation. Not only are people upset about Annie, but they are upset about your blog and your sermons that are so political. The church isn't supposed to be political."

"That's where you're wrong," said Mo. "The gospel is not partisan, but it has clear political implications. Christ is Lord. And being disciples of Christ means that Christ makes claims upon our entire life as people, and that means Christ has something to say about the public policies and politicians we support and do not support. There are difficult and important decisions that must be made, and our faith should be guiding those decisions. We read over and over in the Bible about God's care for the hungry, the sick, the oppressed, the vulnerable, the immigrant, the children, the imprisoned, the lonely, and the poor. So, shouldn't we be having honest and open conversations about what constitutes ethical politics as Christians? And shouldn't we be talking about what politicians, especially President Trump and his administration are doing that is so unethical, destructive, and deadly?"

"Well, all I know," said Mildred, "Is that people are starting to grumble, and I'm concerned about our church."

"Then they should come and talk to me face to face as a brother in Christ," said Mo.

"People don't like to do that, because it makes them uncomfortable," said Bill.

Mo wanted to scream, "Uncomfortable?! Too bad! Do you realize what's at stake here?" Instead, he answered in a level tone. "Jesus commanded us to talk to each other face to face when we feel we've been mistreated. It's right there in the Bible, Matthew 18:15-20. He also said that being his disciples would not be easy. 'Take up your cross and follow me,' he commanded."

The meeting ended with little progress as far as Mo was concerned. He told the committee that he would write a letter to the congregation reiterating his policy of speaking out about social justice issues and his policy of face-to-face communication, rather than anonymous complaints. He would say nothing about Annie because it was none of the congregation's business.

Chapter 55

But Melvin Anderson, a member of a local White supremacist group felt that Mo's blog was most definitely *his* business. Melvin was not a member of the congregation. He was a 52-year-old tobacco-chewing, country guy, six-feet tall and a 180 pounds (thirty pounds of it beer gut), who had cheated his way to receiving a high school diploma. Melvin briefly considered military service after high school, but when he visited the local recruiting station for information and met a Black U.S. Army staff sergeant working there, he decided he had no interest in going through basic training and military service where he might have Black soldiers ordering him around. And though he would never admit it, the prospect of going to war terrified him.

So, the local "militia" aka White supremacist group, was a perfect fit for him. He and his friends could drink beer and do pretend military maneuvers, running around firing weapons at targets in the woods, and there was never the problem of people on the other side firing back at them. They could also march around town with loaded weapons and Confederate battle flags, yelling and chanting racist nonsense and making people nervous. It was heady stuff for him, and his face beamed with a happy malice any time the militia got together.

If you did a little background study, Melvin's temperament and inclinations were unsurprising. He'd grown up with a father who beat his mother, his little sister, and him on a regular basis for "looking at him wrong," or not doing chores to his satisfaction or a host of other excuses for him to be violent. Melvin's father had been an active member of the KKK, and the entire family was racist to its rotten core, undergirded by racist friends, a racist culture, and even racism taught and accepted in their fundamentalist church.

In his regular life, Melvin worked on the line at a local plastics factory, but had been passed over for promotion a couple of times. Most recently the position he wanted was filled by a young Black woman. Melvin claimed it was because of "reverse discrimination," but, she was simply an excellent worker, and he often came to work drunk or buzzed.

For years, Melvin had heard about Mo, this fake minister who complained about President Trump on his blog and even in a few of his sermons. Mo had called out Trump's racism, bullying, constant lying, criminality, and cowardice. He had warned about the rise in hate groups and militias during Trump's time in office. And he had said that Trump was giving permission

188

for these groups to come out of the shadows and be proud that "one of theirs" was in the highest office in the land.

Melvin celebrated when Trump went on television after the White power rally in Charlottesville where counter-protesters were beaten and one of them killed, and Trump had said "there were fine people on both sides." When Black Lives Matter protesters rallied in several U.S. cities, the militias went in and did what they could to stir up violence and even to destroy property, knowing that Trump and his allies would blame the Black Lives Matter people for all of it. And Trump and his supporters in Congress could then say that they were all about "law and order," even though Trump was perhaps the most lawless president in U.S. history. Melvin and his White supremacist friends were thrilled. It was like the good old days coming back when Blacks, Hispanics, Jews, Muslims, homos, and women would relearn their place. And the White man would be on top again where he belonged.

Melvin knew that Mo was one more tiny, stupid obstacle and threat to that hope, because he wouldn't shut up, and people listened to him, because he was a fake minister. And as Melvin said to his militia friends in private, "He uses fancy words, like his shit don't stink. He's forgot where he come from and who he really is. But as far as I'm concerned, he's just another libtard. And I know a way to shut him up."

Chapter 56

Mo decided that maybe a good way to address the conflict at Memorial Drive Presbyterian Church would be to preach a "talk-back sermon." That is, he would preach a sermon about what was going on. Then, after the service there would be an opportunity for interested congregation members to meet with him in the fellowship hall and, over a light lunch, to ask questions and make comments. Mo did not run the idea by the session or the Personnel Committee, but he felt it would be a great way to state some important truths and get the conversation out of the shadows and into the open for healthy dialogue. Surely, the light of truth would cleanse and heal.

When Annie heard the idea she said, "I'm not so sure, babe. But I know you must try something."

Mo advertised the upcoming sermon talk-back in the church's weekly newsletter three weeks in advance. He billed it as "What's going on at Memorial Drive? Come and find out the truth. Join us for worship at 11:00 a.m. and a sermon talk-back on Sunday, January 19th at noon for a light lunch and a respectful dialogue."

January 19th arrived and at 11:00 a.m. the sanctuary wasn't packed, but it was more filled than usual. As Mo waited for the service to begin, he noticed the faces of a few disgruntled members he had not seen in months. On the other hand, many of the discontented still were not there. For the scripture readings that Sunday, Mo had selected three passages—the first on Christian unity, the second on how Jesus commanded Christians who felt offended to talk face to face, and the third about the need for justice and truth to be proclaimed and lived by the church, including the need for the church to speak to politics.

After the readings, Mo attempted a little bit of humor to begin the sermon. It fell flat, and he felt his mouth getting dry. He then moved on to a point about Christian unity, and how it was based not on agreement about every issue but agreement about the attempt to follow God revealed in Jesus. Then he moved to his second point, the necessity of following Jesus's command to talk to one another face to face whenever we feel wronged by another. Finally, Mo turned to his last point; the church can and must speak the truth in love and practice justice, and this would be difficult and dangerous, as it had always been. Mo mentioned how God called the Old Testament Prophets to speak the truth to elected leaders who did not want to hear the truth and who sometimes responded by attacking the Prophets. Then Mo said, "Jesus, our Lord, himself spoke out against evil policies and evil leaders in his day. He did not call Herod 'a fox' because he thought he was attractive but because he was weaselly and wicked. Remember, Jesus was crucified by the Roman Empire because his idea of God's reign of love was a threat to Rome's idea of reigning by terror and torture.

"I know there's talk these days about 'the purple church.' If that means we recognize that our congregations do indeed contain Republicans and Democrats, that's fine. Unfortunately, for many people it has come to mean that the pastor must never take a stand for truth and justice if it offends people in one political party or another. It has come to stand for a bland gospel that never calls out lies, injustice, and cruelty. It has turned the gospel and proclaimers of the gospel toward heresy and cowardice. Just imagine, if only Jesus had known about 'the purple church' he might have avoided that whole 'crucifixion thing.' You'd think he could have said, 'Well, I was going to declare the urgency of God's inbreaking shalom and humanity's call to respond immediately, but there was a Pharisee party, and a Sadducee Party, and the Roman Emperor Party, and I didn't want to offend anyone connected to a party and be accused of being partisan. So, I said nothing. And it really worked out much better for me. See? No crucifixion!'"

As Mo continue to speak, several congregants stood up and stomped out of worship while shaking their heads and grumbling under their breath.

After worship was over, Mo delivered the lunch blessing and benediction from the back of the sanctuary. He skipped shaking hands at the sanctuary door so that he could get to the fellowship hall and grab a quick bite before the dialogue began. Mo had asked a middle-aged clergy friend known for her calm listening skills, the Rev. Susan Nettles, to facilitate the dialogue. Mo introduced her to about 25 people who had decided to stay for lunch and the conversation. She thanked Mo for the invitation to assist. Then she offered a brief prayer, set the ground rules for the dialogue, including "no name-calling or personal attacks," and then she walked to a large pad of paper set on a foldout easel with markers.

"Let's begin," Susan said, "by talking about what you found most helpful about the scripture readings and sermon this morning."

Responses included: "It showed us the tension between unity and truth-telling." "I liked the joke at the beginning." "It really emphasized how we have to talk to each other face to face, instead of gossiping behind people's backs."

Susan wrote the various responses on the newsprint. Then she tore the paper off the pad and taped it to the wall.

"Now," she said, "what did you find most challenging or even troubling in the scripture readings and sermon?"

"I was surprised to realize that the Prophets and Jesus reprimanded political leaders. I guess I should have known that, but I had just never thought of it that way," said one woman in her thirties.

"I felt everything was just an excuse for Mo to complain about Trump and the GOP. I'm so sick of it, and I know others are too. I've also heard through the grapevine that our fabulous Music Director, Gerald Offenbacher, and our beloved Christian Education Director, Amy Hutchins, are very unhappy with the way they've been treated by the pastor. But they're afraid to say anything in public for fear of reprisal" said Sheldon Davidson, putting on a show of great dignity, but barely suppressing a smile, and finally getting his chance for revenge against Annie who had dared to set boundaries with him.

Mo was stunned, and Susan broke in to say, "Folks, we need to stick with the conversation about the sermon and the sermon topics, not rumors, please." Her reminder made no difference.

"Ditto Sheldon's remarks," said a woman in her early 60s. "I know quite a few members who are not here today, and their membership in this church is just hanging on by a thread. If they wanted to go to a rally for the Democratic Party they would have done so. I hate to say this, but I wonder if you should go."

The rest of the comments were just as negative. At the end of the meeting, Susan asked if Mo wanted to respond to anything that had been said. "No," he said. "I have told you what I believe and where I stand. Some of what I've heard today is encouraging. Much of what I've heard makes me very sad, but I committed to listening today, not talking. You've given me a lot to think about."

Mo and Annie drove home together, neither saying much, just trying to absorb and make sense of what had happened. Their anger and heartache only increased that evening when Mo received an email from the Personnel Committee. They had met without him, which was against the congregation's bylaws. But their message was clear. "Dear Mo, after much discussion and prayer we have voted unanimously requesting the session to ask you complete your service with us and to leave on his own as soon as possible, of course, granting you a few months to find a new position. If you refuse that, our suggestion to the session is that a congregational meeting be called, and you be voted out for the good of the church."

After reading the email, tears dripped down Annie's face and she said, "I'm just so angry. All these years we loved them, and it meant nothing to them, nothing. All these years, all that we've shared, and our love was wasted."

Mo sighed, nodded to agree, and then said, "I'm furious too. This bunch of hypocrites and backstabbers just doesn't get it. But it's not the whole church. It's a powerful group in the church. And I still believe that even though love is not always reciprocated, it is never wasted. I think that somehow God keeps that love and it means something in God's keeping. It counts for something in eternity, even when it's not always appreciated here on earth."

Annie said nothing as she wiped some of the tears from her face. Then finally she asked, "You really believe that?"

"I do," he said. "It doesn't feel like it right now, but I do believe it."

"Well, you may be right, but I'd still like to scream at a couple of 'em."

"Me too," Mo said. And they laughed through their tears.

Then Annie took her hands and touched Mo's face on each cheek, looked into his eyes and said, "I want you to know something. You could have backed down when people started complaining about your message. You could have apologized and shut up. But you didn't. You were brave. And no matter what happens, I'm proud of you."

"I love you, Annie," he said. "And thank you for standing with me through all of this. We'll figure something out."

"I love you too," she said. "I know we'll figure it out."

Chapter 57

2020

So, Mo did meet with the Permanent Judicial Commission (PJC) of Good Shepherd Presbytery. This was the group designated to deal with disciplinary cases involving elders and clergy. Unlike some other denominations, Presbyterians did not have bishops with the power to handle such disciplinary problems; they had the PJC. Discipline within the Presbyterian system was meant not to be punitive but restorative, at least that was the stated intention.

At 2:00 p.m. the Rev. Malcolm Compton, Moderator of the PJC, looked around the small conference room at the presbytery office, noting six people, not counting Mo, with paper name plates placed on the table in front of them. This was the Permanent Judicial Commission tasked with handling Mo's case. Compton said, "I see that everyone is here. Thank you all for coming. Though this is a formal meeting, with your permission, we'll be on first name basis." He looked around the room, as everyone nodded in agreement. "I'll call this meeting to order with prayer. Lord, you have not made us to be alone in this life. Instead, you call us into relationship, and we are grateful for that gift. But you know being in relationship is sometimes difficult for us and we struggle with how to relate to each other in appropriate and uplifting ways. So, as we come together this day, grant that we might be given the wisdom and compassion of Christ. We pray in his name. Amen. Again, thank you everyone for attending today. I'll ask that the clerk keep our minutes today. The Rev. Luis Mendoza will read the charges."

Malcolm nodded at Luis who began to read, "The Rev. Dr. Moses Witherspoon Campbell is charged with violating the commands of Scripture and the Book of Order with outbursts and vulgar language in a meeting of this presbytery. He has failed to uphold the standards required for being a Minister of the Word and Sacrament in the Presbyterian Church (USA). Mo, do you have any comments? And have you brought counsel with you?"

"No, I haven't brought council. Yes, I do have comments," said Mo, "I am simply amazed that this presbytery is too cowardly to speak up clearly about the evil and dangerous behavior of President Donald J. Trump. For heaven's sake, we're Presbyterians with a proud history of standing up to tyrants. What happened to our prophetic voice? I'm embarrassed by our inaction."

Some members of the PJC squirmed in their seats. Others crossed their arms and shook their heads in disagreement.

"Mr. Chairperson, may I speak to Mo's assertions?" asked Elder Diane Lawson.

"You may," said the chairperson.

"Mo, we've been friends for a long time, and I really respect you and the ministry you do. You are a kind man, a conscientious pastor, a person of integrity, and you're also a good friend I've shared lots of laughter and fun with."

Mo nodded and gave a small smile in agreement.

Diane continued, "But do you think you're the only one in this presbytery who has noticed Trump's behavior? Do you have any idea how arrogant you sound? I am especially reminded of the story I'm sure you know, 1 Kings 19 when the Prophet Elijah flees from Jezebel and hides in the cave. God comes and speaks to him and, I'm paraphrasing, Elijah says to God, 'Everybody else has forsaken your covenant, Lord. I'm the only faithful prophet left.' And God says, 'Get up and get to work. There are about 7000 faithful who will join you.'

"Mo," Diane said, "Forgive me for being blunt. You're not the only prophetic voice around. Stop being so arrogant."

Mo's face turned red, and he took a deep breath.

"Diane, I appreciate your kind words as well as your challenge. I've also been grateful to have had you as a friend and colleague for decades now. But friends tell each other the truth in love. You know there's some 'bad language' in the Bible, crude, and sometimes obscene language in the Hebrew of the Old Testament. Remember Jeremiah 3:2? And then there's the Greek of the New Testament. Remember Philippians 3:8? That 'bad language' is used to shock and make a point. Can you not see that my 'arrogance,' as you call it, is profound grief, sadness, and loss turned to righteous anger? And the problem is not my arrogance, as you say, it's the failure of this presbytery to take a public stand about what is going on with Donald Trump. Do you not see that he is attempting to set himself up as a dictator? He acts like a miniature Hitler, and this presbytery is too busy trying not to offend anybody. So, it doesn't make a firm statement for the rest of the church and the world to hear. It's disgusting. And I cannot remain silent," said Mo.

"Mo," said the Reverend Neal Turner, "With all due respect, you are welcome to your opinion, but you are not welcome to disrupt the presbytery meetings with foul language. It must stop now. Will you offer a sincere written apology to the presbytery, and will you promise not to have any more outbursts?"

"I will not," said Mo. "I am not offering my opinion. I am speaking God's truth and the presbytery damn well better listen whether you like my tone and language or not. For heaven's sake, you've been to seminary and passed your ordination exams. You know how the Hebrew in Jeremiah 3:2 "lain with" would be translated more accurately into English, and you know how the Greek in Philippians 3:7 "refuse" is a tidied-up translation of the crude word for human excrement. But you are so worried about *my* bad language? Are you not in danger of doing what Jesus warned the scribes and Pharisees of? 'You strain a gnat and swallow a camel.'"

"But you are not an Old Testament Prophet or Jesus. You are simply a Presbyterian minister who promised to abide by our discipline. That's not straining a gnat and swallowing a camel. That's what community is built upon—Christian respect and courtesy," said the chairperson. "And you really don't leave us many choices as far as the decision of this PJC. Do you have anything more to say to us?"

"No."

"Then we'll tell you about our decision by the end of the day."

The meeting adjourned with prayer.

It occurred to Mo that one of the great struggles of his life was how he would respond to an evil voice that kept telling him to be silent in the face of injustice. The voice said, "Be silent because it will be dangerous and costly to speak out when dealing with bullies. Be afraid. Be silent."

But this time, at least, he had chosen not to be afraid and not to be silent.

As promised, by the end of the day, he was informed that the PJC would be recommending he receive a formal rebuke from the presbytery.

Good Shepherd Presbytery did vote to rebuke Mo. It was their softest form of formal disciplinary action, and he was not stripped of his ordination. Yet it was still a public and permanent blemish upon his career and upon him.

After weeks of conversation, the session of Memorial Drive Presbyterian Church and Mo also came to an agreement that he would be given nine months to find a new position. But at his age Mo knew his opportunities were limited. At least Annie still had her job, though after the word of her abortion in college had gotten out, she began to be treated with subtle contempt by some of the teachers and staff who were fundamentalist Christians.

The last time Mo led worship at Memorial Drive, the congregation had not had in-person worship and Holy Communion in a several months due to the COVID-19 pandemic, made immeasurably worse by Trump's lies, delays, and failure to provide national strategic leadership. Mo looked out at the little band of believers, mainly older folks, all wearing masks, all spaced at least 10 feet apart from each other in the pews. He saw many people with teary eyes, people lonely, tired, and afraid. Mo began to read the familiar words in the communion liturgy, a quote from Jesus, "Come to me all you who are weary and heavy laden, and I will give you rest…" And as he said the words, Mo's own voice quavered and caught for just a second before he recovered. He hoped nobody in the church noticed, but someone probably did. It hit him that the reason his voice broke was the recognition that the people before him were 'weary and heavy laden,' and needing rest. And he himself, with his broken heart was 'weary and heavy laden,' and needing rest too.

Chapter 58

Early one Saturday morning in the spring, Mo went out running in the quiet countryside. Exercising was one way he tried to find some calm in the storm-tossed life he and Annie were enduring. He was also trying to knock out his five-mile run in the cooler semi-light before the day turned into a sunlit sauna.

Mo took a familiar route that he had run hundreds of times before, starting back when he was a younger man. And he was coming to his favorite part of the run, climbing three long hills in a row, several hundred feet of pushing himself, his heart rate hitting around 180 beats per minute. And finally, he would reach the top where the road leveled off to reveal over his right shoulder rolling hills, a reddish rusty-roofed barn in the distance below, pastures dotted with brown and white Jersey cows, and farmland as far as you could see for twenty miles. The view at the top was the reward for the effort. And Mo always looked out over the scene, grateful for nature's beauty and for the ability still to run and push himself.

Whenever he could, Mo ran on the left-hand side of the road, against traffic, as he did that morning. Dripping sweat in his eyes and breathing hard as he crested the final hill, he looked to his right. And through the light morning mist, he took in the scene stretched out before him, a land that looked peaceful and whole, so promising.

A car pulled alongside him from his right side, something that happened occasionally when out-of-town people might ask for directions to the local ball field for Little League Baseball games or soccer matches. This morning the car kept pace with him. The driver's side window came down and a friendly voice called, "Hey, Mo. How's it going?" As he continued to run, Mo turned his head toward the voice, and he leaned down a little to see who it was. And at that moment, the car drifted from the lane, closer toward him, and the driver lifted a sawed-off 12-gauge shotgun from his lap and fired both barrels at the same time, hitting Mo in the neck and face. He fell to the pavement, gurgling, most of his face, and neck blown off, just a bloody mess left still attached. The driver stopped his car to admire his handiwork, and then he said, "I guess you don't have anything to say after all, do you?" He laughed and started to spit some tobacco juice out the window, but then thought about the cops finding DNA. So, he just drove away giggling, careful not to speed.

Mo died in under a minute. His body was found five minutes later by an ICU nurse on the way to work at the Dover Hospital. She stopped her car along the road, emergency blinkers flashing, and called 911. Then she threw on her facemask, grabbed a medical kit from her trunk, and rushed to Mo's side. She felt for a heartbeat—nothing. And then she saw the extent of his injuries and she knew he was gone. So she sat beside Mo's body, weeping, waiting for the ambulance to arrive. There was really nothing else she could do.

Annie had gone for a long walk early that morning and then met some girlfriends for breakfast at a local restaurant. Shortly after she arrived at home around mid-morning, she was surprised not to see Mo back from his run, but she figured he was running late again. She looked in the dirty clothing hamper and his sweaty running clothes were not there either. And then she saw a police car pull into the driveway. "Oh," she said in a quiet voice. A male and a female officer got out of the car and came up the walk onto the front porch. Annie opened the front door, and she could see their somber expressions.

"Mrs. Campbell?" said the female officer.

"Yes," said Annie, her heart beginning to thump. "What's going on?"

The officers stepped a little closer. The female spoke again. "Ma'am, we have some very bad news to tell you. We regret to inform you that your husband, Mo, was killed this morning."

In that instant Annie felt Mo and their life together, all that they had lived, all that they had planned to live, slip from her grasp into the hands of God. And then the pain was upon her, enveloping her like the sound of a freight train too close, drowning out anything else. Just pain and loss and confusion remained.

"No!" cried Annie. "Killed? Are you sure? What happened?"

"Ma'am, he was shot."

Annie felt her legs go weak, and the officers reached out to steady her. "Ma'am, may we come in?" he asked.

"Yes. Oh, my God," she said.

The officers and Annie talked a few minutes, answering questions. "Where did it happen?" "Who found him?" "Did he suffer long?" "Which funeral home do you use?" "Are there some people you need to contact?" "What are the next steps?" Then the officers drove Annie to the morgue to identify the body. As they zippered open the body bag, Annie touched what was left of Mo's face and she cried out again. "Oh, my God. Who did this? Why did they do this to you?"

After the identification, she called Sarah and told her the news. Sarah and Terrance and their two children, Allen, and Sasha, packed and drove from DC to Sidwell for the funeral that was held at Memorial Drive Presbyterian and conducted by one of Mo's friends, the Rev. Carl Kingsley. As Mo had always requested, though he was briefly mentioned in the service, the funeral focused mainly upon the goodness of God and God's promises, especially the promise of the resurrection and God's final victory of love for all the world. Sarah spoke for a few minutes about her dad and what he had stood for during his life on the earth. Annie was too overwhelmed to speak, except to thank everyone for coming.

Terrance drove the children back to DC the next day, but Sarah decided to stay with her mom a few extra days and fly back later. She and Annie spent some time thinking about Mo and his life, his peculiarities, irritations, and humor, but especially his kindness and sense of justice. Sarah felt some guilt that she had not been more active in church, but she cherished her father and the time they had had together. She also was grateful that the previous Christmas she, Terrance, and the children had been visiting her dad and mom. And after they had opened presents, Sarah had gone out with her dad on Christmas morning to visit shut-ins, just like the old times. She had no way of knowing it would be the last time they went, and one of her final memories of her dad.

The murder of an outspoken pastor was rare, and it made the news across the state. As standard procedure, the police had to rule out Annie, or some secret spurned lover as suspects. Because there had been some threatening blogposts, the police were also interested in that angle, but the White supremacists in the area were tightknit and tightlipped. So, after a few months the investigation stalled.

However, there was someone who had lived in the wider area his whole life and who met the full gamut of the public. This someone who had an ear close to the community was Michael, the owner of Michael's Burgers and Ice Cream in Dover, the next town over. He had heard some quiet gossip, but he did not share it with the police. He shared it with someone else, someone who did some digging around to confirm it, someone who then made his own plans.

Chapter 59

A warm, sticky summer morning, 5:45 a.m., and Melvin Anderson was running late for work at the factory. So, after throwing on clothes, skipping both a shower and brushing his teeth, he hurried to the kitchen. He set his cellphone on the counter, reached into the fridge, and with one hand grabbed the bag lunch his wife had made for him the night before: a ham sandwich, an unopened bag of potato chips, an apple, and some peanuts. Looking both ways and seeing that his wife was still in the bedroom, with the other hand he grabbed a can of beer, headed out the front door, and called over his shoulder to his wife, "Bye! See you tonight!"

And then he was moving across his yard, lunch in one hand, beer in the other, out to his car parked along the street. He set the lunch on the roof of his car, opened the unlocked door, pushed aside some trash on the seat and added it to the other trash on the floorboards in the front and back, put the lunch on the passenger seat, and set the beer in the beverage holder. He popped the top on the beer can, cranked the car, and sped up the road figuring that if he went about 15 over the speed limit, he wouldn't be that late. Melvin looked around, took a long swallow on the beer, burped, and sighed, glad to have something just to take the edge off and make the day go faster. When he realized he'd left his cell phone on the kitchen counter, he cursed but said to himself that it didn't matter. He'd rather have the beer anyway.

Melvin had traveled about four miles and was speeding down a long hill towards the Tomcat River, the car radio blaring Hank Williams, Jr., Melvin humming along, taking in the scenery, looking all around before sneaking a sip of beer from time to time. He'd almost finished the whole can when his right leg exploded with such blinding pain that Melvin lost control of the car. It flew over an embankment into a culvert toward a jungle of several acres of thick, green, viny kudzu, already ten feet high, and growing almost a foot a day. The last thing Melvin saw as he looked down at his leg that seemed to be on fire, was a six-foot Eastern Diamondback Rattlesnake whose fangs had just sunk into his right calf almost to the bone. Shrieking in terror as the car crash-landed in the kudzu, Melvin, wearing no seatbelt, flew through the windshield and died instantly. He and his car were not found until the late fall when the annual frost had killed the kudzu and it had shrunk from its towering height down to about ankle level to reveal the vehicle and what was left of Melvin's body after the animals and insects had had their share of him.

The rattlesnake was uninjured in the crash and slithered out one of the shattered car windows to safety. Melvin had never heard a warning from the snake, because Mr. Merriweather had carefully removed the rattles from its tail, knowing that they would grow back over time. He had also chilled the rattler in the refrigerator for a little while to make it lethargic. Then he had placed a loosely tied burlap sack containing the hungry creature underneath the driver's seat earlier that morning. As it warmed, the furious snake managed to slither out and it struck the first thing it identified by heat and movement as prey--Melvin's right calf.

At church the Sunday after Melvin's body was finally found, Mr. Merriweather sat in the pew of First Baptist Church with his family and said a silent prayer to God. "Lord, I apologize for killing one of your children, but you know he'd turned so evil that there seemed no other way to stop him from doing even more evil. And you know he had killed one of your messengers, Mo, who was my friend, and like a son to me. I hope you'll forgive me for what I've done."

Chapter 60

Annie got a phone call from Sarah a few months later. She said, "Mom, I've made the craziest decision. You're not going to believe it."

Annie said, "Let me guess. You've decided to have another baby, and you're pregnant."

"No. Try again."

"You've decided to go to seminary to become a minister."

"Mom! How did you know?"

"I knew that you didn't stay away from the church because you hated it but because you were so frustrated by it. Now I think you're ready to jump in and let God use your passion for justice in the messy and wonderful church. Your dad would be so pleased. Better, I think God is pleased."

Almost a year after Mo's death, Annie was finally cleaning out his bedside table. In the top drawer were a cellphone charger, some spare change, a Bible, some prescription medicine, and a tiny flashlight. There was also a small notebook, and on the cover, in Mo's handwriting it said, "Sermon and Writing Ideas." These were the recorded thoughts that came to Mo sometimes at bedtime or when he awoke in the morning, and sometimes it included thoughts he had when he awoke from a dream or even a nightmare in the middle of the night.

In the second drawer down, surrounded by a box of tissues on one side, and the latest John Sandford murder mystery on the other side, was another notebook, this one from The Dollar Store. On the cover pre-printed it said, "Composition 100 Sheets, College Ruled" but written on a blank line, Mo's handwriting said, "Marriage Thoughts." Early in their marriage, Mo and Annie had begun writing in this notebook various positive things about their marriage and about how they appreciated each other. They did this off and on for a several years, but gradually neglected the practice as they got busy. Finally, years ago, the notebook had been put away entirely, taking its rest in Mo's bedside drawer.

Annie's eyes filled with tears, and she took a breath as she lifted the book from the drawer and opened its pages. In the first entry, Mo had written, "I love the way you like to dance to the music on the radio. October 11, 1982" Then Annie had written, "I'm thankful for how you listen, _really_ listen to me.

October 13, 1982" The entries were steady for several months, then trickled away, and finally stopped altogether. But then starting in September 2020, without telling her, Mo had resumed his entries. "I love how you grow old, not with the fake hair color, but with the real you. September 5, 2020." "I'm so grateful that in spite of your aches and pains, you age gracefully not grouchily. September 6, 2020." Annie laughed at that one.

One of the last entries was September 15, 2020. "Annie, I have a feeling that my time here with you might not be as long as we had hoped. With all the hatred and vitriol coming from the so-called militias, (nothing more than domestic terrorist groups with high-sounding names) I get a feeling that my time with you now is short. Maybe I'm just being dramatic and silly. I hope so. But if my time here with you ends soon, I do want you to know how much I thank God for you. If I had a thousand lives to live on the earth, I would always choose you to spend those lives with me. If I had to weather any storm, enjoy any sunrise, make love with any person, it would be you. Just you, my love. And if my time here is over soon, I will wait for you in the world to come. And then no one will ever separate us again."

Annie's face collapsed and the sobs came heaving. Her tears dripped from her eyes onto the pages she held in her hand, as if watering thirsty flowers.

The last entry was simply, "What a wonderful conversation partner you have been during these difficult months of isolation due to COVID-19. Here's to many more conversations! September 25, 2020"

People say the dead continue to live on in an existence some call heaven, and Mo had believed that eventually all people, all God's children, no matter how good or evil, will eventually be forgiven and somehow transformed into the people they were meant to be in the end. At the last, God's love unfiltered by our human suffering, pain, and stubbornness, will be irresistible. And God will not finally fail with anyone. We will all go home. For now, those who love us have gone ahead to wait for us and cheer us on. And some days when we feel a strength we had not known, a hope that seems unjustified, a tenderness that melts away an icy grudge, they are the ones sending us that strength, hope, and tenderness.

The old farmhouse seems too large and empty without Mo sitting in the rocker beside her. Jürgen, their dog, died years earlier, but Annie still has her old cat, Fee-lion, to help keep her company. Annie continues to teach English at the high school. The energy of her smart and creative students inspires her, and lately she has turned to writing short stories and poetry as a kind of self-therapy.

Sarah and Terrence and the grandchildren visit a few times a year, little ones holding on to one of Annie's legs, hugging and saying, "I love you so much, Grandma," shouting "Play with me!" and sometimes still asking "Where's Grandpa?"

Nights alone are the hardest. "From dinner until dawn" says Annie "is fifty hours, sometimes." But then there are the times when Annie dreams at night. And every now and then Mo comes to her in those dreams. He looks young again. Restored. Smiling. Laughing. Calm. He says, "Don't be afraid, Annie. I'm okay. I love you. And we will be together again. Forever. Forever, my love. And it will be beautiful."

Works Cited

Bonhoeffer, Dietrich, *The Cost of Discipleship*, New York, Macmillan, 1980.

Dostoyevsky, Fyodor, *Crime and Punishment*, New York, Signet Classic, 1968.

The United Presbyterian Church in the USA, *The Worshipbook—Services*, Philadelphia, The Westminster Press, 1970.

Tillich, Paul, *Dynamics of Faith*, New York, Harper & Row, 1957.

Zim, Herbert S., and Smith, Hobart M., *Reptiles and Amphibians: A Guide to Familiar American Species*, New York, Simon and Schuster, 1953.

www.ingramcontent.com/pod-product-compliance
Lightning Source LLC
Chambersburg PA
CBHW061303210726
48293CB00003B/1093